The
Wedding Deal

HEART IN
THE GAME
SERIES

The Wedding Deal

HEART IN
THE GAME
SERIES

CINDI MADSEN

Entangled Publishing, LLC
2614 South Timberline Road
Suite 105, PMB 159
Fort Collins, CO 80525
rights@entangledpublishing.com

Amara is an imprint of Entangled Publishing, LLC.

Edited by Stacy Abrams
Cover design by Bree Archer
Cover photography by Manuel Faba Ortega and undefined undefined/
Getty Images

Manufactured in the United States of America

First Edition March 2019

To all the sports fans out there who ride the rollercoaster, cheering and swearing and often uttering the phrase: "There's always next year." I promise to never make you wait a year to get your happy ending.

Chapter One

As human resources manager of the San Antonio Mustangs, Charlotte's job was to manage the humans who worked for the NFL team, and her history of doing so in a calm, firm-yet-kind manner was impeccable.

But then Lance Quaid happened.

Charlotte hugged her notebook, folders, and the book she'd grabbed off the bookshelf in her office tighter to her chest, her heels clacking out a steady rhythm on the hardwood floor. *Just what I needed. To go from a stable work environment where I finally feel like I'm on top of my game to having to deal with the ego and unpredictable moods of a former quarterback, who's obviously too used to people worshipping him instead of keeping him in check.*

The guy had been the owner of the Mustangs for all of one week, and he'd already stacked up multiple complaints, as if he was determined to break as many records for that as he had on the football field before an injury cut his career short.

Being well versed in all things football, along with having

a freakishly good memory and a penchant for stats, simply thinking his name called up his info sheet.

Lance Quaid: former quarterback of the Tennessee Titans. Six foot four, two hundred twenty-five pounds, round-one pick ten in the draft. Sixty-five completion percentage and once voted offensive player of the year. He came from football royalty, made a huge splash from his very first year in the NFL, and played solidly for six years until an ACL injury took him out.

Charlotte had no idea what he'd been doing for the past three years, but when his grandfather—and the previous owner of the Mustangs—had passed away, Lance had inherited the team. And she, in turn, had inherited the stubborn, privileged, foul-mouthed pain in the butt.

This is what you've been trained for. Her footfalls grew more determined, her chin lifting another inch. Unfortunately, it didn't magically untangle the knot of nerves that'd formed in her gut at the thought of the confrontation. Growing up, change meant something was about to suck even more, and she wasn't a fan. She liked structure. Give her predictable any day.

But changes inevitably happened, and she was doing her best to deal with it while wishing she didn't have to.

Owning the team doesn't mean he's above all the rules. People who felt the rules didn't apply to them irked her, and then there was common decency, which Lance Quaid had apparently never heard of, either. *He has to figure out how to practice restraint and learn some respect, especially when it comes to talking to coworkers.*

And it was her job to remind him of that.

Her stomach dive-bombed as she neared his office, a sarcastic *lucky me* breaking into her internal pep talk.

She'd already put off having this uncomfortable conversation with him for too long, telling herself she needed to attend to emails and other paperwork first. Because how exactly did one go in and tell their new boss that he was…well, wrong? The complaints had come flooding in immediately after Mr. Quaid took up the helm, and while it was technically her job to listen to them, she'd sort of cursed how accessible she'd made herself. Before now, her most challenging tasks had been keeping up to date on ever-changing laws and double-checking payroll while trying not to feel a pinch of jealousy over the bloated salaries compared to her modest one.

A quick glance at her watch told her the big staff meeting was in thirty minutes, and she simply *had* to talk to Mr. Quaid before then. To say the transition in ownership had been rocky would be an understatement. Everyone was still grieving a bit—a pang rose up, one she quickly tamped down—and that exacerbated the situation, too. Honestly, things had been on the grim side for the Mustangs for a while. After several lackluster seasons, including the last one where they hadn't won a single game, they were quickly turning into the joke of the NFL.

But that was a different problem for a different day.

A section of her hair fell forward as she glanced at the door, the brown fringe obscuring the stainless steel knob for a moment. *Just forget who he is and who he was and talk to him like you would anyone else.* After all, she'd had to reprimand countless employees for breaking the rules in the seven years she'd worked here. In all but a few cases, the people involved corrected their bad behavior, and the work environment was better for it.

She sucked in a big breath, transferred the bulk of what she was carrying into her left arm, and rapped on the door, nice and loud.

A muffled "come in" filtered through the wood, and she opened the door and stepped inside the large office.

Nothing had changed. The windows still boasted a nice view of downtown, the large flat screen TV was tuned to sports highlights but on mute, and every dark wood surface gleamed. Two cushy chairs that looked like they were meant for giants sat facing the large desk, and awards and trophies from decades ago, when the team had won a fair amount of games, were in a large glass case that lined the far wall.

The scent was different, though. Woodsy and masculine, not a hint of that spicy cologne that Mr. Price had worn. The pang she'd smothered returned and morphed into a sharp twinge she couldn't as easily ignore. He was really gone, the man who'd taken a chance on her at a time she was afraid no one would. Sure, he'd been a tad dismissive of the few ideas she'd lobbed his way during meetings, but his kindness more than made up for his old-school ways. It hit her all over again that he would never stop by her office to ask how her day was going or toss her one of those hard caramels he always kept in his suit pocket.

Lance Quaid glanced up, the full impact of his blue eyes hitting her. "Did we have an appointment...?" The vague hand gesture he added made her realize he needed her to fill in her name.

Of course he didn't remember. He'd met a lot of people over the past week, so she tried not to take it personally. Tried not to compare him to his grandfather, who made it a point to catalog every staff member's name, no matter how big or small their position with the Mustangs. It wore a little shine off the famous ballplayer, too, which would make it easier to be firm. "Charlotte James. I'm the human resources manager."

"Right." He ran a hand through his nearly black hair, although the strands were short enough it didn't make a mess of it. Guys had it so easy. A dab of hair gel and they were done, whereas she had to use three-point-five products, decide whether to go curly or straight before her hair refused to do either, and the lightest breeze or hint of humidity could destroy all her efforts in two seconds flat. That was the nice thing about a pretty pair of shoes—they always looked good, and since she was a short woman in a world of tall men, they also gave her a few inches' boost. "Sorry," he said. "This past week's been a bit of a blur."

"Understandable." Time to get on with what she came here to do. "While I didn't make an official appointment, Mr. Quaid, there are—"

"Lance. Please."

She wished he hadn't interrupted, since it'd been so challenging to just start that sentence, but she could roll with it. "Fine. Lance. There are a few things I need to talk to you about before the meeting. There've been...complaints. About you. And the way you talk to people."

One dark eyebrow arched, but the slight twist to his lips made him appear more amused than worried. "I'm sure there have been. Gotta break a few eggs and all that."

While she'd wanted to give him the benefit of the doubt, he didn't seem to be taking this seriously. And people weren't eggs; they were human beings with valid feelings that shouldn't be cracked and discarded. She highly doubted Mr. Omelet-Maker had ever worked in an office before stumbling into ownership. Sure, he knew the game, but there was so much more that went into it. She'd been born and raised a Mustangs fan, and she'd hoped the new owner would care about the franchise and work hard to make it better. She didn't want to have to say "there's always next year" from now until the day she died.

To keep her fan side in check, she focused on her business side and strode closer to the desk, her noisy footsteps getting swallowed up by the tacky black and white rug you could lose a zebra in. "For instance, it was inappropriate last meeting when you told Coach Hurst that the only first down he's completed lately is shoving his head that much farther up his ass."

Lance chuckled. *Chuckled!* "One of my better ones."

Charlotte glared at him, lips pursed. "Well, it was also against section two of the employee handbook. As was asking the guys, uh"—she cleared her throat—"where they'd stashed their balls. Or if they had any to start with."

"So let me get this straight..." Lance leaned forward and folded his forearms across the top of the desk. "People came to you to complain about these things I said to motivate them to pull their heads out of their asses?"

"I think they considered it insulting as opposed to motivating. And just an FYI, saying 'pull their heads out of their asses' also goes on the inappropriate list. In addition to being on the vulgar side, to build a happy and productive workplace, we need to treat others well and help them feel safe. Try more carrot versus stick in your approach, and I believe you'll get better results."

The line of his jaw tightened, and his words came out clipped. "You think I don't know what it takes to rally a team? To push them into action?"

Charlotte ignored the instinctual flight response coursing through her and held her ground. "On the football field, yes, but office dynamics are different. I brought you a copy of the employee manual, and I'm sure that reading over the policies will help you better understand." She slid the thin book off the top of her pile and tossed it in front of him. "Since we've got a meeting in a few minutes, I'll just hit the highlights: we *politely* discuss differences of opinions; all employees deserve respect; and we work hard to ensure that relationships between employees are appropriate and harmonious. A *please* and *thank you* never hurt, either— kindness is catching."

Lance picked up the manual and flipped through the pages so fast he couldn't possibly have read a single word. It dropped back to the desk with a *thud*, and he placed his hand on top of it. "Thank you for bringing this to my attention, Charlotte."

Something inside of her flickered at the way he'd said her name, all deep and a pinch intimate, and she quickly snuffed it out. So he had a sexy voice to go along with his drool-worthy looks, which she absolutely wasn't going to let throw her off. In fact, she wasn't going to think about his sexiness at all. Nope, she'd simply ignore how snuggly his crisp white shirt fit across his built chest and the way his Mustangs-appropriate red and black tie hid the fact he'd undone his top button, giving him a slightly disheveled edge. She definitely wouldn't think about the dark scruff covering his chiseled jawline or how underrated the rugged businessman look was.

All those were merely observations she'd catalog along with everything else in her brain about Lance Quaid.

The important thing was he'd said thank you without sounding even slightly sarcastic. Even if he didn't mean it, a lot of workplace etiquette was faking it till you made it. "Just doing my job."

"I assure you that I'm going to straighten everything up at the meeting. That way you can get this off your plate and focus on the more important parts of your job."

The urge to explain that employee relationships were an important part of her job was strong, but she figured it was one of those pick-your-battles situations. The biggest battle was over, and as that sank in, tension leaked out of her neck and shoulders. "Oh good. I was worried this would go a lot rougher."

"Not at all." He picked up a pen and spun it through long fingers she presumed came in handy when gripping a football. "I'm a perfectly reasonable guy."

"Glad to hear it." All that worry over nothing. She backed away from the desk, her steps much lighter with the pressure of scolding her boss officially off her shoulders. Maybe the transition wouldn't be so bad once they all got more used to each other. She probably shouldn't have judged him so harshly, either, simply because she hated change and was missing her old boss. "Okay, so I'll see you at the meeting."

He inclined his chin. "Until then."

• • •

Lance strolled into the meeting room with its theater-like layout and cushy seats that faced a screen where the team often watched film. The facilities had recently been upgraded, and as much as he loved his grandpa, he didn't understand why he'd poured so much money into frivolous things that his staff hardly deserved.

The head coach, general manager, offensive and defensive coordinators, director of pro personnel, CFO, and director of scouting sat in the front row, shooting the shit and not even bothering to look up when he came in.

There were a dozen or so other people in attendance—the specialized and conditioning coaches, who were seated in the second row—as well as a few members from the front office, including the brunette HR manager who'd stormed into his office earlier. Despite the looming meeting, he bit back a smile at the way she'd reprimanded him for his insults and vulgar language, tossed an employee handbook at him, and demanded he read it.

He wasn't sure how he'd missed her in the blur of introductions, but his eyes lingered on her now. Her long, chocolate-colored curls contrasted her pale skin and perfectly framed her almond-shaped eyes, pert nose, and lips he'd bet were pursed more often than not. She gave him an encouraging head nod from her seat in the second row, and he walked to the center stage area of the room.

A little over three years ago, he'd been carried off the football field, and he'd known in his gut it'd been his last game, even as he tried to tell himself he could come back. He'd already had surgery on his torn ACL his senior year of high school, and instead of giving it time to fully heal, he'd pushed through the pain in order to play in college. After his second surgery, the doctors warned him that if he pushed much more, he could lose most of the mobility in his knee.

That almost hadn't been enough to keep him off the field, but months after the surgery and a lot of physical therapy, he still couldn't move as fast as he needed to, and he put what was best for the team above what he wanted. Now that his mom's father had left him the Mustangs, he planned to do the same thing he had back then and make decisions that would be the best for the team. This was his second chance to do what he loved, and he wasn't going to kowtow to his staff's fragile feelings.

Seriously, what a bunch of overgrown babies.

He fastened the middle button of the suit coat he'd thrown on before the meeting and cleared his throat, impatiently waiting as the chatter in the front row gradually died down and all eyes finally lifted to him. "We've got a problem—a big one. Everyone's gotten a little too comfortable, and a lot too complacent, and this whole organization's turned into a total shitshow."

Charlotte leaned forward, a finger in the air, and when he glanced at her, she mouthed, *"Nice, remember? Be nice."* She mimicked waving something in front of her face, her way of reminding him to use the dangling carrot method, he was sure.

"It's an unorganized mess," he revised, and she gave him a thumbs-up, along with an encouraging smile. She had a great smile, too, one that made her cheeks stand out and softened her uber-serious, all-business edges. For a second, he forgot he was in the middle of a speech.

That's it. No more looking her way.

She probably wouldn't be smiling for much longer, anyway.

"I tried to give you all a chance and tell you what I thought you'd need to hear to light a fire under your asses, but instead you decided to whine and complain, and that's not who I want for my team. You think it's funny to have a fucking parade to celebrate a so-called perfect season without a single win? Well, now you can parade yourselves on out of here." He narrowed his eyes on the front row. "Jimmy, Steve, Mark, Scott, John, Thomas, and Clint, you're all fired. Thank you for your time with the Mustangs, but I've decided to go another way."

Jaws dropped, and silence fell.

"Is this a fucking joke?" Jimmy asked.

Charlotte stood, a panicked gleam in her eye. "Now if we can all just keep calm, I'm sure—"

"This whole team's a fucking joke," Lance said. "And I refuse to be a punch line. So, as I said, the entire front row's dismissed. Gather your things and go. Security will escort you out if necessary.

"As for the second row, you're on thin ice. Prove yourselves or you'll be looking for jobs with other teams as well. And if any of you'd like to resign"—he gestured toward the exit—"there's the door."

With his big speech delivered, he turned and strode out of the room. His heart beat faster, not from nerves but adrenaline. And okay, maybe a little bit of nerves. He had five months to restructure an entire team and have them up and running for preseason.

But he had contacts. There were plenty of guys waiting

for a chance—both players and coaches—ones who wouldn't squander it. This should've been done years ago, honestly. The older he'd gotten, the kinder and more sentimental his grandfather had become, and luckily Lance didn't have those things to get in the way and cloud his judgment.

Once he was back inside his office, he reached for the whiskey decanter and glasses Grandpa Price had kept in the minibar behind his desk. Now he knew why.

The door to his office burst open and Charlotte stormed inside, none of the hesitation she'd done her best to hide during their earlier interaction. This time she was all fire and fury, and as his heart beat faster for another reason entirely, he again wondered how he'd missed her before.

The lid of the decanter clinked against the top of his desk as he discarded it. "Hello again, Charlotte. I'm guessing you came to commend me for taking care of things so thoroughly?" He shouldn't stoke the flames, but he couldn't seem to help himself. She claimed to want professionalism, so he'd go over-the-top with it and see how much she liked it then. "I told you I'd fix it so you wouldn't have to deal with it anymore, and I always keep my promises."

"That's not how... You can't just..." She pressed her fingers to her temples and began to rub circles there. "You said you were a reasonable guy."

"I am. I gave them a chance to get it together. Instead they complained to you about my methods and how I'd dared to demand they do their jobs, which shows me they were too far gone for second chances. And considering our pathetic record, it's more like their fifth or sixth chance." The only reason he'd given the coaching staff a shot at all was for his grandpa, and he was almost glad they'd failed because now he could do what he'd wanted to do in the first place. "In order to make the Mustangs a team we can be proud of, we need to start over." He picked up his glass and tipped back the contents, sighing at the way the honeyed liquid burned and soothed on the way down—it was the good stuff. He set down his glass and met Charlotte's gaze.

Laziness was nearly impossible to overcome, but passion could be shaped and molded, and this woman had it in spades—even if he'd love to point it toward other areas of the company. "I'm hoping you'll stick around to help me with that."

She crossed her arms, emphasizing her curves and her frustration at the same time. "Because you suddenly have a whole mess of job postings to make that'll result in hundreds of résumés to sort through?"

"Yes. And because of all the people in that room, you're the only one who's been bold enough to tell me what you thought to my face. I have a feeling you're very good at your job."

"Oh, I am, but I'm not sure you want to hear *all* of what I'm thinking."

He poured a couple more fingers of whiskey before glancing at her. "Did you want a glass?"

A semi-insulted sound came out. "Drinking on the job? That violates section three of the employee handbook."

He bit back a smile, because there was stoking the flames and then there was asking for something to be hurled at his head. Idly he wondered how good her aim was. "So that's a no?"

"No, thank you."

He lifted his glass, swirling it to keep his hand busy, even as his eyes remained on the woman across from him. "But a yes to helping me restructure the organization, I hope."

Exasperation creased her features. Uptight wasn't his usual type—although, it'd been long enough since he'd dated that he wasn't sure he even remembered what his type was—but there was something about her buttoned-up manner and the way she recited the sections of the handbook that sent a flicker of desire through him.

One he quickly smothered, because he had a whole organization to restructure and he knew better than to get involved with someone from work. A big ol' spotlight was being shined on him now that he'd taken over the team, and from here on out, he wanted to make headlines for winning games, not for ridiculous reasons.

He'd had more than enough of that to last a lifetime, and he'd be perfectly happy if he never had to speak to a reporter again.

"I need this job," Charlotte said. "I've been with the team for seven years and worked my way up, and I don't want to have to start over somewhere else. More than that, I love my job. Like I said, I'm good at it."

"And you'll have plenty of chances to prove that to me by posting the listings and helping me sort through the replies." She hadn't been wrong about him needing help with that. He'd prefer someone familiar with the organization and positions involved, but if she wasn't willing, he'd find someone who was.

She gave him a saucy head tilt. "Oh, I have to prove it to you?"

"Sure you don't want that drink? You seem kinda wound tight." He lifted his glass in unreciprocated cheers, and she scowled at him. After downing the contents, he tugged at the knot of his tie, loosening the silk noose. "I'd rather not fire you, Charlotte. What I'd like for you to do is channel all that frustration, turn it into positive energy, and"—he smacked a palm on the desk for emphasis—"help me do what's best for the team." He gave it a beat to sink in before adding a disclaimer. "But I'm not handing out guarantees, either."

The tactic he'd often used while on the field didn't have her standing straighter and hopping to it. Instead his inspirational speech earned more of an eye roll. "Let me guess, there are no guarantees in football?"

"Exactly. More crying than you'd expect, though. Possibly more than in baseball."

The corner of her lips quivered slightly, so she'd obviously understood that he'd thrown her modified movie reference right back at her. Clearly she wasn't ready to fully give up her anger quite yet, either. "Fine, I'll help you restructure the staff. But this doesn't mean you're above the rules. You can't simply yell 'you're fired' at someone and be done with them. There are forms and certain protocols, and I hope you're prepared for severance pay requests and wrongful firing lawsuits that might be brought against you."

"I'll take your suggestion under consideration. But for now, I think we'd better get to work on those job postings."

"I'll grab my laptop." She took a few steps toward the door and then abruptly spun around. "I really hope you know what you're doing."

He kept his indifferent mask in place, but he couldn't help thinking: *I really hope I do, too.*

Chapter Two

"Sorry I'm late," Charlotte said as she took the stool next to her roommate. Wednesday nights at the bar were how they dealt with the hump day, the *weekend's still too far away* blues. It was a tradition they'd started about six months ago when they'd become roommates. They'd forged a friendship based on necessity at first, but it'd quickly moved into genuine territory in spite of not having much in common. "Work was the worst today."

Shannon spun toward her, her blond curls swishing with the movement. "Did you lay down the law with Lance Quaid?"

Charlotte loosed her hundredth sigh of the day as she let her head fall back. "I did. I'm just not sure it took."

"Well, now that you got all up close and personal with your new boss, let's get to the important details first." She propped her cheek on her fist as a dreamy look overtook her features. "Is he as handsome in person as he was on TV?"

"He's…" The irritation she'd felt in his office—especially after the meeting where he fired everyone—drifted to the surface again. "Frustrating. Pigheaded. Impossible."

"So yes."

Charlotte glanced around, since they were in a sports bar and you never knew who might be listening in, then leaned closer and whispered, "He's even hotter in person. Like, I accidentally ended up ogling him a few times and forgot to listen to whatever he was saying— I'll deny that if you tell anyone."

Shannon squared her arm as if she were about to swear an oath in court. "I promise not to reveal any of your secrets. Although the fact that Lance Quaid is hot is hardly a secret. The *Locker Room Report* ran an article on him today and added him to the NFL's most eligible bachelor list." She grabbed her phone, tapped the screen, and swiveled it to Charlotte.

A quick scan revealed his picture—he was tossing a ball, his arms gloriously bare and sporting a sheen, the strong profile she'd stared at for way too long highlighted along with the confident smirk that drove her crazy in more than one way—the news about inheriting the team, and his eligible bachelor status.

Considering his temper and his obstinacy, he might be a bachelor for life. Actually, Charlotte knew that was far from true. Most women wouldn't care about that, especially when they factored in his net worth. But the guy had impulsively fired the front office, and now he wanted *her* to cover his ass.

And my, what a nice ass it was.

When they'd been working on the exact right wording of the job listings and he'd been putting out feelers via a hundred phone calls, he'd paced his office. Her eyes needed a break from the computer screen, so she'd glanced up and accidentally noticed how nicely his backside filled out his tailored pants.

Luckily a minute or so later he'd spoken, effectively

downgrading his hotness a level or two.

"Look at the comments." Shannon scrolled down. "This one says, and I quote, 'the Mustangs have been out to pasture for years, but this guy looks like he could give me a decent ride.'"

Charlotte leaned over the lit screen, sure Shannon was making it up. But nope, there it was in black and white, and another person had added she'd happily try her hand at taming him. The next person escalated the thread with her remark about riding bareback, and Charlotte's cheeks warmed with embarrassment on behalf of someone she didn't even know.

Who posted that kind of stuff on a public page? Judging from the slew of similar comments that were mixed in with statements about his quarterback career and how they were upset/glad/doubtful/hopeful about where he could take the Mustangs, several women and a couple of men, none of whom were overly concerned with things like online etiquette or proper grammar.

Then again, it'd be rather hypocritical to fault them for losing their minds a little over the guy when she'd had trouble keeping hold of hers when they'd been in the same room.

Which was why, after giving herself a mental scolding for ogling him as he was pacing, she'd made a strict decree.

There'd be no checking out any of his assets.

No sniffing the cologne that lingered in the air of his office.

No thinking about how he was still in really good shape.

And her kryptonite—scruff-covered jaws that screamed all-man—was also off-limits.

The bartender asked for her order, jerking her away from dangerous territory where she was slipping on the *thinking about Lance's scruff*. She asked for the whiskey that she'd refused to drink at work—it'd been a long day, and she'd just have the one and then she'd go home and prepare for tomorrow.

Silver lining, at least she still had a job.

For a few minutes in that meeting, after Lance had fired everyone, she'd worried she was getting the ax, too. Not that it'd stopped her from doing her job and demanding to know what he was thinking, but that was because she was as good at what she did as she'd claimed to be. Her exceptional knowledge of every rule and regulation and attention to even minor details had earned her promotion after promotion until she was the director of HR, which was a huge accomplishment and a goal she'd worked toward since day one.

But she really did need the job. A huge chunk of her savings had gone toward her dad's expensive rehab bill. Which was something she worked to keep hidden, even from her roommate, who'd once told her that she allowed the men in her life to walk over her far too much. She'd stated it as nicely as possible, saying they shared the weakness and it was something they were working on together.

What was she supposed to do, though? After nearly a decade of begging her dad to get help for his gambling addiction, he'd finally come to her and admitted he had a problem.

Because of his history and the public repercussions, she needed a rehab center with a stellar reputation for being successful *and* discreet, and about three weeks ago she'd checked him into one that would treat his addiction and the resulting depression. If it worked, it'd be worth it. And she *had* to believe it'd work.

"Earth to Charlotte." Shannon snapped her fingers in front her face.

"Sorry. I'm here now. No more work talk."

"At least tell me I can hold my head high as a Mustang fan this next season." Shannon was more of a casual fan, cheering for the team now that she was a local. Her football knowledge was spotty, but she'd picked up a lot the end of last season when Charlotte had been standing on their couch screaming at the TV.

"Yet to be determined," she said, then quickly glanced around like a paranoid lunatic. While she'd never go into details, she had to be careful talking about the team in general. She'd signed a nondisclosure agreement she'd personally ensured was up to par and took it deathly seriously, to the point she sometimes felt like she couldn't even cheer for the Mustangs in public for fear she'd slip and say too much.

Working for the team had been a dream come true, one she'd been scared to actually believe for quite a while. After everything that'd happened with Dad, she'd worried people would take a look at her last name, put two and two together, since it'd been a huge story in the news around that time, and reject her without even giving her a chance. Worried she'd end up in a boring office where she didn't feel as much passion for what she was doing.

Luckily Mr. Price had told her that he judged people on their own merits. Kind of funny for a team that practiced a bit of nepotism, but when you owned enough companies to make you a billionaire, you got to dabble in hypocrisy.

After this afternoon with Lance, she could at least say he obviously cared about what happened to the team. Over the past few years, it'd been more and more difficult to remain a fan. Not that she'd hop on a shiny bandwagon when it passed on by, but it would be nice to not spend every Sunday during the season disappointed.

"Okay, so I guess it's time to move on to another depressing subject." Shannon glanced around the bar. "There is a severe lack of guys out and about tonight, and this was the only social outing on my calendar all week."

Charlotte was glad her drink arrived, and she took a swig before Shannon could say what she was 99 percent sure she was going to.

"That means we're going to that speed dating thing next door."

"Tonight?" Charlotte shook her head, cursing that her drink hadn't had time to work yet. She was exhausted. She also wanted to point out that even if the bar was chock-full of guys, they'd all be marked off the possibility list because she had a new rule against meeting guys at sports bars. It always ended badly. Technically, every one of her relationships had ended badly, but again, football was to blame in a surprising amount of them.

It'd all started with her first boyfriend, who'd found out her dad was the assistant football coach at the college he wanted to attend. Where he also hoped to play after he graduated high school, of course. She'd gotten him his in, and for her efforts she'd acquired her first broken heart.

You see, football kept him too busy for a serious girlfriend. It did not keep him so busy that he couldn't have sex with a lot of coeds, though. Funny the way that works.

"It's happening," Shannon said, undeterred. "We're going to take advantage of this hot, ballbuster-businesswoman-meets-retro-pinup-girl thing you've got going on while you're already out and about."

The compliment cracked Charlotte's resolve to remain firm, despite her best efforts. It had been the exact look she was going for, fashion the one area where she liked to bend the rules a little—not to mention that vintage styles flattered her curvier figure far better than modern ones did.

"Really, you brought this on yourself," Shannon added, chasing away the warm fuzzies and resealing those cracks.

"How?"

"You refuse to go out after you get home, kick off the heels, and flop on the couch. Remember how we decided we were going to get back out there?"

"I remember *you* decreed that you were." Charlotte still wasn't there yet, but if she'd voiced that when Shannon was on her tear about it last weekend, her roommate would've only debated why she should be, and she hadn't wanted to hear it. This was the problem with simply nodding. People thought you were agreeing and committing.

"We both are. Just like we're both looking for more accessible guys, ones who want the same things we do. And you have that no-football-guys rule, although I still don't really understand it. Shouldn't you have similar hobbies?"

"It's a precise system. They can enjoy watching a football game now and then, but if they go all starry-eyed when they find out I work for a team or if they start prodding me for insider information, I walk away. No more thinking that eventually they'll understand I can't get them access to the players, the field, or what I know about the games before they go down." It wasn't easy, trying to find guys not obsessed with football in Texas. Even the ones who were Cowboys or Texans fans weren't immune to the idea of a behind-the-scenes tour or tickets to games when their teams played. *As if* she could date a guy who cheered against her team.

"Oh yeah. Makes perfect sense now." Shannon glanced at her phone. "Eight minutes."

The last of her drink hit the back of Charlotte's throat, and as her pulse skittered under her skin, she debated going back on her decision to only have one. It'd help with speed dating but might also not so much help, and she needed to be fresh for work tomorrow and *ugh*. "How about we go speed walking in the park and see if we can meet a nice serial killer instead? That sounds like more fun to me."

"You promised to be my wing woman," Shannon reminded her, and Charlotte groaned. Her roommate's decision to take more risks and meet more people would've been fine if Charlotte didn't have to go along for the painful ride.

"Painful" was also a good word to describe her last relationship, and it definitely fit how it'd ended. After her year-long relationship had crashed and burned over issues she should've realized were too big to overcome, she'd had a hard time convincing herself that love—the true, intense kind she used to dream of as a little girl when spending far too much time alone—existed.

Everyone always wanted something. Wanted you for what you could do for them. Each relationship had taken a piece of her, and thanks to the way she'd grown up, she didn't have that many to give. Her first boyfriend took another piece, and Ian had taken more than one.

Right now she was using the leftovers to help keep Dad afloat.

Maybe after she'd had more time to heal and Dad was on steady ground, she could find a bit of that shiny optimism she used to have. Maybe then she'd be ready to sincerely date.

But thirty minutes later, as she was sitting across from a guy, not nearly buzzed enough, she thought she'd rather go back to Lance's office. Regardless of it meaning he'd be over her shoulder, watching her post job listings and insisting on different word choices, as if that would make the best coaches and general managers leap at the chance to work for a team that hadn't won in so long that most of their fans and even some of their own players had given up.

• • •

Lance tossed his keys on the counter of his penthouse apartment. It'd been his grandfather's as well, and he recalled all the times he and his brother, Mitch, had been scolded for running through the halls, both from Mom and his older sister, Taylor, who'd often thought she was the boss of them growing up. The five bedrooms and two floors had been convenient whenever they visited and needed a place to stay but seemed extravagant now that Lance was living here alone.

All the space accented how alone he was, too, and he wondered if it'd gotten to his grandpa during those past few years, after Grandma Price had passed away.

Maybe after Mitch and Stacy get married, they'll come visit. Taylor can bring her kids, too, so they can help breathe some life into the place.

Added bonus, he could teach his nephews to race through the house. He chuckled to himself as he thought about how Taylor would have to retrain them after they returned home. Kids should be kids, after all.

Lance walked over to the couch, shed his suit coat, and yanked off his tie, glad to be rid of both. For now he'd dress up and look the part of an office flunky, but before long, he was going to loosen the dress code.

Something Charlotte James would undoubtedly take issue with. She'd probably even tell him exactly which section of the employee handbook it violated. A smile crept across his face as he thought about the way she sighed when he was telling her to reword the job postings.

For a rule follower, she certainly was feisty. Honestly, he was just glad he'd have help to sort through the mess, which yes, he'd made himself. Though really, his grandfather had let things slide these past few years, too worried about keeping up appearances to let show that he was tired and rundown, and he forgot things now and again, ones that made running the team difficult.

Not even the family had known the extent of it.

Obviously they'd known the best decisions weren't being made as far as the team went, but Lance could still remember voicing his opinion about a player they'd traded when he was a sophomore in college, and how Grandpa had told him that it was his team and he'd damn well do what he wanted. He'd added that when Lance ran the team, he could do the same.

It was something he'd occasionally dropped into their conversations, but Lance never thought he'd be running the team so soon. At one point he'd actually thought he'd pass. That was back when he figured he'd be playing quarterback into his early forties and maybe coach a while before Grandpa passed away.

But between Lance's second knee injury and his grandpa's stroke, life made it clear that it didn't respect set plans. Things happened, and you had to read the field again and come up with a new play.

Right now he was searching for open players for his staff, trying to determine who'd be able to catch the ball and help lead his team to victory. He sure as hell wasn't going to deal with a bunch of babies who'd go crying to HR if he raised his voice or swore over an incompetent move. If he'd done that back when he'd been playing ball, he would've been dropped in a hot minute.

I hope the Stangs players haven't grown soft along with the staff.

His phone buzzed in his pocket, and he smiled when he saw his brother's name.

Mitch: *I hope you're not getting a big head now that the Locker Room Report has given you most eligible bachelor status. I'm gonna be a total diva about you stealing the spotlight during my special time.*

Lance huffed a laugh. He'd heard about the article from one of the PR people who was safe for the time being, but he didn't put any weight to it. Since his athletic glory days had been a study in how little control he had over what journalists said about him, he simply hoped it'd be good for the team. Maybe extra publicity would make it easier to rebuild.

Sure. He'd grasp at any straws right now.

His phone vibrated again, the ring splitting the quiet. He moved his thumb over the decline button but didn't tap it when he saw it was his mom. You didn't ignore calls from Mama Quaid, especially since she'd just keep on calling.

"Hey, Mom."

"You haven't responded to my texts about the wedding." Mitch's wedding was a week and a half away, which was why he'd joked about his "special time." And boy was he taking a lot of it, milking the event for all it was worth—he'd expect nothing less from his baby brother, though, and he was happy for him. He just wished the timing was better.

"I've been busy."

"We're all busy," she replied. He had no doubt she was overloaded with the endless wedding planning stuff, and there wasn't any point in arguing his busy—trying to rebuild a team—was a different kind. "We've been planning this for a long time, and I expect you to arrive the same day the rest of us do."

He plopped onto the couch and leaned back against the cushions. No one knew how to throw a celebration like his family, which meant it wasn't just a wedding but a destination wedding with events starting the Monday before the ceremony.

"I understand that, but there are things you can't plan for." *Like Grandpa's death*, but he didn't say that. Not when it'd been her father and she'd had such a hard time saying goodbye—she'd cried for a week straight, the funeral bringing on a wave of tears he'd never seen from her before. The upcoming happy event was most likely what was helping her hold it together, so he'd go along with anything she wanted.

"And there are things you'll regret missing for the rest of your life. Now, as for your plus one…"

Make that *almost anything* she wanted. "I wasn't kidding

when I told you I'd be married to my job for the foreseeable future," he said. "That's going to be my priority for the next year at least."

"Pish posh. Your brother managed to get engaged *during* the season, when he was traveling nonstop for games." Their parents were college sweethearts who'd been married for almost forty years, and his mom had been obsessed with marrying off her children since the time they hit twenty. Taylor made her happy by getting married shortly after college and immediately popping out a few kids, and now Mitch was ten days away from joining the land of the wed. Lance wasn't anywhere near there, nor did he want to be. You'd think after ten years she'd give up, but nope. "You don't want your life to be empty, do you?"

He had way too much experience with empty days, ones where he looked around and found that everyone he'd thought were his friends were long gone.

Maybe that was why he was having trouble adjusting to the giant penthouse in a mostly unfamiliar city. He'd grown up in Raleigh, played for the Tarheels, and then was drafted by the Titans. While there'd been plenty of busy months he'd hardly seen his family, he'd never lived quite so far from them.

"You have to try again someday," Mom added, as if he needed a reminder of how close he'd been to being engaged before he'd been injured and every single part of his life fell apart. "If you need a push, I'm happy to provide it. Along with the names of a few lovely ladies who'd be happy to attend the wedding with you."

"Oh, so I get a plus *two*?"

She clucked her tongue at him, but she was also trying not to laugh, he could tell. At least he'd managed to add a smidge of happy to her night—he honestly was worried about how she was coping with her grief, and what would happen once the wedding stuff wasn't there to distract her anymore.

"How about I give you their phone numbers and you can call them up and see if you click with one of them? Then we can take it from there."

Saying he didn't have time to chat up anyone between calls that involved rebuilding the Mustangs was useless. Mom wouldn't hear it or believe it. Even now, this conversation was cutting into time he should be dialing up associates.

For his mom, he'd take the time.

Cold-calling girls she thought would be perfect for him and getting stuck in awkward, too-long phone conversations? Not so much.

He could only imagine how much worse it'd be when he arrived back in North Carolina, where his entire family would also be "helping" to set him up. His family had always been close, but sometimes they were close to the point of being intrusive.

If he were smart, he'd find a nice girl to take with him so he could skip all the painful forced interactions with women they were definitely planning on springing on him. Then at least he'd get a choice.

Of course he hadn't been on a date in months, and asking a woman to travel with you on a first date—to a wedding, no less—seemed either crazy or desperate. Or both.

"Don't worry about me," he said.

"Not an option. It's a mom thing that never goes away."

He smiled, in spite of it meaning she wouldn't be giving up her matchmaking attempts. "I'll see you on Monday, Mom. Just don't book too many activities. I'll have to do a lot of work while I'm at the hotel."

"I'll talk you out of that when you get to the beach," she said with a laugh, and he shook his head, even as affection wound through his chest.

You'd think his family would understand, what with their football legacy, but like the staff he'd recently fired, they'd grown complacent. Too comfortable. And he wanted that for his family.

But for himself…he wanted something more. He wanted to take control of that legacy and not only return it to its former glory, but to prove he was more than a washed-up quarterback whose career ended way too short.

If he couldn't break any more records on the field, he'd do whatever it took to ensure the team he'd just inherited did it on his behalf.

Chapter Three

Charlotte reached for her coffee cup, only to find it empty already. Her voicemail was completely filled, and her email inbox was spilling over as well. On top of all that, she was tired, her speed dating night to blame for the exhaustion and residual grumpiness. You'd think by now she'd be used to it. How almost any time a guy found out she worked for the Mustangs, they decided to quiz her on football facts, as if to test how well she actually knew the game.

She always passed; they did not.

Why, oh why, did I let Shannon talk me into going along? At least she *got two numbers for prospective hopefuls.*

Since her brain made it clear it'd be on strike until it received more caffeine, Charlotte grabbed her mug and headed to the breakroom. The office was like a ghost town this morning, so many of the rooms dark, and the remaining staff walked around on eggshells, barely speaking above a whisper.

Naturally there was only a splash of coffee left in the gurgling pot, and in spite of the fact it'd be burned and taste like crap, Charlotte poured it in her mug before starting another batch. She downed the sludge, grimacing when the lukewarm substance formerly-known-as-coffee slid down her throat.

So not worth the caffeine.

She grabbed the box of Texas Tasters Buttery Crackers and shoved a handful in her mouth. Breakfast of champions right here. Bonus, they could double for lunch, and she had a feeling they probably would have to with how much work she had to do today. It was sad how often she skipped lunch, and how little effect it had on her tummy and hips.

Unlike Shakira's, her hips did lie. They said go ahead and eat that, it won't matter. And then they'd get bigger, and her clothes would get tighter, and with that in mind, she decided to go ahead and believe her lying hips anyway and eat more crackers.

Footsteps sounded behind her, and she glanced over her shoulder, freezing when it was Lance.

"There you are," he said, and she automatically glanced around the room to see if she'd missed someone else's presence.

She shoved the crackers to one cheek, cursing how dry they'd left her mouth. "Me?"

He cocked his head, one corner of his mouth turning up. "Yes, you. I was looking for you."

"Why?" she asked—the coffee needed to hurry up with its brewing because she wasn't alert enough to respond intelligently. Or better yet, keep her internal thoughts inside her head where they belonged.

"We have a lot of work to do."

"I certainly do. People have been calling nonstop, and the words 'wrongful termination' have been tossed around."

"You can forward those to our lawyer."

"You didn't fire her?" Yep. That was another inside

thought. What was it about this guy that made it hard to hold back her snark?

"Not yet, but I will if she doesn't do her job. As I said yesterday afternoon, I'm well within my rights to fire anyone who doesn't do their job."

"And as I said yesterday afternoon, there's a lot of paperwork involved in all the firing you did. Between answering calls and emails, I've been compiling it, and I'll need your help getting it filled out so everything can be properly documented as soon as possible."

"That can wait. Have any applications come in yet? From the postings we listed?"

"Actually, it *can't* wait, because you can't hire people without completing the paperwork terminating contracts. But yes—that's the other reason my inbox and voicemail are overflowing. We've had a lot of people respond, but I haven't had the chance to sort through them, so I'm not sure if we've had any qualified applicants. I was going to dig in after I grabbed more coffee."

"Print it all out and bring it to my office. I'd like to go through them with you."

Every cell in her body froze. In his office. Where he'd be looking like that, all tall and muscled, a teasing of tanned skin left exposed by the top few undone buttons.

Walking a fine line there, Charlotte.

It'd be impossible not to notice his hotness, but she wouldn't let herself dwell on it. Before long she was sure she'd get used to the way he looked and how her pulse quickened— part of that was because he was her boss and he'd fired everyone. Yeah. That was the *only* reason.

"Charlotte?" His deep voice caressed her skin and sent a zip through her core. She didn't really have a good reason for that, but it wasn't like she'd act on the misguided hormonal surge.

Focus on how much harder he's made your job. How he came in here and fired everyone. She cleared her throat. "I'll print them out—along with the termination forms—and be in your office shortly."

He gave a quick nod and gestured to the coffeemaker. "Are you going to share?"

The *glug, glug, glug* slowed, and she glanced at the full pot. "I have a feeling I'll need about this much to get through the day. But I suppose it'll get cold and gross before I can drink it all, so I'll share if..." She raised an eyebrow. "You make the next pot."

He stepped closer, and her heart pounded harder, the jolt she needed from caffeine coming from his nearness instead. "Deal." He reached around her for a mug and poured coffee into it, filling her mug as well.

Then he lifted the box of crackers and studied them. "Are these shaped like Texas?"

"What else would they be shaped like?" she asked, as if it was a ridiculous question—which it was.

"Is this another one of those lavish expenses we've been spending money on?"

She shook the last of the sugar out of the five packets she'd ripped open to pour in her mug. "That's just how the yummiest crackers come down at the local H-E-B. I bought them myself, and they're the store brand. Please don't tell me you've been eating your salsa with boring circle or triangle chips?"

He blinked at her. "The *chips* are shaped like Texas?"

She intoned her best accent, although it wasn't nearly as strong here in the city as in the smaller towns and the southern end of the state. "Honey, you can get most anythin' shaped like Texas here. Crackers, chips, slices of cheese. Cookies. Even trucks 'round these parts have a Texas edition option—although I wouldn't recommend eating them."

She chuckled at her own joke. "Feel free to try some," she said as she pivoted to the fridge where she kept the good creamer. She poured a generous amount into her cup, the dark liquid turning light brown. She extended it toward him. "Cream? It's not Texas shaped, but it's Southern butter pecan flavor, and it's delicious."

"No, thank you. I prefer it black."

"Of course you do. Guys think that drinking their coffee black makes them more macho somehow, but that's just silly when you could have coffee that tastes good instead."

"Or maybe I just prefer coffee to taste like coffee."

"Not buying it." She moved to put her beloved creamer back in the fridge—she was a bit of a snob when it came to the International Delight brand, too. It was just better than other brands. "I'm gonna head to my desk, and if you decide to pour some in while you're in here alone, no one will know. Just saying."

"Can we apply that same idea to not filling out the paperwork? No one has to know."

"Nice try," she said, shaking her head as she walked past him. Typical male, wanting to act brashly and leave someone else to deal with the consequences.

That was probably unfair. But she was a stats girl, and when it came to the males who'd been in and out of her life, the figures backed her up.

. . .

"Okay, and reason for termination." Charlotte's fingers paused their tapping on her laptop keyboard as she peered over the screen at him. She'd slid on a pair of pale pink, cat-eye glasses, and the lenses reflected part of the never-ending questions in front of her.

Lance dragged a hand down his face, beyond done with

this process already, regardless of only being halfway finished with the first of many termination forms. "Head lodged too far up his own ass to see reason."

Her mouth flattened into a tight line. "I can't put that."

"Why not? It's true and seems like a valid reason to fire a coach to me."

She gave him a sharp smile. Her foot went to bouncing again, the black stiletto adding an air of extra impatience. He'd thought they were kind of sexy before he worried she might use the spiky end on him.

"Did you go to college to learn what paperwork and forms are necessary when terminating an employee, as well as all the labor laws?"

He knew better than to answer that. Not that he really had to.

"I'm trying to cover your ass, and you've already had complaints lodged against you for derogatory remarks." The tightness in her voice made it clear she was running out of patience as fast as he was. "Best not prove the point in a document he could use against you."

"Just tell anyone who questions my motives to watch any game last season—that should be explanation enough."

She sighed. "It's called due diligence, which is especially important for a billion-dollar company. Why must you make it so difficult?"

"Here I thought *you* were making it difficult. Who even looks through the paperwork?"

"I do! And if a lawyer needs it—and ours is definitely going to—they will. Which means a judge might also see it. I'm not going to do a crappy job because you want to impulsively fire everyone and not have to deal with the consequences."

"Trust me, if I knew this was going to be part of the consequences, I might've just decided to forgo a shot at winning a game ever again."

Her eyebrows lowered, those full lips pursing in the way they too often did. As frustrating as she was with all her dotted i's and crossed t's, he kept getting caught up staring at her pretty features. Her big green eyes practically glowed, and right now it was with irritation aimed at him.

And he found himself experiencing a clashing mix of annoyance and attraction.

Those damned black pantyhose with the dark line up the back that occasionally flashed when she crossed her legs certainly weren't helping matters. They, along with her shoes, were the only things about her that didn't scream sensible, and his brain kept getting snagged on them when it should be focusing on everything else. About her, *and* about the massive amount of work they had to do.

"Section seven of the handbook states that the termination procedure typically starts with the employee's supervisor or manager—you—who discusses the matter with human resources—that'd be me. Once they determine if termination is necessary, they schedule a meeting with the employee and explain why ending the employment relationship is the best solution for all parties."

He simply stared. Partly because an intelligent response refused to come to mind, and partly because she'd just rattled off another set of rules he'd gotten lost in. It pretty much boiled down to him not having a leg to stand on, he got that much.

"But you didn't do any of that," Charlotte continued, an admonishing pinch to her expression. "So I need you to help me out so I can help you. Help me help you."

"Just put down incompetence."

"Great." The aggressive *click* of her keyboard filled the room. "I'll also look through his contract later and reference any pertinent sections to further justify letting him go."

Damn politics and rules and never-ending piles of

paperwork. No wonder the team sucks. Everyone spends too much time tiptoeing around, trying not to hurt delicate feelings.

Well, Charlotte could get as mad as she wanted to, but he wasn't tiptoeing around. Football wasn't about preserving feelings. It was about teamwork and taking hits and pulling off insane plays as you poured your blood, sweat, and tears into every workout. Every game.

He wanted his staff to be willing to lay it all on the line so he could ask the players to do the same. He wanted to get to the fun part, where the team was gelling and finding their groove and grinding it out on the field. That needed to happen as soon as possible, because this year, the Mustangs were going to make the playoffs for the first time in over a decade. A lofty goal like that meant he wasn't going to slow down or mince words until they'd put together a team that could make that happen.

He picked the top résumé off the stack, but his phone rang, interrupting before any of the information he'd read sunk in. It'd rung nonstop, but when he saw one of his former teammates' name flash across the display, he quickly answered—finally, someone he *wanted* to talk to.

"Foster, how the hell are you?"

"Still handsome and as talented as ever," Foster said, because humility was never his cross to bear.

Lance snorted, and after exchanging some typical give-each-other-shit remarks and taking a minute or two to properly catch up, switched into business mode. "So, find anything out from your contacts? I could use some good news."

"I poked around a little. Talked to Billy Mulroney and he was very interested. He's the only one I've been able to talk to so far."

"Billy Mulroney could be good."

"*Really?*" Charlotte said, and at first he thought she

might be mad because he'd answered the phone, but then she muttered, "Sure, if you want to keep on losing."

He almost ignored it but decided he might as well give her the chance to speak her mind—not that he could stop her from voicing her opinions anyway. Might as well let her do it in a more official capacity. "Hey, I'm gonna put you on speaker. I'm in my office with my human resources manager, Charlotte James." He clicked the speaker icon. "Charlotte, I'm talking to Kevin Foster. You know him?"

"Sure. Wide receiver, round three draft pick, over eight thousand receiving yards, sixty-four receiving touchdowns and counting. You two played really well together."

Lance took a moment to pick his jaw off his desk. "You followed my career?"

"Slow down there, Mr. Ego. I follow football."

Foster laughed, and Lance decided to charge on through. "Okay then, let's hear your opinion on Mulroney. From the sounds of it, you don't think he's the coach we need."

Charlotte shrugged. "He's too cautious."

"Cautious can be good. We want someone who makes smart calls."

"Smart and cautious aren't the same thing. Sometimes taking a risk is the smart move. He always plays it safe, and that means field goals when there could've been touchdowns. It means not making the big plays that catch the defense off guard. Don't tell me that when you were playing and it was third and three or four that you didn't think you could get the first down. Especially if you were behind and the clock was ticking faster and faster toward the end of the game."

His eyes locked on to hers, and the challenge inside of them sent a heady thrumming through his veins. "I'd go for it. Hell, Foster and I've gone for it plenty of times."

"Converted most of them, too," Foster said.

Charlotte smiled at the phone on the desk between them,

and Lance experienced a pinch of…he wasn't sure what. He didn't get smiles like that. Why did Foster's *voice* get one? "Exactly. It's the perfect example of high risk, high reward. Everyone expects you to give it to your running back in those situations, and most of the time, it's the right move. But when you switch it up, throw one of those amazing passes, and get an extra ten or twenty yards…? Those are the times the fans go extra crazy. That's what fills the seats—which isn't something we've done for a while, as our budget attests. If we're going to restructure, let's put together a team that'll get fans in seats." She glanced at him. "I mean, that's what my vote would be. Not that I get a vote. I'm just saying."

"I appreciate your input," Lance said, and he meant it. He drummed his fingers on the desk. "Who else is out there?"

They threw out a few names, but most of the well-known coaches had been snatched up, and it'd take digging to find out whose contracts were up when.

Lance tapped the speaker icon, picked up the phone, and told Foster he'd circle back around, but if he could spread the word and let him know if there was any interest, he'd appreciate it. If his former teammate was a free agent, he'd push for him in an instant, but he also knew Foster was eyeing retirement. Maybe eventually he'd recruit him as a coach, but that didn't help the here and now.

As he paced, he kept glancing at Charlotte. She typed away on her computer, occasionally pausing to readjust her glasses, and he couldn't stop thinking about the way she'd rattled off those stats earlier. Her point about Coach Mulroney being too cautious.

When Lance hung up, he tossed out the name of one of the greatest running backs in NFL history, curious to see how extensive her knowledge truly was.

Charlotte rattled off his stats in one long stream, just like she'd done with Foster, and then asked, "What about him?"

He walked around the desk and glanced at her computer screen, sure she'd pulled up Google. But the only thing onscreen was one of those stupid termination forms she insisted he fill out for every single person he'd fired. "I...just..."

"Wanted to see how much I really know about football?"

"No," he said, a hint defensively because it'd been part of it. So far he'd mostly seen how much she knew about HR, rules, and foods shaped like Texas.

"Let's just go with a lot, and I'm crazy good with numbers, especially where stats are concerned."

"There's good with numbers and then there's...whatever you are. You could make a killing in Vegas."

Her face dropped. "I don't gamble." Tension crept into the room, and her shoulders lifted a bit higher.

He hadn't meant to upset her. Even though he wasn't sure how he'd managed to with such a simple statement, he softened his voice and worked to undo it. "It was more an observation and one of those things people say, not a suggestion."

She nodded, her posture relaxing slightly. "Right. Of course."

So they would stay away from Vegas, but he mentally patted himself on the back for keeping her around. The weight pressing against his shoulders even lightened a bit. He'd felt so responsible for every part of the team and rebuilding the staff and had wondered how he would possibly do it all. Sure, he knew the game and how to play, but there were so many moving parts, and there was always a mix of skill and luck involved in every game.

Speaking her mind had allowed Charlotte to keep her job—and yes, he'd needed someone to help with all the hiring as well. But he realized that she could be an asset to the team in more areas than HR.

In fact, he was starting to think she was his ace in the hole.

Chapter Four

A mug was thrust into her line of sight, and Charlotte glanced up, bleary eyed, from her computer screen.

Lance had been on the phone and had walked out of his office about ten minutes ago—for privacy she assumed—and she was surprised he'd noticed she was out of coffee. "I added a shit ton of your fancy creamer, too, since you don't have to pretend you're macho like I do."

"Yeah, if gross coffee is the price, I'll pass." She returned his smile as she took the warm offering in her hands and inhaled the delicious aroma. She took a sip, and her entire body perked up.

"I know we had a deal—you shared your pot with me, so I made more—but full disclosure, I'm also hoping to get in another hour or so of work. I've got to head to Nag's Head, North Carolina on Monday, and since I'll be there at the beach for a week, I'd like to get as much as possible done before then."

She frowned. While there was definitely a string attached to her perfectly made cup of coffee, she was more concerned about the last part. "Let me get this straight. You fired most everyone on the Mustangs staff, and now you're just going to go on a beach vacation?"

"It's my brother's wedding," he said, and she wished she hadn't voiced her incredulity.

"Oh. Well, a valid reason—"

"Gee, thanks for validating me," he muttered, and she glared at him. Apparently their momentary truce was over.

"I wasn't quite finished," she said. "What I was going to say before you interrupted was, '*But* this stuff is never going to be done before you go.' Even if I stay the extra hour or so this coffee will help get me through. Not to mention that with the draft coming up, we're under a huge time crunch as it is." Thanks to their horrible record last season they had first pick, so it was an even bigger deal than usual, one they couldn't afford to waste. These kinds of decisions affected everyone involved in the entire franchise from the staff to the players and everyone in between. *Plus* their families.

"Which is why I'll be working most of the time I'm in North Carolina."

"I'll try to hold down the fort here, but *full disclosure*, I'm going to have to send you a ton of paperwork to sign so I can get it all filed and we can get started on new contracts."

His phone rang, and he sighed, a completely exhausted, frustrated noise.

She'd forwarded her desk line to her cell, and between paperwork and sorting through résumés, they'd both been on calls all day, so she understood. If she had to talk to one more person over the phone, she might lose the calm and collected manner she prided herself on. Even when people called to yell, she always kept her cool, although she did get firmer and sharper if necessary.

Lance answered with his name, already off and pacing around his office. After all day of doing so, she noticed he was favoring his right knee. She assumed he wouldn't want her to ask about it, even if it would be to see if he needed ice or pain meds or something.

"Oh, she did, did she?" Lance glanced at Charlotte, and she fought paranoia. What did she do now?

I'm innocent! I've been in here with you the whole time!

Admittedly she'd thought several times about how nicely his slacks fit—he kept putting his hands in his pockets and stretching the fabric tighter across the ass she was filling out all this paperwork to protect. He'd also rolled up his sleeves, and she'd accidentally ogled the enticing line of his forearm, and okay, she wasn't *totally* innocent. Maybe it was a good thing he was going to be out of town for a wedding. It'd give them time to get more people into the office and give her some distance from the guy, which would help tame her improper thoughts about him and his ridiculous body. And his deep voice, which continually affected her, regardless of whether he was being nice or completely impossible.

Although for the record, she'd behave either way.

Just to ensure she didn't go thinking too much about things she shouldn't, she promptly pulled up the inter-office dating policy. Despite already knowing it by heart, she read it to herself. Not only was dating in the office highly discouraged, section three, paragraph four clearly stated that supervisors must not date their direct reports. The restriction extended to every manager above an employee, and Lance was the very top of everything.

Not that she thought he would have a problem with wanting to date her—and she definitely didn't want to spend any more time than necessary with someone so frustrating—but it was inappropriate for her to think about her boss in any way besides the guy who was making her life hell but she had to report to anyway.

Maybe there should be an inter-office ogling policy. I'll

write it up, and there will just be one word: don't.

Lance muttered a few mmm-hms and pinched the bridge of his nose. "Well, it was lovely to *meet you*, but I can't really talk right now." Pause. "Later. Sure." Pause. "Goodbye."

He lowered the phone and glanced at her again, and her spine automatically straightened. "What?"

"My mother is giving out my number to women she wants to set me up with and telling them to call me."

"Didn't she hear that you made the most eligible bachelor list? No need for her to play matchmaker—soon you'll have all sorts of women beating down your door."

"Oh, I don't think I'm in much danger of that." A horrified expression crossed his face. "Unless my mom gives them my address."

"Or maybe I will," she teased, acting like she was pulling up his information. Then she stuck out her pinky and her thumb and mimicked being on the phone. "Yes, you can go right on over to his place. He *loves* unexpected guests."

He scowled at her, and she probably shouldn't enjoy ruffling his feathers quite as much as she did, but she owed him after all his complaining about her forms, while being so useless at helping to fill them out. "Wouldn't that be a violation of privacy?" he asked. "That's gotta be in the handbook somewhere. I'm guessing you and your photographic memory even know which section."

"I don't have a photographic memory, but yes, yes I do know. I'm not going to spoil the read for you, though. You're going to have to look it up yourself."

He shook his head, but the corner of his mouth kicked up. Then his phone rang again. His brow furrowed before he answered it in his usual way. His posture tensed. He plopped into his seat and dropped his head into his hands. He was polite but short and made his apologies about needing to go.

"Another one?" she asked after he'd disconnected the

call. Too late she realized that wasn't any of her business, and asking was crossing a line she'd meant to keep firmly taut and far away from.

"Yep. Apparently my mom's determined for me to have a date for the wedding, and her way of ensuring that was to give all of her friends' single daughters my number."

Charlotte laughed. "I'm sorry. It's totally not funny," she said, but then she laughed again.

His head tilt was slightly chiding, but a faint glint of humor lit his eyes. "I'm glad you're enjoying this. Even though it's cutting into time we could be using to fill out more of your ridiculous forms."

"I do love me some forms," she said, in spite of it being the least favorite part of her job. Under other circumstances, she might even agree some of them were overkill. "It's just kind of nice seeing that even star football players have to deal with things like having their mothers attempt to set them up. Dating is…" She shuddered. "Last night my roommate convinced me to go to this speed dating event."

"On a Wednesday?" he asked.

"She thinks the people out and about on weekends are fake single."

"As in they're in committed relationships but pretending otherwise?"

"More like they must not want a relationship enough if they only go looking on Friday and Saturday." She waved a hand through the air. "I gave up trying to understand her theories a few months ago." While her brain was saying this was another gray area path, her mouth kept on going anyway. "I'd say in those type of situations, the day of the week doesn't much matter. Every time there are three times as many women as men. It's like the dating *Hunger Games*, and the odds were not ever in my favor."

Evidently he didn't read a lot of young adult novels or

keep up on popular culture, because there wasn't so much as a flicker of recognition. "So, no luck?"

"My roommate ended up with two numbers. I ended up with a headache."

Instead of the laugh she'd hoped for after her awesome joke, his eyebrows knitted together. "Were there a bunch of idiots there? Or were they just too scared to ask for your number?"

"I think they were uninterested as opposed to scared."

He ran his gaze up and down her, and the temperature in the room shot up a couple of degrees. "Doubtful," he said. "Did you recite all the rules to them? Quote the dating handbook?"

"Oh, so you're saying it's my personality. Maybe I should've turned on the charm and told them the only first down they'd ever make was shoving their heads up their asses."

He huffed a laugh. "Hey, if you're into that type of kinky stuff, go right ahead."

She felt herself blush, and with her pale skin, there was no chance he wouldn't notice. "I'm…that's inappropriate. I'd never discuss… Pursuant to section three of the handbook, any discussion that would make fellow employees uncomfortable is to be avoided."

"Jeez. What were you, raised by robots?"

"Nuns," she said. "And a gambler father who inadvertently taught me that it was much safer to follow the rules." The nuns comment was an oversimplification, but he'd stabbed at a raw spot.

A flicker of some sort of realization, along with a hint of pity, flashed through his features, and she cursed herself for reacting too strongly, the same way she had over the Vegas suggestion he'd made earlier. She was revealing too much, things she was usually so much better at keeping in the vault.

Lance held up his hands. "I don't want to have to file any more paperwork than I already do, so I'm officially surrendering on this. That doesn't require any special forms, does it?" He patted his pockets. "I seem to have misplaced my white flag."

"Ha-ha. And don't tempt me, because I could totally draw up a surrender form, one long enough it'd make you cry before you got to the end of it to date and sign."

"Of that I have no doubt. Just plenty of fear." He gave her a teasing smile, one that reanimated the long-dead butterflies in her stomach. Solidarity butterflies aided by appreciation over the fact that he'd let the subject drop, that was all. "Now, where was that résumé you wanted me to look at?"

She sorted through her stack of papers to the college coach she'd spotted in the mix. Usually the general manager would be heavily involved in this process, but considering they didn't currently have one…

Honestly, it felt nice that he was giving her input some weight. Although it added a bit of pressure, too. It was one thing to sit on her couch on Sunday afternoons and the occasional weekday evening and yell that she could've done a better coaching job, but it was another thing to actually help pick who would be making the hard calls.

Lance's lips moved as his gaze skimmed down Sean Bryant's résumé. It was kinda cute how he muttered to himself as he read—in a *buddy ol' pal* way. Not in a *dang, his lips are rather sexy and I like the way they move* way. Just to be clear.

"I assume you already read through his résumé?"

She nodded.

"Thoughts?"

"He's a risk, no doubt about that. But he doesn't play it safe, either. Yeah, I read his résumé, but I've also seen the way he works magic from the sidelines. In the six years he's coached, his team has gone from one of the last in its division to one of the top."

"But is he ready for the pressure of an NFL team? I could see him as maybe an assistant coach, but I'm not sure it's a good idea to just toss him the reins of our runaway horse."

"Funny. Wild mustangs and all."

His forehead crinkled for a second before it smoothed. "Pun not intended." He sat back and ran his fingers across his jaw, and she forced her eyes to return to her screen so she wouldn't go and start thinking about his nice jawline.

Now her anxiety was kicking in, making her worry about how many times she'd overreacted this afternoon—he was going to think she was an overly sensitive mess. Not far from the truth sometimes, but *he* didn't need to know that. "Hey," she said, and he looked up, and she wished she would've said her piece without getting his attention on her first. "Sorry I sort of snapped about the dating thing. And the robot thing."

"I shouldn't have said that."

"Sometimes I think it would be easier to be a robot." A mirthless laugh slipped out. "A lot of guys have disappointed me, and admittedly, I wasn't trying very hard during the speed dating event. I mostly go along with my roommate's plans because it's what she wants. A relationship isn't even at the bottom of my priority list."

"I hear that. I've told my mom that I'm going to be far too busy to date, but obviously she doesn't get it."

"I do. Especially after working here. There are times when it's too crazy to think about anything else. Anyway, I just wanted to clear the air."

"Air cleared." A smile slowly spread across his face, a hint of mocking to it.

"Okay, now I'm going to get mad about being the brunt of whatever joke's going through your head."

"It's just...that chair is so big, and you're so little it almost swallows you right up."

"Yeah, because they're built for football players."

"I've known some big guys in my day, and even they wouldn't be able to fill one of those chairs."

"Well, you know what they say. Everything's bigger in Texas."

He laughed, and they were okay, and even better, she felt like they'd struck the right kind of balance. Friendly without going too far, the respectful vibe still there.

The clock at the top of her screen was blurry when she checked the time, the numbers letting her know how late it'd gotten. "My lunch barely counted as a lunch, and I need to go eat and get some sleep so we can cram in another long day tomorrow."

"I understand. I'll see you first thing in the morning."

She nodded.

"You might as well leave all of your stuff. The chair can certainly accommodate it, and then you won't have to lug it back in here."

Sure. It made sense when he put it like that, but the thought of another day working so closely with him tugged at her already fraying nerves.

But what could she say? Not only was he the boss, the close quarters situation would only be for one more day...

Chapter Five

Day two of nonstop forms, calls, and résumé sorting with Lance was coming to a close, and Charlotte was powering through what little reserves of caffeine and sugar from the cookie she had for lunch were left.

Lance's phone chimed with a text, and for a moment, it was dead silent. Then his sigh carried across the space, and he muttered something she didn't quite catch.

"Everything okay?" she asked, glancing up from her computer.

"My mom wants to know if I've heard from any of the women she gave my number to, and if so, what I thought. As if talking to someone on the phone for a few minutes would be enough to tell."

"With the right person, maybe it would be," she halfheartedly said, and Lance shot her a look packed with a heap of skepticism.

"You don't really believe that." Not a question.

Earlier he'd gotten another call from one of his mom's prospective hopefuls, and like yesterday he'd been polite but brief. Unlike the other women, this one hadn't gotten the hint and had rattled on and on while Lance kept pointing at the phone and Charlotte tried to bite back her laughter. It was the first time in her life she'd thought maybe she was lucky her dad only cared about her if he needed her to crunch numbers. Which was hardly fair now that he was semi-trying.

Finally, Lance had mouthed "help," and Charlotte had stood, clomped across the office as loudly as she could, and said, "Did you forget about the meeting? Everyone's waiting on you, and if you don't come now, the deal's going to fall through."

"No, I don't think a conversation with someone is enough to tell if you're compatible," she admitted. Thanks to experience, she knew hundreds of them weren't enough. Her last boyfriend had felt like her best chance at happily ever after, but after investing all that time and effort, he'd still wanted her more for what she could do for him than wanted her for her. "Believing in love at first sight—or first listen, as the case may be—and all that other fairy tale-type stuff is just setting yourself up for failure. It's like expecting a perfect season. Bad weather hits. People have off days. Players are injured."

He nodded. "And I'd way rather have even a good season than a great relationship right now. It's refreshing how much you get it."

Refreshing wasn't the word she'd pick, but it did sound better than jaded.

"If it's this bad now," Lance said, "I can't imagine how bad it's going to be once I get to the resort. She'll probably schedule a date a night, and I just don't have time for that. I don't have time for this week-long wedding madness as it is."

He began typing a reply, and Charlotte almost advised him to be nice but reminded herself it wasn't any of her business, and hopefully he already knew to be nice to his mother.

He lifted the stack of papers in front of him, the one she'd sorted from most to least qualified after disregarding the completely unqualified ones they'd received. "How long does it usually take to fill a position?" he asked a couple résumés in.

"Anywhere from a week to a month."

His disappointment and sense of urgency was palpable. "We need stability. I need this all wrapped up in a matter of a week—two at most. Which would still only give us a little over a week to get the new staff up to speed and working together by Draft Day."

"I'll do my best, but with you being gone, it's going to be tricky. I'm sure you'll be harder to reach with all the wedding festivities, and waiting for your input before I can add someone or cross them off the list is going to be super time consuming."

"Unless…" A lightbulb dinged on over his head, and she wasn't sure why it sent trepidation tiptoeing down her spine, but it definitely did.

"If you're gonna suggest we go recruit coaches, GMs, or players with solid contracts in place, it's a bad idea. There are rules and—"

"Come with me to my brother's wedding."

It took her a few seconds to rewind the conversation and sort through the words he'd actually said instead of the ones she'd expected. "Come again?"

He stood and circled the desk, stopping right in front of her. "You want this wrapped up as much as I do. Like you said, going back and forth over the phone is going to take extra time we don't have. And if you come with me as my plus one, my family will leave me alone about finding a date."

"Is this a joke? We haven't known each other long, and you don't strike me as a joking type of guy, but…if this is your attempt at a joke, I've gotta say you're not very good at them."

He pointed a finger at her, and she jerked, her head hitting the extra tall back of the chair. "*That's* the kind of brutal honesty I need. I also need the thing you did earlier, where you bailed me out of that conversation with the woman my mother told to call me."

"But won't the ref—or your mother in this instance—flag me for interference?"

He cracked a smile. "I can risk one penalty easier than I can risk hours and hours of my time being sucked away." His smile widened, and he reached out and nudged her knee. "See? When I make a joke, you can tell."

"Are you saying that was one?" she quipped, and he pressed his lips into a contemptuous line. It probably said something about her tired mental state that it caused an intoxicating zing instead of a surge of annoyance.

"Charlotte. I'm sincerely asking you to come with me. I'll even add a please if that's what it takes."

Professional lines are about to be blurred—abort, abort, abort. She put a hand to her chest. "I can't be your date for your brother's wedding, Mr. Quaid."

He made a face like he'd bit into a sour lemon. "*Mr. Quaid*?"

She stood, her heart beating too fast. She wanted to say she wasn't tempted, but she knew it was a bad idea, and more than that there were rules. Rules she'd stick to, even if he accused her of being a robot again. "Section three, under the seventh subheading about employee relations, 'while this policy does not prevent friendships or romantic relationships between coworkers, it does establish boundaries as to how relationships are conducted within the working environment.'"

"There you have it—it's fine."

"I'm not finished," she said, and she remained undeterred when he muttered "Of course you're not." "Individuals in managerial roles—AKA, me—and those with authority over others' terms and conditions of employment—AKA, you—are subject to more stringent requirements and are not to date their direct reports."

"Right, but I'm not asking for you to jump into a romantic relationship with me. I'm not even asking you on an official date. I'm asking you to attend a wedding with me so that we can get more work done."

Of course he wasn't asking her on a date—she'd never thought that, although he didn't have to make the idea sound so preposterous, especially since she didn't want to go out with him, either. There was something about the words "attending a wedding" that struck fear in her, though.

Family. All that time together. No break to build up her walls or space in general. Not to mention a big ceremony and several days of having to be "on" nonstop.

Then again, they really did need every spare hour they could get...

. . .

Charlotte blinked at him for what seemed like an eternity, pausing the hasty exit he was sure she'd been about to make—he would've let her, too, and he'd even backed up a step so she didn't feel trapped.

He realized what he'd proposed was a crazy idea. But he was also fully aware of how much he needed to accomplish these next few weeks. The wedding couldn't come at a worse time—again, not that he wasn't happy for his brother. He wanted Mitch to get started on his new life as much as he wanted to get started on his own new life. Ever since he'd been injured he'd felt stuck, and inheriting the team had lit a fire inside of him that he hadn't experienced in a long time.

"Given who your family is, won't it look bad for me to

come along?" she asked. "Everyone will assume it's a date even if it's not."

"I'll set them straight. Strictly business."

She bit her lip, and it gave him thoughts that were far from business minded. Was he jumping out of the frying pan right into the fire? Maybe. A trip where she'd be by his side, pushing up her glasses in that adorable way she did, always crossing her nice legs or biting her lip... Leaving every room smelling like that vanilla perfume he kept inhaling and holding in might also lead to temptations he knew better than to give in to.

Luckily, she was all about the rules. And because the team was his highest priority, he could smother his general attraction to her and focus on how much he needed her help. The past two and a half days had beyond proved that.

"Did my grandfather ever ask your advice on the team stuff?" he asked.

She shook her head. "While I did impress him with my stats knowledge during my initial interview, it was my passion for the team and my qualifications in the human resources field that won him over and eventually led to my promotions. He was very kind to me, but he was definitely in the old-school, *leave the football to the men, darlin'* club."

Lance closed the distance between them again so that he could look her in the eye. Even with her tall heels on, he had a good foot on her and ended up tipping his chin down. "You were underutilized."

"Giving me lines to get me to go to a wedding? I'm not sure that's allowed in the handbook, either."

"I notice you didn't cite a section."

"It's a bit of a gray area," she said, and he smiled.

"Those are my specialty." He wanted to reach for her hand, but he was afraid that'd do the opposite of assure her that he understood her boundaries. "It's not a line. If you hadn't been in my office yesterday, I might've offered the coaching position to Mulroney, and after watching highlights from more of the games he's coached, I just kept seeing how right you were."

"I appreciate that. And I do think I can help—my fantasy football league kills every year. I can't play an official one of course, conflict of interest and insider information and all. But even before I started working here, I knocked it out of the park, if I do say so myself."

"You've convinced me."

Her lips quirked up on one side. "I thought you were supposed to be convincing me."

He took a step closer, and that vanilla perfume hit him again. "I'm pretty sure I already did."

"Cocky much?"

"Confident. Like you said yesterday, high risk, high reward. Don't tell me you're going to play it safe."

"I want a raise," she said. "If I'm going to be consulting, too, it's only fair."

"Ballsy. I like it." He extended his hand. "Deal."

Instead of taking his hand like he'd expected, she only stared at it.

"We're also going to need to fill out some forms before we go—not a joke this time, just to be clear."

"For the love of God, woman, you love your forms."

She narrowed her eyes. "It's important to document everything and have the extra checks and balances. No surprises, we've followed the rules, and I don't have to call myself into my office—that'd just be super awkward."

He bit back a smile, thinking she was definitely better at the jokes than he was. "Fine. I'll sign whatever forms you want. Now, do we have a deal already?"

A slight jolt went through him as she finally slid her much smaller hand into his. "Deal."

Chapter Six

Over the weekend, Charlotte had tried to keep up with her inbox and had gone shopping for beachwear and a wedding-appropriate dress, because everything in her wardrobe was out of style or no longer fit or both.

When Lance had pulled up to her house in a silver Jaguar earlier this morning, she'd had a beat of panic where she asked herself what the hell she was doing. But she kept going back to that moment when he'd told her she'd been underutilized.

Over the years she'd often felt unappreciated, and for him to recognize there was more to her... Well, maybe it was a line and she was a sucker, but she was choosing optimism.

As they maneuvered out of the heart of the city, Lance still talking away on his earpiece, she had her second moment of doubting she should've come.

"Let me know what you find out," Lance said, and then he tapped his ear, disconnecting the call. He swerved around a car, and Charlotte braced a hand on the dash.

"Listen up, Edward Cullen. I'm sure you think highly of your reflexes, but I'd like my skin and bones to stay where they are, so if you're gonna keep taking calls and speeding, I'm gonna have to insist on driving."

"What did you call me?"

"Don't act like you don't know who Edward Cullen is."

"Does he play football? For which team?"

She burst out laughing. "Technically he plays baseball. In thunderstorms."

Lance glanced across the car at her. "You lost me."

"Never mind your lacking pop culture references—we have enough to work on right now, so those will have to wait. Basically, I'm offering to drive so you can take all your important calls without wrecking."

"*Pfft.* As if I'd wreck."

"I'll take 'famous last words people say before they wreck' for one hundred dollars, Alex."

"You say such weird things."

"Thank you," she said. "What it boils down to is that people think they're really great at multitasking, but they're really just half-assing everything."

"Half-assing? Let me get this straight, I can't tell my employees their heads are shoved up their asses or call what they've done to the organization a shit show, but you can tell me I'm half-assing stuff? Do I get to make a complaint to you about you now?"

"I'm not swearing *at you*, especially not in a derogatory way that'd violate section two of the handbook. Swearing is permissible when there's not a better word to describe a situation."

"I think you just know how to twist the rules so they don't apply to you."

She gave him an innocent smile and shrugged. "You have to know the rules to break them. And speeding applies to everyone, as I'm sure a cop will tell you if he pulls you over."

Lance eased off the accelerator. "There. Better?"

"Yes."

His phone rang, and she picked it up and read him the name on the screen, not to be intrusive but to be helpful with the not-wrecking thing.

"I'll call him back when we're in the air so I don't have to endure any more of your cryptic responses and lectures."

"I appreciate that." She really was trying not to be a backseat driver—or side seat driver, as it were, especially since he'd slowed down as requested—but wasn't he going to get over? She pushed her foot down on the nonexistent brake pedal on her side of the car and sat forward, unable to help herself. "You're going to miss the exit."

"I'm not."

"Okay, but you just did." She flopped back in her seat. This was why she should've driven—why she liked control. Guys always thought they knew the way, too stubborn to listen. Sure, she occasionally got disorientated enough to not remember which way was east or west, but at least she didn't miss giant exit signs with airplanes on them.

"Relax," Lance said, passing a car on the right when the left side was blocked by other cars, another show of thinking the rules of the road didn't apply to him. "We're going to the local airstrip, not the airport. I assumed you knew we'd be taking the company jet."

"For a private trip?" She bit her thumbnail. "That's way too fancy for me. I can just take a regular old airplane."

Lance turned off the freeway. "It'd take longer for me to book you a ticket through one of the airlines, then I'd get there way before you and have to wait, and I plan on using the time in the air to go through résumés—in other words, I'm planning on using our time in the jet for business. You're the one who made me sign a document that declared our arrangement was strictly business."

After searching through the many forms stored in her

laptop, she'd revised the consensual romance in the workplace agreement. Even though there was no romance, it was the closest fit. She'd ended up titling it the Wedding Deal.

There was verbiage about recognizing that they'd entered into an agreement where she was his plus one for a wedding in a strictly business capacity, where she'd be in close proximity during the festivities for the purposes of consulting and performing her work duties. There was a section about not engaging in public displays of affection that would create an uncomfortable work environment for others, and while it didn't apply, it felt wrong to completely delete the rest of the form. It also stated they'd act professionally toward each other at all times, even after the—she'd changed "relationship" to "work trip agreement"—had ended.

She'd even notarized it and made Lance a copy. Not that he'd appreciated it. He'd jammed it into his desk drawer, most likely never to be seen again. Still, it made her feel better.

As they pulled up to a hangar, those better vibes were quickly dissipating. "Don't tell me *you're* flying us there."

Lance slid his sunglasses into his shirt pocket and gave her a sidelong look. "Will you relax?"

"Depends on if you're pretending you're also a pilot."

His signature *you're exhausting* sigh carried across the space. "While I do have my pilot's license, we also contract with several qualified pilots, and I plan on working while we're in the air." A mischievous gleam entered those blue eyes. "But if there's an emergency, I'll be ready to take the controls and fly us to safety."

"So reassuring," she muttered, and he laughed.

Charlotte began gathering her purse and extra bag, and somewhere between picking them off the floor and checking for her sunglasses, Lance had rounded the hood and opened the door. He extended a hand.

"While I appreciate you opening my door, it feels too

relationship-y. Would you do the same for a male consultant?"

"For the love…" He grabbed her hand and tugged her to her feet. "You're going to meet my Southern mother, who raised me to be a gentleman and would skin me alive if I didn't open the door for a woman, so get used to it."

She could feel her features wrinkling into an expression that would've earned her a remark about *getting stuck that way* when she was a kid. "You're so grumpy this morning. Did you not get enough coffee?"

"*Me?*" he asked, exasperation filling the word. "You're telling me how to drive and how you don't want me flying the plane and questioning every damn move." He popped open the trunk and reached for her suitcase. "So if I'm grumpy, it's because you're driving me crazy."

Her mouth dropped. "Excuse me for being cautious."

"You told me the other day that there was a problem with being too cautious." He set his suitcase on the tarmac next to hers.

"Yeah, for a coach. Not for my life."

A low grumble sounded in the back of his throat, and she wondered again if this was a bad idea. Somehow over the weekend she'd forgotten how much he tested her patience. They managed to get along for the most part while going through résumés and discussing stats, but the little between moments…they clashed a lot.

"Maybe this is a bad idea," she said. "I don't want to create drama at your brother's wedding."

"Then stop being dramatic."

She gritted her teeth. "Then stop being a bossy ass." Yep. In this situation, there was no other word for it, and if he filed an official complaint with HR, she'd simply judge it was completely justified.

Lance opened his mouth like he was going to snap at her, but then he took a deep breath and slowly let it out.

"Charlotte dear—"

"Terms of endearment are a little close to crossing a line and hardly fall in the super-professional range." It just sort of popped out, her frustration and nerves taking the wheel. Part of her wanted to push hard enough for him to tell her never mind, he'd simply go to his brother's wedding himself.

Lance lowered his voice, and it had a deadly calm edge to it. "Hey, human resources manager person."

She hitched her chin. "Jokes on you. I think that's perfectly appropriate."

"Get your perfectly appropriate ass—*self* on that plane," he said, and she reached for the handle of her suitcase. He grabbed it before she could and started toward the plane, striding so fast with his long legs that she practically had to run in her heels to keep up.

Apparently this truly was happening. At least it was okay to curse a lot in her head.

• • •

Lance ducked inside the plane and guided the suitcases into the bins so they wouldn't roll around during the flight. Admittedly, he'd also wondered if this trip with Charlotte was a bad idea. It was like the more used to each other they got, the more they meshed on discussing football—and the more they clashed on everything else.

He'd never met anyone so by the book, and his mom could—and often did—quote Bible verses at him. He wasn't kidding when he said she'd be appalled if he didn't open doors and act like a gentleman, either.

With everything situated, he turned to make sure Charlotte had followed him on the plane instead of stormed away—to where, he had no idea. Not like there was anywhere to go. Unless she drove off in his car, which he wouldn't put past her.

No, that'd be too close to stealing, so I'm probably safe.

Her dark eyebrows arched as she took in the cushy interior, a bit of an Alice-in-Wonderland awe on her face. He'd been born into money, and while he tried to stop and be grateful, he sometimes forgot how things that were ordinary to him were extraordinary to other people.

Charlotte smoothed her hands down the form-fitting floral dress she had on. He didn't understand the big belt, since it clearly didn't hold up anything, but it did accentuate her waist and the flare of her hips. Today her shiny brown hair hung in loose waves, and the cool air had pinked her cheeks, adding to the stunned innocent look.

The pilot stepped out of the cockpit, and Lance told him hello and introduced him to Charlotte.

"Charlotte's a bit nervous—she's never been on a smaller plane like this."

She shot him a scowl, and then the red lips that matched the roses on her skirt curved up as she turned to the pilot. "It was more that I was nervous when I thought *he* was flying us there. And I've been on one of those little prop planes before. It was stormy and super bumpy, and I had to grab the puke bag out of the seat in front of me, but luckily I didn't have to use it and…" A nervous giggle came out. "Okay, now I'm feeling a bit nervous."

"You're in good hands, Miss," the pilot said, giving her a wide grin. While Lance wanted her to feel safe, he experienced that slight pinch in his gut again, the same one he'd felt when Foster had been on speaker and she'd so happily talked to him.

She's my *strictly business plus one.*

"Wheels up in ten," the pilot said, and Charlotte walked past Lance to check out the rest of the plane. He, in turn, took the opportunity to check out the back of her outfit. Her sky-high heels emphasized her ass and her calves, and the straps around her ankles made his fingers ache to unbuckle them.

For a rule follower, she was dangerously sexy, something he definitely shouldn't be thinking about.

And reason number two why this might be a bad idea rears its ugly head.

But they needed to work, and with his brother getting married, Mom's pushing for him to settle down had dialed up into the obsessive range. Charlotte would make a good buffer, and she was a safe one at that—not only was she as uninterested in a relationship as he was, she was so set on not crossing the lines that he couldn't even sarcastically call her "dear" or open her door for her without getting a lecture.

The pilot announced they were about to take off, and Charlotte rushed over to the seat next to his. She fumbled with the seatbelt for a few seconds and exhaled as soon as she finally got it secured in place. She glanced around, her eyebrows drawing together—they did this cute upturned thing in the middle that he'd never seen before, and now he was studying her eyebrows?

Snap out of it, Quaid.

He rested his arms on the cream-colored leather. "What's wrong?" he asked when Charlotte continued to fidget. "Looking for a puke bag?"

"No." She wrinkled her nose. "Do they have them?"

Yeah. This flight might be a mistake. He needed her next to him so they could go through résumés, but he wasn't sure getting barfed on was the best way to start off their trip. Strike that—he was sure. "Under the seat."

She bent and studied the underside, and then popped up, her hair halfway over her face. "I don't think I'll need them." She fixed her hair, tucking it behind her ears. "I'm just…"

"I'd say *a bit nervous*, but I got in trouble for saying that earlier."

She fired a dirty look at him. "I didn't want everyone to know."

"Me and the pilot are everyone?"

"In this plane, yeah."

He covered his smile with the back of his hand, sure it'd get him in trouble, too. The whine of the engine grew louder, and her green eyes widened to the point he worried they might pop out of her head like some kind of deranged cartoon character.

"I just hate the takeoff part. And the landing part. Even in big planes." Her fingers curled around the armrests. "Usually it helps for me to see Goliath. I wish on him, which I know is weird, but it's my process."

"Goliath? Does he also play baseball in the rain?"

Another dirty look—at this rate, she'd set a record by the time they arrived in North Carolina. "The horse at the airport? The giant statue with the glowing eyes? I call him Goliath, and I know a whole bunch of people want to remove him because they think he looks demonic, but I like that he looks all badass. It makes me think of what the Mustangs used to be. How they could be again."

He vaguely recalled a horse statue in the familiar Mustangs red and black colors but hadn't ever paid much attention.

"I'll be fine once we're in the air." Her breaths came quicker and quicker, and she winced as the plane rolled into motion. "Just consider this my ten-minute break, okay?"

"Okay, but I'm timing you," he said, twisting his wrist like he was checking his watch. She didn't laugh, though, and her skin paled.

It was no fun to tease her if she crossed into freaked-out territory.

The plane quickly gained speed as they accelerated down the runway, and her grimace grew. Unable to help himself, he gently placed his hand over hers, readying himself for a lecture on how it wasn't professional, and then he'd get to discover which section of the handbook it violated.

She lifted her hand and he thought, *There's the brush-off I expected*. But she simply twisted her wrist so their palms met. Then she squeezed his hand so hard that if it were back in the day, taking a flight before a big game, he'd worry he wouldn't be able to throw the football.

Since those days were long behind him, and he found he liked being her lifeline, he squeezed back. He even decided to pretend not to hear the tiny squeal she made as they lifted into the air.

Chapter Seven

The giant window in the hotel room was a huge distraction, one Charlotte was having more and more trouble not focusing on. The blue sky went on forever, water lapped the sandy shore, and the sun shone on the people who occasionally wandered past, all of them looking happy and perfectly at peace with the world.

She and Lance had worked through the flight and arrived at the opulent hotel about two hours ago, only to discover her room wasn't quite ready yet. They'd ordered lunch and set up camp in his suite, which had a large front area and a door to the bedroom that made her feel much better about using the space as a temporary office.

Finally, she couldn't stand it anymore. "It's my job to make sure you get the breaks required by labor laws."

Lance barely glanced up at her, his gaze immediately drifting back to the papers in his hands. For a second or two, she got caught up staring at the big hands and long fingers that'd wrapped around her palm as they'd been lifting off from San Antonio. She'd grabbed his hand right before landing, too. It was okay, she told herself, because she would've grabbed a stranger's hand on the plane as well—had done that before.

She supposed now that she'd experienced the brush of his skin, callused from years of holding and throwing a football, it didn't matter how many times she touched it, as long as she didn't linger. She ripped the papers from his grasp, gripped his hand, and tugged.

He didn't budge, the jerk.

"Come…on." The grunt that came out as she tugged again was extra attractive, so good thing she didn't care about being attractive for her boss. "I demand a fifteen-minute break. I've never touched this side of the ocean."

"The ocean has sides?" Finally, he stopped fighting and let her pull him up.

"Totally. Only pretentious people call them coasts."

He laughed, low and deep, and a swirl went through her gut. Since she'd noticed the accidental reaction, she forced herself to drop his hand. Mission achieved and all that, so any longer would've been lingering anyway, and she absolutely wasn't going to let herself do that. To further keep herself on track, she rushed over to the patio door and slid it open. Ocean-scented air hit her, the breeze swirling her hair around her face. So much for the time she'd spent with her straightener this morning—the humidity was already bringing out the wave, and soon it'd be on the frizzy side.

"You're lucky you're pretty, ocean," she mumbled.

"What?" Lance asked from right behind her, and she jumped. He'd moved faster than she realized, and apparently he didn't make any noise when he walked. Good to know, although she wasn't sure why, and her overactive thoughts only proved how much she needed a mini-break.

"Nothing. Come on."

"Don't you want to change first?"

"I'm afraid my boss would subtract the minutes from my break."

He shook his head, but a smile spread across his face. "This from the woman who's constantly spouting rules."

"Not for the next fifteen minutes," she said, unbuckling her shoes and kicking them aside. Her skirt kept her from moving as fast as she would've liked, but she managed to take the steps down to the beach without tripping, and then her toes were digging into the warm sand.

Stress melted off her as she inhaled the salty air, her cares and worries drifting somewhere far away, to be dealt with later. She closed her eyes and tipped her face to the sun.

She felt Lance step up next to her, and having her eyes closed made other things about him stand out. That hint of rich cedar cologne mixing in with the breeze, the way his hulking presence thinned the oxygen surrounding her—or maybe that was because she was at sea level.

Wait. Air got thinner the higher the elevation. And it wasn't exactly a huge change from Texas. Whatever. She was sure there was some type of science to explain it.

"You can go ahead and say it," she said, cracking open her eyes. "This was a good idea." She craned her neck to peer up at his face. Without her shoes, he was that much taller now, practically dwarfing her like the chairs in his office. His dark hair was too short to be affected by the wind, but the sun played on the planes of his face, highlighting the slope of his nose and the way his scruff accentuated his lips.

The trick on this trip wouldn't be ignoring the way he looked—she'd already discovered that was impossible. But more accepting he was beautiful in a rugged, devastating sort of way that made her ovaries react. The important thing was overruling them with her brain. To help with that, she put extra space between them, moving toward the frothy waves that were calling her name.

"Eep, it's a bit cooler than I expected. Refreshing, but I have goose bumps now." Usually she didn't go down to the Gulf of Mexico to play in the water until the summer. "Guess I'm going to have to wiggle around to keep myself warm." She hiked up her skirt a few inches and spun, and Lance moved closer, the hint of a smile on his lips.

The smile didn't fully catch, though, which meant he still wasn't letting go of his work thoughts—not getting the break they both needed. So she did what any logical person would do and kicked a stream of water at him.

He dodged out of the way, dang it, and flashed her a reprimanding look.

She kicked harder, the water hitting his legs this time. A laugh spilled out of her, so loud she nearly startled herself. It'd been a long time since she'd laughed that loud.

He stepped into the oncoming tide, the water drifting up to mid-calf range and lapping at his rolled-up pants—they were both going to be wet by the end of this, but she couldn't bring herself to care. Why travel all the way to the beach if they weren't going to get a few minutes of ocean and sun?

The bikini she'd thrown in her suitcase on a whim needed to be broken out and worn, in theory. Wearing it was another story, especially if she thought about wearing it in front of her boss. *Maybe I should've bought a one-piece.*

Too late now.

Lance pushed up his sleeves a few more inches, exposing more of his forearms to the sun and her disobedient eyes. "It seems you're assuming that as a former quarterback, I don't know how to tackle. If you want to find out how good I am at it, go ahead and kick more water at me."

"Tackling definitely breaches section two of the handbook," she said with a grin, and then she swung her foot through the water, sending another stream at him.

He lunged for her, and she squealed, the same way

she'd accidentally done as they'd taken off in the plane. Her dang skirt kept her legs bound together, and she wobbled. Her stomach dropped as she flung out her arms, her hands searching for purchase.

Lance snagged her wrist and steadied her.

Water seeped into her skirt, the wave soaking the fabric before the tide took the swell away.

"Don't tackle me, okay?" she said, her eyes imploring his.

"Like you stopped splashing me?"

"You can splash me."

He leaned down like he was going to cup the water, and she threw up her hands. "No, wait!"

"That's what I thought."

She laughed again, happiness floating through her as she stared at him. Regardless of whether or not he would admit it, she could see his shoulders were looser, and the corners of his eyes crinkled with his smile. Another, stronger wave crashed into them, and she gripped his biceps to keep her legs from getting swept out from under her, gasping as the water hit high on her thighs. "I got a little wetter than I meant to."

"I'm sure there's a section of the handbook that would advise me against turning that into an innuendo and delivering a line about how that happens a lot when women are around me."

A combination of embarrassment and surprise twisted through her, but she covered it the best she could and rolled her eyes. She carefully removed her hands from the biceps she couldn't help noticing were quite firm. "Thank you for not tackling me or letting me fall. This outfit isn't really meant for swimming."

"Hey, I suggested we change."

"I was trying to save time." A piece of hair stuck to her lip gloss, and she swiped at it—or what she thought was it. "And patience isn't exactly my strong suit."

"No," he said, putting way too much fake shock into it.

"I'm going to splash you again." She took another swipe at the stubborn strand of hair stuck to her lip, but she couldn't find where it was coming from and—

Lance reached out and swept it off her face. His fingers brushed the shell of her ear as he tucked the hair behind it, and in a low, challenging voice, he said, "Bring it."

A shock of awareness traveled down her spine, and she was caught in his gaze, unable to look away.

"Lance? Is that you?"

His spine straightened, and he dropped his hand like she was a hot coal that'd burned him. A group of people was coming toward them, a lean dark-haired woman at the front of the crowd.

Lance made his way toward the shore, and she followed. As they neared the group, the woman's sharp eyes moved from him to Charlotte. Instinctually, she wanted to wrap herself around his arm and use him as a shield, but she knew that'd give everyone the wrong idea.

The woman threw her arms around Lance and squeezed him tight. "How long have you been here? And why didn't you text to say you'd arrived already?" Her features softened as she peered over Lance's shoulder at Charlotte. "And who is this beautiful woman by your side?"

"We haven't been here long," Lance said, giving his mom a tight squeeze before breaking the hug and angling his head in Charlotte's direction. "Charlotte and I have been working since we checked in, but we decided to take a quick break and get some air."

"I'll bet," the guy in the group said. If she was the betting type—which she wasn't, for the record—she'd put her money on the dark-haired guy being Lance's brother and the groom-to-be. He stepped forward, and they exchanged a bro-hug. Then he gave the woman holding his brother's hand a quick hug before turning to the couple with two young boys and embracing the female in their group, who also had dark hair and matching blue eyes.

He squatted to talk to the boys, and Charlotte couldn't help grinning as they called him Uncle Lance and immediately began regaling him with stories of seagulls and sand castles.

Lance straightened and made introductions, confirming the group was comprised of his mom, Maribelle; his brother, Mitch, and fiancée, Stacy; as well as his sister, Taylor, her husband, and his two nephews, Aaron and Austin. "...and this is Charlotte James, my *business associate*. Charlotte is the Mustangs' human resources director. I tripled her workload by shaking everything up, so I figured the least I could do was bring her along to the beach where she could get in some sunshine and catch a few waves while we worked."

"Lovely to meet you," Maribelle said. Charlotte extended a hand, but the woman made a *pshaw* noise and pulled her into a hug. "We're a family of huggers."

Charlotte gave Lance a teasing glance. "I never would've guessed."

"That's because you have rules against everything," he muttered so just she could hear, and she barely resisted sticking her tongue out at him.

"You both are joining us for dinner, right?" Maribelle asked, her expression all expectant.

"Oh," Charlotte said, panic surging forward and abrading her senses. "I've got a lot of work to do, and I don't want to interrupt your family plans."

"Nonsense. Tell your boss to give you the night off." Maribelle patted Lance's chest. "Dinner's at Basnight's at six o'clock. It wasn't easy to get reservations for such a large group, so don't be late."

Well that was that. Apparently Charlotte would be having dinner with Lance's entire family.

Chapter Eight

At the soft knock, Lance crossed the living room area of his suite and swung open the door.

His breath caught as he took in Charlotte, her hair pinned up in one of those twisty things women did. Her dress was black and came all the way up to the neck, but her sleeves were sheer, and there was something really hot about that. He still couldn't believe what she'd said about the guys she'd met at the speed dating event, and how they weren't interested in her. Did she not realize she was beautiful? Not that she'd allow him to tell her, because it'd break the rules.

To keep himself from blurting out something he shouldn't, he focused on finishing up the knot in his tie. "You could've just used the key I gave you instead of having to knock. This is our office for the time being."

"Yeah, but it's different since our actual office doesn't usually have a bedroom on one side, and there's not a possibility of me walking in on you changing."

"I could change in my office in the city."

"Which is why I'll knock on *both* your office doors before

entering," she said, a self-satisfied smirk to her lips, as if she'd proven her point.

He strode over to the table to grab his wallet. "How's your room?"

"Exceptionally nice. I sort of feel like I don't belong there—maybe you should've booked me at a different, less fancy hotel. Or do they have a room in the basement or something? I'd feel more at home there."

He scrunched up his forehead and stared at her, trying to figure out whether or not she was joking. Maybe a little bit, but he got the feeling she truly wasn't that comfortable with being treated well, and that scraped a nerve. Why did she always downplay what she did, how she looked, what she deserved? "Between all the long hours and being willing to come along on this trip, you deserve that and then some."

"Thank you." She reached up and rubbed the side of her neck. "I didn't mean to interrupt your family time, either. If you need a break from me, just say the word and I can make myself scarce."

"The whole point of you coming along—besides getting all our work done—is so my mom can't play matchmaker. I don't have time for that nonsense. Not the matchmaking, not the dating. None of it. So I'm going to need you by my side at family functions, too."

"Oh, so I'm your beard?" she asked with a laugh, way too amused at herself.

"Funny." He ran a hand across his jaw. "I've already got a beard. One my mom will probably tell me I need to shave before the wedding."

Charlotte took a few steps closer and examined him. "It's a nice beard. It suits you."

"Oh, hey. An actual compliment."

"Compliments aren't against the rules," she quickly said.

He couldn't quite figure her out. Most of the time she was

the uptight rule follower—and spouter—but there were these moments she'd suddenly be surprisingly laid-back. Like on the beach earlier when she'd been laughing and kicking water at him, her hair swirling around her smiling face.

It'd caused an oddly pleasant tightening sensation inside his chest, and he wasn't sure if he was experiencing residual affection or if he was softening toward her in general. It was like the ocean water had swept away some of her seriousness and revealed a hidden side to her—the same side that wore those tights and heels. "Noted," he said. "You ready?"

She nodded, and without thinking, he lifted his hand to put it on her lower back as they exited the room. Last second he dropped it, sure she'd take issue with it. As he pulled the door closed behind them, he remembered the phone call he'd taken right before she'd shown up.

"I made a few inquiries about Coach Bryant and have decided to conduct a phone interview with him for the head coach position. Do you want to be on the call, too?"

Her eyes lit up. "Yes, that'd be awesome." The excitement faded, and two creases formed between her eyebrows. "Unless you think... I know there have been some big changes and even a few female coaches signing with NFL teams, but there's still a lot of pushback. The good old boys' club isn't exactly open to a woman weighing in, and even though he's on the younger side, I'm not sure what camp he falls into. What if the fact that I'm part of the interview process makes him decide not to take the job?"

"Then screw him. I don't want someone like that on my team."

Utter astonishment flickered across her features.

He meant it. If someone was stupid enough not to take a job because of that, he didn't want to work with him. He wanted open-minded people. People willing to shake things up enough to take a losing team to one they could all be proud of.

"That means a lot," she said, her voice soft.

And that damn tightening sensation went through his chest again.

· · ·

Charlotte watched Lance's family interact with each other, smiling as they jibbed and reminisced and caught up on each other's lives. While the tablecloths in the private room they'd reserved were white linen, and there were candles—that quickly got blown out by Taylor when one of her sons reached for them—the room was far from quiet, the mood far from swanky.

Austin was five and did his best to behave, but clearly sitting still was akin to torture for him, while three-year-old Aaron needed constant appeasing. He kept demanding more drink or Goldfish crackers, standing on his chair to announce his wishes so the entire room could hear.

Taylor and her husband, Scott, would be in the middle of a sentence one minute, then shifting gears to mommy and daddy mode the next. Maribelle, Lance's father, Chuck, and Mitch and Lance pitched in as if it were second nature, asking the boys a question that drew their attention and made them forget how restless they'd been moments ago.

Charlotte had always wondered what it'd be like to have a big family. The raised-by-nuns retort she'd made to Lance seemed a little too true at times.

Her mom passed away when Charlotte was ten, and Dad had pulled her from her familiar school and enrolled her in the Catholic school right next to the college campus where he coached football. Even though they weren't exactly Catholic—apparently Grandma James was, and that counted. That and paying tuition and following the rules.

Dad was forever late to pick her up, so she'd end up sitting in the cathedral with one of the few nuns on the staff. Sister Margaret was super strict and put Charlotte to work, because "idle hands are the devil's workshop."

If she didn't do a job 100 percent perfect, Sister Margaret would make her do it again. If she stepped out of line, the doled-out punishments were harsh. Charlotte quickly learned that the easiest way to avoid getting in trouble was to follow the rules to the letter.

It wasn't all bad, though. She managed to make a handful of friends, and occasionally Sister Agnes would be at the cathedral instead. She mothered Charlotte, showed her the meaning of charity, and kept her hopeful by telling her that one day she'd look back and see how much she'd learned and how strong it'd made her.

That was what she clung to when Dad only paid attention to her as it suited his whims. When she could finally drive herself home and constantly arrived to find it empty.

Even when he came home, it still felt empty.

A strange sort of longing wound through her as she watched Lance's family interact so easily. Every word, every gesture showed how much they cared about each other, no strings attached.

It's okay. I have Shannon. Her roommate had become her support system these past six months, and she still had Dad, along with her hopes of repairing their strained relationship. Surely he'd be easier to get through to after he finished treatment for his gambling addiction, too.

"Charlotte, you look so familiar," Maribelle said, pulling her out of her thoughts. Lance's mother was seated opposite her, her husband on one side and Aaron's booster seat on the other. "Were you at my father's funeral?"

"Yes, I was. Mr. Price was a great boss, and I'm so sorry for your loss." She should've said something sooner, but she'd been so caught up in the buzz and all the people.

"Thank you, dear." Unshed tears glistened in her eyes, and her husband wrapped a supportive arm around her shoulders. She leaned into the support, but her gaze remained on Charlotte. "How long have you worked for the Mustangs?"

"Seven years." She glanced at Lance, who'd gone quiet at her side. His attention was on his mom, concern creasing his features.

Maribelle's smile turned watery. "I loved my father like crazy, but he gave his life to that team. He could get so cranky about football."

"Can't we all?" Charlotte automatically said, and she swore the room quieted. "Or…am I the only one?"

Snickers went around the table, and Lance said, "I think you're in a safe place when it comes to losing your mind over football."

"You should see how grouchy Mitch is when the team loses," Stacy chimed in. "I can hardly stand him." She quickly kissed her fiancé to soften her statement, and he lightly pinched her side, making her laugh.

Maribelle shook her head. "I tried to avoid it. Swore I wasn't going to marry anyone who liked the sport. But then I met Charles…" Her gaze turned adoring as it drifted to him. "And somehow ended up *married* to a football player. My dad never let me hear the end of it, either. Now I'm surrounded by football fanatics."

Guilty smiles bounced from one person's face to the other, and then an object flew through the air. Lance whipped up his hand and caught the projectile sippy cup, flinching when some of the liquid dripped out and hit his face.

"Future baller right there," Chuck said, laughing, while Taylor told him to stop encouraging him. She took the blue and yellow cup Lance extended her way and set it out of Aaron's reach. She explained to him that he wasn't getting it back until he stopped throwing it, but as soon as she turned to see what Austin needed, Chuck scooted it close enough that his grandson could pick it up.

When Taylor noticed, she asked who'd given him his cup, but the waiters came in with the food they'd ordered, saving anyone from having to rat out Chuck.

No wonder Lance wasn't a rule follower, although it was sorta endearing from Chuck—probably because she didn't have to cover him by law.

"You said you've been working for the Mustangs for seven years?" Chuck asked, and she nodded. "That's about the time the Mustangs started losing more than winning."

Charlotte sipped her water. "It almost sounds like you're blaming *me* for their losing streak."

His laugh held a whole heap of false innocence and mischief. "Of course not. Just making an observation and giving you a bad time."

"I'm afraid Lance has you beat in that area." She nudged him with her elbow. "He's made my job a bit of a challenge as of late."

Lance gave her a sidelong glance, as if to say *careful, I'm watching you.*

Undeterred and finding she enjoyed flipping the script and putting him in the hot seat, Charlotte leaned across the table, closer to his parents. "If you have any tips on how to best handle him and his moods, I'll happily take them."

"Oh, he's always been rather stubborn." Maribelle's fork clattered against the plate as she set it down. "When he puts his mind to something, there's not much changing it. Really he was a good kid for the most part. Naturally he got into trouble here and there…"

"Then I'd get grounded from football usually. Sorry, that won't work in your case," Lance said, draping his arm over the back of her chair. "I've already been grounded for three years." He said it lightly, but there was an edge to the words.

Her eyes met his, and he faked a smile, one so at odds with the easier, natural smiles that'd spread across his face since they'd arrived at the restaurant.

A pang went through Charlotte's chest on his behalf, and she opened her mouth, hoping the right words would come out.

"Hey, Mr. NFL's-most-eligible-bachelor, stop hogging the salt and pass it over here." His brother sighed, extra loud and dramatic. "I knew it'd go to his head, all the fame and fortune."

Lance picked up the salt shaker and hurled it, hard and fast. While Charlotte automatically winced, sure it'd hit Mitch in the nose and he'd end up with a black eye for his wedding, he caught it with a laugh.

"Boys!" Maribelle's voice echoed through the room. "What have I said about throwing stuff at the dinner table? And if you tell me that Aaron got to do it, I'll show you what I can do."

Both of her sons hung their heads as if ashamed, but then they started kicking each other under the table. The trash talking started, along with flung-out challenges that would evidently be settled at a football game on the beach tomorrow afternoon.

Charlotte had only seen hints of this more lighthearted version of Lance—really only the two or three minutes he spent on the phone with Foster and during their mini-water fight in the ocean. His family obviously brought it out more. It was probably something most families did, come to think of it.

"Is Charlotte going to play?" Mitch asked, and she nearly inhaled her bite of potatoes.

She coughed to dislodge the food and wheezed, "Oh, I don't *play* football. I just watch it."

"It's just a fun family and friends game," Stacy said. "No tackling—well, the guys sometimes get carried away. But we've got flags, and we always have a blast."

Everyone looked so encouraging that Charlotte hated to say no, but she didn't have a choice. "I was born without hand-eye coordination. Or any athletic ability at all."

"I'm sure that's not true," Lance said.

"Oh, I assure you it is."

He smiled down at her, a genuine smile at least, but this one sent a prickling across her skin.

"What?"

"You're going to play football with us tomorrow. When it comes to my passes, you don't even have to work to catch them. Just open up your arms and I'll put it right inside."

"Not if I duck and close my eyes as I throw my hands over my head."

He laughed as if she'd been telling a great joke. "Well, don't do that then."

"It's instinctual." Her voice pitched higher as she tried to convey that she wasn't kidding, and she definitely didn't want everyone to witness how truthful she was being about her lack of athleticism.

Lance dropped his arm and squeezed her hand under the table. "We'll work on it before the game. Trust me."

Dangerous words.

"If you want to see something really impressive," Lance said, raising his voice, "you should see what this girl can do when it comes to stats. Charlotte, tell my brother his football stats."

The prickling from a few seconds ago spread, along with a flush of heat. "I'm sure he knows them."

"Come on." Lance squeezed her hand again, making her realize they were practically holding hands, and she told herself it was a friendship sort of hand-holding so it was fine, even if it made her voice come out wobbly.

She rattled off the facts and figures that summarized his career so far, and when Mitch asked for one of his teammate's stats, she demonstrated her party trick again.

Lance twisted toward her and bent his head. "See. It's impressive."

Yeah, she'd impressed people with it before, and they'd used her for it. At least this time it was to advance her career and so that her football team could have a chance at improving, but still. "I feel like your dancing monkey."

He didn't move, his face so close to hers, and the apprehension her past had stirred up faded to the background. "You dance?" he asked.

"Nooo," she said with a laugh.

"Might have to teach you that, too. For the wedding."

She patted his shoulder. "Let's take it one impossible task at a time, champ."

His low laughter traveled across her skin and settled deep in her core. She had no idea how long she'd been grinning at Lance, her hand on his firm shoulder, when she realized his mother was watching them extra closely.

Maribelle was utterly beaming at them, and from that twinkle in her eye, Charlotte was pretty sure she had the completely wrong impression of their relationship.

Chapter Nine

Moonlight danced across Charlotte's twisted-up hair as she bent to remove her heels. She hooked them in her fingers and straightened, several inches shorter than when they'd exited the restaurant. "There. Much better."

He extended a hand. "Need me to carry your shoes?"

"I've got them," she said cheerily, practically bouncing on her feet. She said she wanted to walk along the beach for the few blocks to the hotel, and he'd offered to go with her. A walk sounded nice, the temperature was perfect, and he found that without forms at her disposal, he liked spending time with Charlotte. Especially the beach version who dug her toes into the sand and spun in a circle for no apparent reason, like she'd done earlier today and was doing so now.

She'd completely charmed his entire family at dinner. Dad liked to tease people, who often didn't get that he was joking, but Charlotte had given it right back. Add in the remarks about football and showing off her stats knowledge, and how easygoing she was about their big, boisterous group, and that couldn't have gone any better.

As he'd hugged Mom goodbye, she'd commented on how smart, kind, and beautiful Charlotte was.

In other words, Mom had decided they should be more than work associates. Which was good. It'd keep her off his back for a while, and Charlotte knew the truth. All in all, this might turn out even better than he'd expected.

"I love the beach. If I was rich, I'd buy a big house right here." She stopped mid-spin and faced him. "Why don't you have a house on the beach? Or *do* you?" She brought a hand up over her mouth. "Never mind. That's really none of my business."

"Yeah, getting way too personal there," he teased. "We lived inland growing up, and my parents still do, but we came to the beach fairly often. We visited my grandfather in Texas now and then, too, and he took us to the beaches down there if it was the off season."

She cocked her head. "Why didn't your mom and dad inherit the team?"

A more personal question than the beach house one. Not that he minded—she seemed a bit like a cat. Curious to a fault, although she tried to stifle it. "You heard my mom say she tried to stay away from the football world. She dealt with my dad doing all the required training and traveling for years, and when he retired, she talked nonstop about how done she was with it and how she was glad they could finally live their lives.

"When my grandfather drew up his will, he asked if she was sure she didn't want it. She said no and made him promise he wouldn't burden my dad with it, either."

A crinkle creased Charlotte's brow, assumedly because she was wondering the same thing he had when Mom let him know about the will and his role in it—how it'd be a burden. Yeah, he understood it involved a lot of big decisions and spending and taking in a lot of money. He didn't fully understand until the weight of it had fallen on him.

"My dad had a minor heart attack a while back," he explained. "It scared us all, and Mom doesn't want him to have extra stress. My ticker's in better condition."

"Because it's made of ice?" she asked, completing another spin.

"Yep, that's me. Cold, calculating."

She held out her arms as if she needed to recalibrate herself. Then she stepped up next to him. "So not true. I thought that at first when you were insulting everyone and firing them, but after seeing you with your family... I was just teasing, you know."

"I know."

"If anything, you've got a football where your heart should be."

"Weird."

She laughed, full out, the happy noise drifting across the breeze and smacking him square in the chest.

"How many drinks did you have at dinner?"

"None. I'm high on the beach. Plus, I get sorta punch drunk when I'm overly tired and hit my second wind. My body is like, okay, if you're not going to give me sleep, you get three extra doses of adrenaline and energy, and now you'll go super-speed until you crash."

My God, the thought of her on super-speed—it was both terrifying and exhilarating, and for some reason he wanted to experience more of it. "And how long does this normally last?"

She shrugged. "It's been a while since I've hit this point. An hour or so." She shimmied her hips to music only she could hear. Then she drifted closer to the wet sand, leaving tiny footprints next to his large ones.

"How tall are you without your shoes, anyway? Five feet?"

Her mouth dropped as if he'd delivered a major insult. "Five-two!"

"Oh, so sorry."

"Hey, those two inches are important."

"And in the shoes?" he asked, jerking his chin toward them.

"They add about four inches." She leaned closer. "I'm not sure we should talk about inches. It might lead to a place that'll get us in trouble with HR." She giggled, and he peered down at her, his amusement growing.

There was a thread of desire as well, but he was doing his best to ignore that. Or there'd be more inches of something else showing, and he'd end up in that trouble she mentioned.

She drifted close enough that their arms brushed. "Hey. About what I said earlier during dinner. Or I guess it was more what *you* said earlier." Her eyebrows lifted in the middle in that way they did when she was confused—he was also slightly confused, no clue what she was talking about. She had the most expressive eyebrows he'd ever seen, and suddenly he was thinking there was something sexy about them, and who knew eyebrows could be sexy? "What I'm trying to say is, I'm sorry about your knee surgery and that it ended a really impressive career."

He shrugged it off. "It's in the past."

"I know, but you said that thing about being grounded from it, and I can't imagine what it's like to lose something you love..."

"Yeah, what would you do if someone took away your handbook and forms?"

She narrowed her eyes. "Very funny. And you're trying to brush it off and act like it's nothing. I'll let you this time, but I sincerely hope you find some of that love again as you're rebuilding the Mustangs. Honestly, when I heard you were taking over, I thought you'd be a spoiled, entitled former player with a huge ego who didn't have a clue about how to run an entire team."

"Wow. Why don't you tell me what you really think?"

"That's why you kept me around, remember? I say it how it is. And I wasn't done yet, so hush."

Man, she was on one. He couldn't remember the last time someone told him to hush—he wondered if he'd lost his mind because it only made him want to hear what she'd say next that much more. Enough that he slowed his pace so they wouldn't reach the hotel before she could finish her possibly insulting thoughts.

"If we'd carried on the same way, we were just going to have another losing season. After seeing your vision for things and how you've made hard decisions... I think you're just what this team needs. Sometimes you have to tear it all down and start over." She bumped her shoulder into his and gave him a smile. "Even if it's made my job harder."

"Thank you, I appreciate that. Not so sure about the entitled ego part, but you got there eventually."

She laughed. "I was doing the tough love coaching thing. Tear you down"—she mimicked an explosion with her hands and then made a fist and pumped it once in the air—"then motivate and rebuild."

"Totally doing it wrong, so we're gonna have to work on it," he said, bumping her back and grinning at her wobble. She was so tiny and pretty, and yeah, he didn't expect this walk, yet it felt like exactly what he needed. "I do like that you always say *we*, not *the team*."

"That's because I'm a true fan. And as a fan who closely follows the Mustangs, I also think we have a lot of good players who are underutilized: Smitts, Crawford, and Carter to start."

"You might be right, and I'll take a look at them and their contracts. But what we need most besides an amazing head coach is a quarterback. A leader. Then, depending on who we choose, we figure out how best to use our number one draft pick. Or maybe that's what our pick should go to, but that gets tricky, too." Pressure built inside, gathering steam and spreading throughout his body. "We can't afford to waste it."

"Well, at least we've got one quarterback on our team." She poked his arm and shot him a grin. "I'm sure we'll find the right one for the field. Just might take some digging."

"And begging."

"And a lot of money," she said.

"And a lot of money," he echoed. That was another worry that only cranked up the stress level. That he'd make all these changes and spend millions of dollars and still lose. But he couldn't think like that, because that was a good way to end up defeated before they even started.

Their hotel loomed ahead, and he decided to shove his worries away for a few more minutes. They'd still be there when he arrived at his room. For now he was going to enjoy walking next to a woman in the moonlight, the waves crashing to his right.

"I like your family, by the way," she said. He wasn't sure how that was *by the way*, but he happily embraced the change in subject.

"They like you, too." His arm grazed hers again, and she sucked in a breath. Earlier tonight he'd squeezed her hand, the same way he'd done on the plane when she'd needed a hand to hold. His fingers itched to grab hold of it again, but he was sure she'd pull away. More than that, he shouldn't touch her more than necessary because it only made him want to touch her more.

She tucked a stray strand of hair behind her ear. "Your mom's getting the wrong impression of us, though."

"We can't control what other people think." Right now he couldn't seem to control what *he* was thinking. There was a tug between them, a push and pull like the tide that came and receded and then came back stronger and claimed a little more sand.

"Says the guy who's been in hot water with tabloids before for what they think." Her teeth sunk into her lip like she thought maybe she shouldn't have said it, but it was out there now.

Earlier in his career he'd often responded without thinking, the whiplash sensation of living and breathing the game to having to answer a barrage of agitating questions getting the best of him. "It took me years of repeatedly telling myself that I couldn't control what they thought to make peace with what they printed. Whether or not I only got the gig because of who my grandfather was, or if I was the hero or the whipping boy that week. And sure, sometimes when a reporter was in my face with a microphone, asking ridiculous questions after a game we lost, I temporarily forgot it and lost my cool."

The PR department and his coaches had both gotten on him. *Don't lash out at the reporters. Remain gracious no matter what they say.* And if he didn't talk to the press, he'd get fined. Slipping up in the post-game interviews hadn't been what landed him in hot water, though. It was the other part of his past he kept in a tightly locked box in the darkest corner of his mind. "Same with my personal life."

A raw mix of anger and old hurts churned through him. His ex had constantly talked to reporters, and then they'd want to confirm with him what she'd said. It put him in a tough spot. If he didn't corroborate what Sage had said, she'd be pissed, but he hadn't wanted them to analyze and rip apart his relationship like they did with the way he played ball. He also thought his relationship wasn't anyone's business. Sage wouldn't stop talking to them, though, and his relations with the press had turned especially ugly when the rumors about her cheating on him with a teammate had come out.

Even uglier when it turned out to be true. He'd threatened to rearrange a guy's face and shove his mic where the sun didn't shine, and every other reporter there had raced to print up everything they could about his horrible temper and how his knee injury had cost him more than just his career. There'd been jokes about how maybe he'd had one too many concussions, too—how maybe that was why he was too dumb to see what'd been happening right under his nose.

"I get that," Charlotte said. "I'm sure it's hard to have that added pressure to say the right thing after hard losses and to have your personal life splashed across the internet for entertainment, and I'm sorry I blurted that out without thinking."

"The past is always harder to outrun than we'd like."

"True that."

A chuckle slipped out. He doubted she had much of a shady past, considering she always followed the rules. "I'd also like to think I'm a different person than I was then." He was, but even that eligible bachelor article bothered him more than it should. Stupid tabloid rags. "So yeah. I'm back to my mantra of we can't control what other people think."

"Again, it's a solid idea and all…" She sighed. "I just hate to disappoint people—that's more what I meant with your mom and her getting the wrong idea. I've never had that family dynamic, and I like your family, so I don't want things to get messed up because of someone like me."

He dragged his finger lightly down her forearm, the back of her hand. "I'm guessing this has something to do with the raised-by-nuns and a gambler father."

She wrinkled her nose. "Maybe. I wasn't actually raised by nuns, for the record. After my mom passed away, I just went to Catholic school and spent a lot of time after school with a few. Mostly because my dad tended to forget he had a daughter. I always had to work so hard for his attention, and when he discovered what my brain could do with facts and figures, suddenly he wanted to spend more time with me. So I milked it and studied stats and percentages like my life depended on it. And if I helped, he also won more often, which left us both less stressed."

Lance frowned, his hand automatically curling around hers so she could hold on if she needed the support.

She faked a smile that looked completely wrong on her features. "It's not a big deal. Thanks to that and my freakishly good memory, I landed a job I love. Anyway, I was just thinking about family dynamics and—"

"That sucks. He sucks for making you feel that way."

She blinked at him and then slowly shook her head. "He… he's trying. Getting help and… Wow, this got real quick." She cleared her throat and increased her pace, pulling her hand from his grasp.

"Oh, look! There's my room." Her voice was too high, and her words had a flighty edge to them. "It'd be nice not to have to walk all the way to the door in the middle, but unlike your room, it doesn't have a fancy walkway, and I'll never be able to climb that balcony in this skirt."

"That tiny balcony? I could chuck you right over it."

She paused long enough to cast an eye roll at him from over her shoulder. "I'm not a football."

"I noticed," he said, his gaze running down her before he reined himself in. "Come on. I'll boost you."

She glanced around as if they were doing something illegal. Her shoes were tossed over the railing and landed with a *clunk*, and she reached for the rails.

He linked his fingers together to make a foothold, and she stepped into it. Halfway up, she was clearly rethinking the plan. "I'm not sure I can get over without flashing you, and this was a mistake."

"I'll avert my eyes. Just throw your other leg over."

A mix of squeaks and grunts came from her, and he forced himself to keep his eyes down. But then a whimpered "help" drifted down to him, and he looked up to see her stuck, the rail under her gut. She'd started laughing and couldn't push herself up—anyway, that seemed to be the problem.

"I'm going to have to shove your…backside."

"That'd violate section three of the handbook. Section four as well, actually."

"I'm pretty sure leaving you hanging on the balcony violates a couple of sections, and people are starting to give us odd looks."

"They are?" she squeaked, and he laughed. No one was really out, although there was a couple a few balconies over that undoubtedly thought they were attempting to break into the room—talk about the worst burglars ever.

He braced his hands on her nice round booty and gave her a firm shove, doing his best to keep his hands flat and in "helping" instead of "copping a feel" range.

She swung her legs over the railing and landed on the other side. Her skirt was hiked up on her thighs, and he told himself to avert his eyes again, but they didn't want to listen. His mouth went dry as she worked her skirt back into place. Then she peered down at him, and for some reason, it made him think of the horrible *Romeo and Juliet* production he was in during high school. He hadn't wanted the role of Romeo, but he was used to memorizing plays and therefore good at memorizing lines.

They were still emblazoned in his memory.

O, wilt thou leave me so unsatisfied? A douchey line by Romeo really, and one Lance wouldn't dare repeat, although he found he didn't want the night to end. He definitely felt unsatisfied at it having to.

"Can we pretend this never happened, and that I did the

reasonable thing and took the main door instead of saving myself another quarter mile of walking?"

"No way. I'm going to cherish the memory of the night you did something slightly inadvisable and climbed your own balcony. Maybe hang it over your head. Bring it up in meetings."

"Jerk," she said, but she said it lightly.

He almost made a joke about how it'd also be faster for him to come in through her balcony and walk to his room a few doors down. But that was courting trouble, and he figured if this night went on much longer, he'd land himself in a mess.

"Good night, Charlotte."

"Good night, Lance," she said. When he didn't move, she added, "Um, are you going to leave?"

"I want to make sure you can get into your room first. You've proven you're not the best at climbing—"

"Ah! In a dress."

"Which you're still wearing. So unless you plan on shedding it if you can't get into your room and have to climb back down, let's play it safe and make sure you're not locked out before I leave you without help."

She sighed extra loudly but swiveled her purse in front of her. She kept digging out different items and saying "not it, not it", and for someone so organized when it came to forms, evidently her purse was an unorganized disaster. "Found it."

She slid the card into the key slot, watched the light turn green, and then pushed open the balcony door. "I'm good."

"Until tomorrow, then. Bright and early, since we've got that football game and need to practice your catching skills at some point."

"Unless I don't play."

He backed away, his gaze still on her. "You're playing."

"Is that an order from my boss?"

"Yep. And don't give me some shit about how it's not part

of your job. Section six of the handbook clearly states that team-building drills are important to the work environment and morale, and all employees are required to take part in them."

She leaned over the railing and adamantly shook her head. "That's not what section six says."

"It will after I make a few changes to it."

"All the employees aren't here, so…"

"You're playing, Charlotte, so prepare to bring your A game." He turned around and walked toward his room before she could argue any further. Not that he didn't expect her to have a bullet-point presentation about it drawn up by tomorrow morning.

Chapter Ten

Charlotte had been on edge all day. For one, she'd climbed her balcony like some kind of lunatic last night, all to save a few measly minutes of being around Lance. Because she'd started to drop her walls. To drift closer to him. To reveal things she hadn't meant to reveal.

So naturally she'd hurdled a too-tall balcony in a skirt and ended up stuck enough that he'd had to put his hands on her butt to help her over the rail. While he'd done it as respectfully as anyone could when it came to palming your ass, it'd made her way too aware of the size of his hands and the strength of his arms.

Even this morning as they'd been working, she kept getting distracted by his rounded shoulders. The dark hair on his corded forearms. Their interim office smelled like him, too, all masculine and divine, and she'd spent the morning on pins and needles, purposely putting space between them.

Now they were preparing to play football, where there'd be no space. Bonus, it'd also probably end with her falling flat on her ass or in an ungraceful nosedive.

The fact that Lance had gone from buttoned up to buttoned down wasn't helping matters. The T-shirt and board shorts brought out his sporty side, and the Mustangs baseball hat managed to highlight his scruff even more.

He tossed the ball in the air and caught it, again and again, his movements precise yet second nature. No thought to the throw. The spin of the ball. The way it made those muscles she kept staring at stand out even more—the short-sleeved T-shirt could hardly contain his arms and pecs and *omigosh stop checking out his body.*

Several beachgoers were sprawled out on towels in scattered groups while others splashed and played in the waves. Families. Single people. Couples. Friends. People everywhere she looked. "So many witnesses."

She didn't realize she'd said it aloud until Lance glanced at her, a crooked grin on his face. "We've been out here for less than five minutes, and you're already contemplating killing me?"

"That implies I ever stopped."

He chuckled, juggled the football to his left hand, and then reached out and squeezed her shoulder. "Relax. We're gonna practice catching and throwing, and like we said last night, we're just gonna play for fun."

"You and your brother were making bets on who'd win. *Expensive* bets." It made her skin itch to think about the dollar amounts they'd thrown out. They were silly bets between brothers, but she'd been around her dad when he'd put a lot of money on the line and lost. As solid as her internal stats calculator was, occasionally players had an off game. Or weather or officials came into play—so many variables, not to mention that bitch, Lady Luck, or fate or karma or whatever you wanted to call it...

She'd been blamed for some of those losses. Thousands of dollars here and there, but then Dad would get up again.

He'd crave that next adrenaline rush and risk more. Her gut sank as she recalled being yelled at over a Super Bowl game he'd lost five figures on. Or so she'd thought, because they'd had a fight about the amount he was gambling.

Then he revealed it was *six* figures, and money he didn't have. His decision making turned from bad to worse, and she didn't want to think now about the snowball effect of that loss.

"Okay, so my brother and I are super competitive. But it's all in good fun, I swear."

A band formed around her lungs, growing tighter and tighter as the memories and pressure began slowly suffocating her. "What if you lose because of me?"

"Wow, now who's got the ego, thinking you can determine the entire outcome of the game?"

She fired a dirty look at him, which was starting to feel like her main form of communication with the guy, but after last night she couldn't throw her usual fire into it, and his grin made it clear he was far from scared. Every moment since they'd dipped their toes into the ocean—even their bickering—was starting to feel less tension filled and more... more.

He stepped a little closer, plenty of taunting creeping into the curve of his mouth. "Haven't you heard the no 'I' in team speech?"

She yanked the ball out of his hands and took a provoking step of her own. "Haven't you heard the one about the HR rep who spiked a football in her boss's face for being so frustrating?" She even cocked her arm as if she were going to follow through on her threat.

"With all these witnesses?" Another smug grin spread across his stupidly perfect face. "Think of the due diligence."

Well, what do you know? He is pretty good at the jokes.

"Also, your form's all wrong." He maneuvered behind

her and nudged her elbow down a few inches. "Think ninety degrees. If all your weight's on the front foot to start, you've already lost your momentum, so"—he gripped her hips and swiveled the right one back—"you want about seventy percent on the back leg, thirty on the front."

She set up, doing her best to ignore the way her blood rushed to his hand on her hip and focus on his instructions. "Take a second to aim, and when you throw, flip the weight distribution, going an extra ten or so percent on the forward leg."

Lance guided her arm forward in a practice throw, his chest bumping her shoulder as his breath warmed her temple. "Make sure to follow through."

A pleasant shiver tiptoed down her spine, and she forgot how to breathe.

Yeah, she'd forgotten how to do something vital to life, even with decades of practice, so she wasn't going to hold her breath on her follow-through magically improving.

Or apparently she was going to, but in an incognizant way that…man, he smelled good.

"Charlotte?"

"Hmm?" His instructions and the reason they were standing so close, his body wrapped around hers, came barreling back to her. "I mean, yeah. That makes sense. Aim, swivel, throw. I think I got it."

He stepped back to give her space, and she set up the way he'd showed her. The percentages on weight distribution helped—she was good at percentages. Silently chanting the things he'd told her in her mind, she hurtled the ball.

It didn't go far, although it was definitely one of her better throws. Never mind that she'd given up on the sports thing as soon as they stopped torturing her with it in PE class.

"Good," he said, and he retrieved the ball and had her try again.

"I'm not going to be throwing in the game, though, right?" Her second toss was better but still rather short in the yardage department. "I'd rather catch. Or better yet, just hold out my hands like I'm going to catch it while you throw to other people."

"Let's see what we've got to work with." Lance brushed the sand off the pigskin and fitted his pinky and ring finger between the laces. "I'll start with a gentle toss."

She lifted her arms, ducked her head, and squinted one eye closed. At the *are you kidding me* expression he gave her, she decided she should've closed both eyes—that way she wouldn't have to see the incredulity.

"Eyes open, chin up. I'll be gentle, I promise. All you've got to do is clamp your hands around the ball when it nears."

"Sure, it sounds easy, but—"

He tossed it, even though she still wasn't ready, and she automatically closed her hands around the football. It wobbled, but she managed to catch it with the help of her boobs. *Ouch.*

"See, I told you it didn't take any effort to catch my passes." The cockiness in his grin kicked it up a notch. "I'm just that good." He blew off his fingertips like one would blow the smoke off a gun after firing it, then he waggled them in a hand-it-over gesture. "Toss it back and we'll keep playing catch as we move farther and farther apart, until we figure out your range. If we have time, we'll practice a few basic plays."

• • •

Lance backed up, the football gripped tightly in his right hand as he surveyed the field—or beach, as it were. Charlotte had missed the two passes he'd thrown at her earlier in the game and had beat herself up after each time. He could probably wait for Jack, one of Mitch's teammates, and the other groomsmen on their team to run his route. She was wide open, though, and if she'd catch just one pass, it'd do wonders for her confidence. He cared more about that than winning the game, in spite of bets and bragging rights with his brother.

Crazy, but somehow true. He couldn't think about why exactly right now, nor did he want to.

Their eyes locked, and Charlotte's practically screamed *don't throw it to me*, her eyebrows punctuating the statement.

Just trust me, you've got this.

He lobbed the ball the five or so yards toward her, a gentle pass with extra arch to give her time to get under it.

She winced but kept her eyes open, her hands reached for the ball, and…

"I caught it!" Her mouth hung open, and she gaped at the ball like it was a foreign object she'd never laid eyes on before.

"*Run*," he shouted, and she seemed to realize they were in the middle of a game. She jolted into motion, and he rushed forward to help block as she sprinted toward the goal line.

Since there were no refs to call holding and all he cared about was getting Charlotte into the end zone, he fisted a handful of his brother's best friend's shirt, holding him at bay. Hunter managed to gain a step on him, dipped his shoulder, and shoved him back.

A few more steps and Charlotte would score.

Lance wasn't going to get to his brother in time to block, but as Mitch dived for her, she completed a beautiful dodge, pivot, and weave move he definitely hadn't taught her.

She crossed the line and slowly spun to face him, shock still written across her pretty face. She glanced at the ball in her hands again. Then she spiked it into the sand and started the cutest celebratory dance he'd ever seen.

"Oh yeah, oh yeah." Her hips shimmied back and forth,

her booty getting in on the action. "How much longer do I have till I get called for unsportsmanlike conduct?"

"Another sixty seconds at least," he said—mostly because he liked watching her dance. Liked the huge grin on her face and the way it made her cheeks stand out.

Warmth and pride mingled inside his chest.

The rest of their team came forward to offer high fives, including the bride-to-be, who joined in with her own set of celebratory dance moves. When they'd been forming teams and Stacy had said she wanted to be on his team as opposed to Mitch's, Lance had said, "Seems like that might cause a fight."

She'd replied with, "That's the point. Then we can have makeup sex after."

Lance's gaze had met Charlotte's across the huddle, his plan to roll his eyes and share a joke about it with her. *Couples, am I right?* But then he'd accidentally noticed her curves in that tiny tank top and thought about how long it'd been since he'd had sex, and suddenly he was ready to start a fight to find a way to make up. Only he knew that wouldn't be the end result with Charlotte.

After doling out high fives to the rest of the team, she was standing in front of him once again. It was his turn to properly congratulate her on the touchdown, only in this instance, he didn't know what was proper.

She surprised him by throwing her arms around his neck. "Thank you. I didn't want you to throw it to me, but that was really fun. Probably the only touchdown I'll ever make, too, so I don't even care if the other team gave it to me."

"No one gave that to you. You earned it." He hugged her tighter to him, basking in the feel of having her in his arms. "That pivot move was amazing."

She pulled back, her forehead bumping the brim of his baseball cap, that amazing smile of hers still curving her lips. The second their eyes met, a zip of electricity shot through him. Another current coursed through his body as she inhaled, her breasts pressing against his chest. Her smile wobbled, and she quickly dropped her arms.

She felt it, too.

She swiped the strands of hair that'd fallen out of her ponytail behind her ear. Then she punched his shoulder. "Thanks, coach."

He lightly punched her shoulder back. "Anytime, James."

As he'd hoped, her confidence grew from that completed play, and he was able to see her celebratory dance one more time before they called the game.

But as they walked back to the hotel, she stayed by Stacy's side, close enough that he wondered if she was avoiding being near him after that moment they'd had in the end zone.

If he was smart, he'd give her the space and follow her lead. He told himself it was good that one of them had self-restraint or self-preservation or whatever the hell it was.

Even as he was also cursing it and the distance between them.

That's it. From here on out, I'm going to shut those stray thoughts about her down.

They were finally getting along, and the business side was coming together. No need to ruin it all for a few days they'd both later regret.

Chapter Eleven

Right as Charlotte was contemplating if she should change into pajamas and watch some TV before crashing for the night, Stacy had texted to say they were hitting the resort's giant hot tub and that she should meet them there. After their football game on the beach, her muscles could use some heat and jets. Plus, she really liked Stacy and her two bridesmaids, Bridget and Grace. They'd taken her right in, and she wasn't quite ready to go to sleep anyway. She was still riding the high of doing better than expected this afternoon.

The good thing about basement level expectations was that something as simple as not falling on her face and managing to catch the ball during an official game—twice—was a win.

As she walked toward the bubbling water of the hot tub, her confidence wavered slightly. The other girls were so tall and beautiful and tan. They looked like they hit the gym on a regular basis, too.

Charlotte rarely saw the sun besides through her office window. She couldn't remember the last time she'd been to the gym, although she often walked to work, which was a good three miles there and back. Of course she usually grabbed a pastry on her way…

"Come on in," Stacy yelled, waving her toward the luminescent blue water. "It feels amazing."

Expelling a deep breath, Charlotte slipped out of her swimsuit cover-up. The halter top of her red and white polka dot bikini supported and hoisted the girls nicely, and the bottom had the mini-est of skirts, so in addition to helping to cover her generous hips, at least her butt cheeks weren't hanging out. She slipped into the water, hissing at the heat.

Immediately a pink drink with an umbrella was thrust into her hands.

On instinct, she nearly refused it. This was a work trip. But she was off the clock, and Lance wasn't here.

"Cheers!" Stacy lifted her cocktail, Bridget and Grace followed her lead, and Charlotte thought *what the hell*. They clinked glasses, and Charlotte fought off brain freeze as the slushy, heavy-on-the-rum drink slid down her throat.

"Wow, that's so strong it'll walk right into your cup," Charlotte said, and the girls laughed.

"I love your cute Texas twang," Stacy said.

"I don't have a twang." She gestured to the girls with her drink. "Y'all are the ones with accents."

"Not here in North Carolina, honey," Grace said, and they all laughed. Yes, she liked these girls a lot. Never before had she clicked with a group of women so quickly, and she wondered if it was because of the situation or the football connection or if it was because she was usually more reserved around new people.

The heat and jets were working magic on her muscles, and complete relaxation had just set in when Stacy sat up straighter. "Oh look. The guys are headed this way."

Charlotte's heart began beating faster as she froze in

place, too afraid to look. She hoped "the guys" didn't include Lance—or at least she tried to, but the amount of anticipation that whirred up at the thought of seeing him told a different story. It suddenly seemed like it'd been a long time since they talked, which was silly. After the game they'd retreated to their individual rooms, and since he had a lot of calls to return, she'd texted to say she might as well complete the paperwork she needed to. She'd given up asking him to fill out the termination forms and began typing in her own answers that she'd simply have him approve later.

The real reason she'd wanted to stay in her room, though, was because she'd hugged him without thinking today, and she needed a little distance to keep her head right. It always got so messy around him.

Finally, she dared a glance over her shoulder, and there he was, next to his brother. He was turned away from her, talking to Mitch as he ever-so-casually ripped off his T-shirt. Even in the dim light, she could see all the grooves and dips. The lean muscled body. The trail of dark hair disappearing into...

Yeah, not going there.

She sipped at her drink, cursing when a sucking noise came out after only one gulp. How dare it be empty when she needed it most! She chewed on the straw, way too aware of each step closer Lance took in her peripheral.

Stacy, Bridget, and Grace scooted aside as the guys stepped into the hot tub, and Charlotte noticed Lance's movements were a bit stiff as he climbed down the steps. He did a double take at her, so apparently he hadn't expected her to be here, either.

Mitch's gaze homed in on his fiancée, and a lovestruck grin spread across his face. "Thought we'd work out our muscles."

"Great minds think alike," she said, standing and giving

him a kiss. Apparently they'd already made up after the game, not that they'd actually had a fight. The love-buzz vibe coated the air around them, drifting over to Charlotte even as she willed it away. It was nice to see such a happy couple who were clearly crazy about each other, even if it also awoke a yearning she liked to pretend didn't exist.

Of course after the rearranging that'd happened to accommodate the guys, the only open space was to her right. As Lance slowly lowered himself next to her, she stared straight ahead. When she'd packed her swimsuit, she'd known that being in it around her boss was a possibility. But she figured it'd be more like a few towels away if he came out to the beach after she'd already set up, and the reality was different anyway. Especially with their thighs so close that one tiny movement would make them brush.

The water undulated as he straightened and bent his right leg.

"Is your knee bothering you?" she asked.

"It's just a little stiff. I've slacked off on my workouts."

Her eyes roamed over his chiseled torso, even more impressive up close, and she bit back the *it certainly doesn't look like it* that'd poised itself on the tip of her tongue.

He draped his arms over the edge of the hot tub. "Don't let me get soft and pudgy sitting in the office too long."

"As you can see, I'm probably not a good person to be in charge of that," she said without thinking, and then he was looking at her and her heart was beating too fast and the heat was making her dizzy—both the embarrassed heat and the water temperature.

"I..." He swallowed. "I'd like to say a lot of things about that, but I'm afraid you'll throw the handbook at me."

"I do carry my pocket-sized edition on me at all times."

He laughed, and she joined in, and it dissipated a dash of the tension. "I'll just say that you look beautiful tonight. Like you did earlier today, and yesterday—like you have since the moment you stormed in my office."

She raised an eyebrow in warning.

"What? You said compliments were okay. Remember how much you like my beard?" He reached up and ran his hand across it, a mischievous twist to his lips.

"So much regret about saying that."

"Can't take it back now, though."

"I can do whatever I want," she retorted, reaching for her drink before remembering she'd already finished it.

Everyone else was chatting amongst themselves, leaving the two of them in their own personal bubble.

Charlotte was wondering if she should break out—simply excuse herself in the name of talking to Bridget or Grace.

But then she glanced at Lance's leg again and the scars crisscrossing his knee. She curled her fingers into a fist so she wouldn't do something stupid like brush her fingers across them. "Does it bother you a lot? Your leg?"

"Here and there it flares up, which is typical of all my friends who've played a lot of ball. We all have that knee or shoulder or joint that makes us say cool old-man things like a storm's-a-coming. I feel it in my bones."

She laughed, but she still hated that he had to deal with it. She was sure it was true—that every athlete did have an injured spot or two that would forever bother them. She frowned as her mind reel came up with the hit on the sidelines that'd ended his career. When none of his teammates were open, Lance had run the ball for a first down. He'd gone out of bounds to avoid the oncoming slew of defensemen and to stop the clock. The hit from the giant player on the other team was late, and there'd been a flag, but it was also too late as well.

"Yeah, but if that guy hadn't hit you so hard, maybe..." The *what if* path was one he'd probably rather avoid. "Is it hard not to be bitter? You gave so much to your team, and they dropped you without even waiting to see if you'd recover."

"Don't go feeling sorry for me," Lance said. "One, they didn't drop me. I told them to find someone else—it was what was best for the team. I'd already had one ACL surgery, and unlike the first one, I wasn't a teenager anymore. Recovery was longer, and with all the added scar tissue and worn-down cartilage, the doctors warned me it'd always be weaker. They told me that if I tore it again, I might not have enough left to fix."

"And two?"

He wrinkled his forehead.

"You said 'one,' so I assumed there was a two."

Understanding smoothed his features, and his mouth kicked up on one side. "I got sidetracked and would've forgotten. This is why I need you around. You keep me on task."

"Truth," she said with a smile he returned.

"Two, every athlete knows the risks. When you're young, you think you're invincible and that you'll be the exception. But we get paid a lot of money for a decade or so, and we're well aware we can't keep at it forever and need to make that money last. I would've liked another eight to ten years, but that's life. It's just like on the field. If the play you wanted to work gets shut down, you regroup and make a new one."

His gaze went hazy, turning to another place and another time. "That also took longer than I would've liked. It didn't help that right when I was losing the team, I also lost—" He clamped his lips and rubbed the back of his neck, clearly uncomfortable. "Well, for a while it felt like I'd lost everything, and I drifted afterward, having a hard time finding my sense of purpose. Until now."

"I'm glad the team's bringing it back."

"Me, too." He twisted toward her, making their bubble

that much smaller. "I... I've never really admitted that to anyone."

"Well, according to HR guidelines, anything employees tell me in confidence, I keep in confidence. As long as it doesn't pose a threat to another employee or the company." She bumped her shoulder into his so he knew she was joking. "I also have something to admit..." She sucked in a deep breath. "I've decided to cut my athletic career short. It was a today-only thing. If I mess up my knee, I won't be able to wear my shoes, and I really love my shoes."

"I'm rather fond of your shoes, too," he said, his voice low and secretive, and it ignited a spark in her gut. That tension was back, the chemistry between them firing stronger as they locked eyes.

It'd be so easy to lean into him. To get lost and forget all the things she needed to remember about why he wasn't a good guy to fall for and how it'd look, and where was her brain with its ever-present list of rules? The rules had kept her safe.

The rules meant she didn't gamble with things she couldn't afford to lose, and she could lose her heart so easily to this guy. If her ex could crush her...Lance would *eviscerate* her.

Desperate to pop their bubble, she turned to address another member of the party, only to find that at some point they'd left them alone. There they were at the bar, getting more drinks. Possibly thinking they should give her and Lance space.

But she needed space *from* him.

She shot out of the water, fast enough that she didn't think about how exposed she'd be until she was standing, water dripping down her body. "I have to go make a call. To my roommate." *So she can tell me all the reasons I need to keep it together and avoid flirting with my boss. Who also doesn't fit the non-football-dude requirement in any way, shape, or form.*

Hell, she'd even agree to let Shannon set her up at this point. That way she'd at least be spending an evening with someone in her league, regardless of if it wasn't the league she wanted to play in.

"I'll walk you back," Lance said, starting to stand.

"*No!*" It came out way too loud, and a few people glanced their way. "I mean, no. Stay with your family and friends. Have a drink. I'll be in our temporary office around nine so we can put in a few hours of work and chat strategy before the call with Coach Bryant."

Instead of waiting for him to confirm the plan, she rushed away, fighting the urge to readjust her swimsuit bottom, since it'd only draw attention to her ass.

After all, she already felt exposed enough.

Chapter Twelve

As Charlotte had been fleeing the scene of overwhelming desire yesterday, she'd noticed a group of pretty women heading toward the hot tub, and the crazy part of her—which was starting to feel bigger and bigger lately—wanted to know if Lance had chatted up any of the women.

What if he'd gone to one of their rooms after? He was of course free to do so, but what if he forgot to be discreet and they had a scandal before they had a full staff?

Charlotte set her laptop aside, her brain morphing into the obsessive level of wondering with Lance seated across from her in their temporary office. "Hey, quick PR chat since the *Times* ran that article on you and the shakeup of the team…" Her Google alerts had lit up her phone at the butt crack of dawn, and she'd read, first with her fan eye and then with her HR, legally-cover-the-team eye. "Since you're now getting to be more of a public figure and are on that eligible bachelor list, there's another section of the handbook we need to cover. Namely section four."

Lance groaned. "Can we give the handbook a rest?"

"It's my job not to give it a rest."

"As your boss, I'm gonna make it your job."

"You can't just change my job description on a whim, and while yes, you can fire me, I'd be legally obligated to file a report it certain protocols were broken. Newsflash, you're not exempt from the rules."

He growled.

As if that would detour her. She crossed her arms and cocked her head, giving him attitude right back. "Is that a frustrated growl or a threatening growl? Because a threatening one would breach section three."

He growled again, no change to the inflection.

"Bet you're regretting bringing me along now," she said. "I told you this was probably a mistake."

This time his gaze actually lifted from his phone screen. "I don't regret bringing you along, Charlotte. I need you here."

Damn it, her heart turned squishy, not being as strong as it should. Perhaps she'd been pushing a tad again, testing where they stood after yesterday. Which was evidently still cordial and friendly until it came to the rules, where they frustrated each other to no end. It was oddly nice to know nothing had changed, even though that mushy organ beating in her chest said otherwise.

He rolled his phone through his fingers, nearly as deftly as he did with pens and pencils, too—he didn't seem to be capable of not messing with whatever was in his grip, a habit she was sure he'd carried over from constantly having a ball in his hands. "And I have a perfectly good time when you're not section this and that-ing me." He'd delivered it lightly, with enough of a teasing edge that it didn't sting. He dropped his phone and leaned back in his seat, his legs spread wide. "Give it to me."

Her throat went dry. "What?"

"The section we need to discuss."

Right. This part wasn't pushing. Just awkward. But the article had mentioned his bachelor status, and a few blogs were speculating about who he'd date—they also suggested women they'd like to see him with, a combination of beautiful actresses, models, and athletes. Good thing she wasn't competing with them. "So, uh, now that there's interest in who you're dating—"

"There's been plenty of interest in that before."

She wound a strand of hair around her finger, suddenly understanding his need to do something to occupy his hands. She took a beat before charging on with it. "I know, but it won't be like before, when there was a whole team of you."

"A whole team of me?" He shook his head. "You lost me again."

"Football players," she said, not doing a very good job at hiding her exasperation. "I mean you were part of a team with a lot of players. Now you're the head of a team, and you're the *only* player in that arena. Does that make sense?"

"About as much sense as usual when it comes to this kind of thing." He looked like he was trying not to laugh.

She was going to straightforwardly smack him upside the head. Deep breath in, slowly let it out. "Section four outlines the way everyone on the team is expected to conduct themselves in the public eye, and I've had to reprimand people for things like Facebook or Instagram posts and tweets before. Along with certain…videos. You need to be careful."

"Videos?" He tilted his head. "I can't have videos of me online? Pretty sure there are a lot of sports highlights on YouTube, and I can't do much about that."

Heat crawled up her neck and settled in her cheeks. "I'm talking viral videos. For not playing sports." *Although they also involve a lot of sweating and grunting and completions.*

Lance blinked at her, confusion twisting his features.

"The sex ones, okay?" Yep, her cheeks were on fire now, in serious danger of bursting into flames.

A slow, self-satisfied smile spread across his face. "Full disclosure, I knew what you meant."

"*Grr.*" She grabbed one of the couch pillows and tossed it at his head. Of course the jerk caught it. "What I'm saying is that while you've experienced a certain amount of scrutiny before, it's going to be different, no matter how cocky you are, or how well you think you can handle whatever comes your way." He'd struggled when the press discussed his personal life as a player, and this would be that on crack. "It'll be a lot more intense from here on out. The spotlight is going to be turned way up. Think eye of Sauron."

"*Lord of the Rings?*" he asked, and a triumphant grin split his face when she nodded. "Hey, I actually got one of your references."

She bit back a smile, a swirl of triumph going through her, too. "Right. And you have the ring. Just you, no fellowship, no Sam."

"Damn."

"Yeah."

He scooted out of the stuffed chair and onto the coach next to her. "I'll be careful, I promise. And it's not something you have to worry about."

She couldn't look at him, and holy crap her cheeks were hot. "I mean it's mostly PR's job, but I just thought, since they're back at the office and you're here. Plus, they're probably too scared to talk to you about it, since you fired most of the staff..." She reached for her open laptop. "Anyway, I just saw the article and felt the need to say something."

"Not that I'm looking to date now, or even in the near future, but why's it always got to be so complicated?"

She shrugged. "You're asking the wrong person." She

smothered the urge to add that he could ask Avril Lavigne if she'd ever gotten an answer, because he for sure wouldn't get the song reference. "I can only imagine the scrutiny you, the staff, and the players are under. I have a hard time simply because I work for the team."

"How so?"

She glanced at him to see if he was goading her, but his expression was sincere. She set her laptop back on the coffee table and tucked up her leg, double-checking her skirt remained in the proper range. "When guys hear I work for the Mustangs, they always want something. For a while I stopped mentioning my job. I'd go on three or four dates and dodge and change the subject if it came up. Which led to guys thinking I was super sketchy. One thought I was a gold digger—considering he worked part-time at a pizza joint, I would've been the worst gold digger ever."

Lance chuckled at that, and since it'd been a couple years ago, she could laugh at it now, too.

"Another dude told me that if I was a stripper, he was totally cool with it." She grabbed the remaining pillow and hugged it to her chest. "As long as I told him where he could come see me dance." She brought the pillow up to cover her face, which was heating up yet again. "That's probably inappropriate, telling you that."

"I…" Lance snapped his jaw closed, and his words came out tight. "Inappropriate would be me commenting on you stripping."

She lowered the pillow and shot him an admonitory glare, and he held up his hands.

"I'm not going to. I know better." He slowly dropped his hands and rested his forearms on his knees. "So you started telling them the truth? Or did you make up a fake job?"

"That's the thing, isn't it? If you lie and you start to genuinely like the person, you're screwed because you've already ruined things. Finally I figured I might as well weed them out as soon as possible. If their first response at hearing where I work is to ask for tickets or for me to introduce them to their favorite players, I move on."

Two creases formed between Lance's eyebrows as he pressed his mouth into a flat line. Clearly he had some thoughts on the matter, and she instinctually knew she wouldn't like whatever they were. And yet curiosity still got the best of her.

"What?"

"My grandpa owned a team, and I've been around players most of my life, and still, if I met a woman who worked for any NFL organization, I'd probably ask that without even thinking. Not so much for tickets, but for an inside look."

She frowned. "I guess that puts you in the nope column. You're already in there, of course, since we work together, but..." She shrugged like it didn't matter. He didn't understand. Her last boyfriend had acted like he understood when she said she didn't cross business and pleasure, but in the end, it was one of the things that tore them apart. When she couldn't "hook him up" he told her it was embarrassing and selfish, and he dumped her.

"I didn't mean to upset you. All I'm saying, James, is that you might end up putting every guy in the nope column."

"So it's expecting too much for a guy to like me for me?" This conversation was getting too personal. "Not that it really matters," she said, scooting forward to grab her laptop again. "Like I said before, I don't believe in that fairy-tale stuff, and I'm not looking for a relationship right now anyway."

He curled his hand around her wrist. "Charlotte—"

The phone rang, and it was go time, and she was glad for it. Even if she also really wondered what he'd been going to say.

. . .

Lance looked across the coffee table at Charlotte. He arched a brow, his silent way of asking if she had any more questions for Sean Bryant, their prospective head coach.

A pale pink fingernail ran down the lines in her notebook, where she'd scribbled answers and thoughts. The *click-click* of her pen filled the air, and she shook her head. Several of the questions she'd asked, he never would've thought to, and they'd given him a lot of insight into the guy on the other end of the line.

Another eyebrow arch from him, along with a thumbs-up, closely followed with a thumbs-down.

Charlotte flashed two giant thumbs-up, her enthusiasm catching. This could actually work.

"We'll let you go," Lance said, leaning closer to his phone. "But we'd like to fly you to the facilities early next week, so you can take a look around and we can talk more about a possible future together."

"Yeah," Coach Bryant said, excitement pitching his voice higher. He cleared his throat. "I mean, yeah, that sounds..." He lost the reins on his emotions again. "*Awesome.* Can we do it Monday? Pretty sure I'm not doing a very good job of playing it cool, so I'm just gonna go ahead and admit I'm not going to sleep until after our meeting." A self-deprecating laugh came out.

Charlotte's grin lit up the entire room, and Lance wondered if Sean could feel it, even from several states away. "Don't worry, we always have a strong pot of coffee in the break room, and if you're not a masochist, I have this amazing creamer that makes it feel like you're drinking a caffeinated dessert. And while Lance here plays it cool rather well, I say squeal and high five and do the type of dance that'd earn you a penalty."

"Oh, I've been dancing this entire time," he joked, and Charlotte laughed.

Her eyes met his, and Lance's heart jolted in his chest. She was such a natural when it came to putting people at ease. Yet she'd also asked the hard questions, pushing and challenging Sean so they could see how he'd react.

"Monday it is," Lance said. "I'll make a few calls and send you the information for your trip once I have it."

Charlotte hugged her notebook to her chest the second after he'd disconnected the call.

"If we hire him, he'd be the youngest coach in the NFL, which will bring extra scrutiny but also extra publicity, and yeah, he's a risk, but I think we could use more fresh blood and people who think outside the box, and you heard what he'd like to do with the team."

"More than that, I heard that he has a plan how to do it."

"I have a really good feeling about him. I think he'd be good for the team, and it'd be great to have his help as we reassess and narrow down our draft picks to fit his plan."

"I agree." His phone chimed, the *groomsmen photos* alert flashing onscreen. "Shit. I'm supposed to meet my family and the photographer in the lobby in ten minutes." He'd put on the tuxedo pants and shirt, but the rest of the getup was scattered around the room. He managed the bow tie, but one of his cufflinks wouldn't snap into place, and with his left hand, it was a losing battle.

"Here." Charlotte took over, easily securing it and reaching up to straighten the bow tie.

"I still think this trend of taking wedding photos *before* the wedding is bad luck." Today the groom and groomsmen were taking photos, and tomorrow Mitch would be banned from a certain area of the hotel as Stacy and her bridesmaids took pictures. In theory it meant getting better staging, more shots, and less hassle the day of. It also allowed for more goofy pictures without the other half of the party impatiently waiting.

"It does seem a bit like tempting fate. What if there's a runaway bride or groom situation? Not that Stacy or Mitch strike me as the running type."

Lance peered down at her. In her heels, she came up to his chin. "I figured a numbers girl like you wouldn't believe in luck or fate."

A hint of anguish flickered in her features, and he kicked himself too late for not treading more carefully on a subject that never failed to put her on edge. "Oh, bad luck is very real. Although it's also not a good idea to rely on superstition or good luck, either. So maybe this is reverse superstition?" Her eyebrows pulled together.

Hell if he knew.

A knock sounded on the door, and Charlotte offered to get it while he slipped on his jacket. Mitch, Hunter, Jack, Mom, Taylor, Austin, and Aaron poured into the room. So much for meeting in the lobby.

"We were afraid we might have to come drag you away from your work," Mom said without him even having to voice his thoughts about the location switch-up. She frowned at him and gestured to his face. "I thought you'd shave for the pictures. Didn't I send that in a text?"

More than one and they both knew it. But he'd been busy, and, well... "Charlotte likes the scruff." How was he supposed to shave after she'd complimented the beard and said it suited him?

His mom glanced at Charlotte, who gave him a sharp smile. "I, uh... It is sort of my kryptonite. Of course now I might kill him for outing me before you get to take any photos." She patted his cheek, hard enough to sting a bit.

Mom ate it up, grinning at the two of them, and he resisted the urge to pump his fist—looked like Charlotte was getting him out of more than awkward forced dates.

His nephews stepped farther into the room, and Charlotte squatted in front of them. "Oh my goodness, you guys look so handsome in your tuxes."

Austin's response to that was to tell her about how he'd found *five* seashells this morning. She oohed and aahed and asked for details, and clearly she didn't realize just how detailed the kid could get—he'd once told him a twenty-minute story about a goose he saw at the park.

Aaron found the football in the corner and picked it up, his face lighting with glee at the discovery.

Lance clapped his hands and held them out in front of him. "Toss it here. Throw it hard as you can."

"I swear, Lance, if their clothes get messed up," Taylor warned, a scary gleam in her eye. "It took forever to scrub off the sand and wrestle them into those suits, and Aaron's hair sticks straight up if you even look at it for longer than a second or two. It's like it senses fear."

"Don't worry, I got it. I break it, I bought it."

Taylor sighed, but her attention was snagged away by Mitch's crooked bow tie, so she went to fussing over that.

Aaron nearly tipped backward with the weight of the ball. He flung his arm forward, and the ball soared through the air, straight and low.

Lance bent to catch it, testing the bounds of his snug tuxedo pants. "Nice." He held out his hand for a high five, and Aaron rushed forward and smacked it. "You're gonna play football for the Mustangs someday, aren't you, buddy?"

"Football," Aaron said, nodding over and over, like a bobblehead doll.

"I decided I'm going to make pretty dresses," Austin said, loud and proud. "Like the one Miss Charlotte's wearing."

Charlotte glanced away from his oldest nephew and up at him, a hint of panic in her eyes. She even moved slightly in front of Austin, as if she might need to block for him. Did she honestly think he'd care?

"Tell you what, buddy," Lance said, equally as loudly and proudly as Austin had announced his possible career choice, "I'll be your first customer. I bet by the time you're blowing everyone away at design school, Miss Charlotte will need a new dress."

The worry in her features drained. She beamed at him as she straightened.

"Okay, everyone," Mom said. "Time to go."

Lance turned to Charlotte. "Oh shoot, I didn't have time to call the pilot to schedule a pickup for Coach Bryant."

"I'll take care of it."

"Oh, and can you also—"

"Call Galen Michaels and see if he'd be interested in the defensive coordinator position?"

Earlier she'd thrown out his name as an option, and when he'd informed her the guy didn't talk to anyone anymore and was hard to reach, she nonchalantly announced that she had his number and they were friends. Evidently back when he'd played for the Mustangs and found out she walked home alone, the huge linebacker had taught her self-defense moves. "Please."

"I'm on it. Now, go."

He turned toward the door, sure that any minute Mom would yell at him to stop dilly-dallying. But he only made it one step before he pivoted back around. "You told me that I was on my own, but you were wrong. I have you. You're my Sam."

It was the nerdiest fucking thing he'd ever said, but he stood by it. Considering the resulting smile, he should say nerdy things more often.

"Are you calling me a hobbit?" she asked.

"If the shoe fits—"

"Okay, that's too far. I might be short, but I do not have big hairy feet."

The hot pink shoes on her tiny feet snagged his attention. The opening across the toe gave him a peek at toenails that were the same bright color. "Fair point."

She reached out and curled her hand around his elbow. "Thank you. That's one of the nicest things anyone's ever said to me."

Her touch sent scoring lines up his arm and straight into the center of his chest. He might've stood like that forever if his brother didn't poke his head into the room and shout that if he didn't get his ass in gear, he was so going to tell Mom on him.

He might call him a juvenile jackass if he weren't practically skipping toward the door, counting down the hours until he'd be back in the room with Charlotte again.

Chapter Thirteen

The words on the page blurred together, and Charlotte took off her glasses, blinked, then put them on and lifted the résumé closer. It was only four thirty p.m., and her eyes couldn't crap out on her already. She and Lance still had a lot of pressing items to discuss as soon as he got back from the photo shoot he'd left for about an hour and a half ago.

Her inbox chimed, and she lifted her phone. The pilot had emailed her an itinerary as she'd requested, and she copied it into a blank email and added a short personal note to it before sending it on to Sean Bryant.

From there she went into the calendar she'd set up for her and Lance and added the meeting with him, along with a couple of alerts. It made her a little sad to think of being in the office by Monday, yet she also needed it to come faster.

Every day—no, every hour—she spent with Lance made her soften toward him. Made her feel other things besides softening. When Austin had said the thing about designing dresses, she'd been so scared Lance was going to tell him it wasn't a job for boys, or that he'd huff and tell him they were a football family. As a girl who'd been obsessed with football, she'd been told she shouldn't be plenty, even in Texas. Or like with the dating thing, where guys would quiz her because her brain couldn't possibly retain football rules or stats. Since she'd had too much experience with that kind of thing, she wanted to protect Austin, and the fact that there'd been no need had sent relief through her.

Along with *way* too much affection. Then Lance had said that thing about her being his Sam, and her heart had swelled so much she thought she might float right up to the ceiling.

You're slipping again. Thinking things you shouldn't. About a guy who doesn't even want a relationship.

Not that she did, either. Except over the past few days, it felt like she kept trying to convince herself of that more than actually believing it. It was the wedding, all that love in the air, infecting her and making her forget about what happened when the tingly vibes faded.

They haven't faded for Stacy and Mitch.

Or Maribelle and Chuck.

Or Taylor and Scott.

But that didn't mean that things would work out for *her.* Maybe she was one of those people who was going to be single forever. Because that wasn't a tad depressing to think about.

Shannon had been far from helpful when Charlotte had called her last night in desperation. Instead of telling her to keep it in her pants, her roommate told her she only lived once and that she should strap on some spurs, hop in that saddle, and enjoy hot sex with the former quarterback tons of women had crushed on—and still were.

"Once more people see that most eligible bachelor list and watch games with him sitting up in the owner's box, tons of women will be vying for his attention—like those aggressive ones in that comment thread—and you'll lose your chance. Do you really want to regret not taking it?"

Charlotte knew Shannon didn't meant it in the way she'd heard it—that if any other women were around, he'd be showing them attention over her. Unfortunately, it was one of her worries about crossing lines.

At first she'd been sure she was the only one experiencing attraction vibes. But right before Lance had left today, looking insanely hot in his fitted tux, she swore there was something in his eyes. Maybe.

Say there was, though. How could they have sex and then just show up at the office and nod at each other? How could she sit across from him without thinking about how he'd seen her naked—she'd had a hard enough time meeting his eyes after he'd seen her in a bikini last night. In the dim light.

And then she'd have to feel jealous over every beautiful woman he dated after.

Hell, she already felt jealous, her gut pitching and roiling every time she thought of all the beautiful women who'd be happy to be on his arm for a night or more. Of the famous women people were already matching him up with.

It'd be good publicity, having him seen out and about in the city. Especially if he did date an actress or an athlete. Every photo they took of the handsome bachelor who owned the Mustangs would mean a mention of the team, and they needed to fill the stadium seats in order to keep their income high and their team continuously growing.

Early draft picks meant jack if they lost seasoned key players because they could get paid better somewhere else.

The knock on the door made her freeze. Who'd be knocking? Lance had a key, and it was his room. Maybe it was one of his family members. Or maybe it was one of those women his mom wanted to set him up with.

Okay, now you're letting your imagination get carried away.

Charlotte set her stack of marked-up papers aside and

padded over to the door, then cursed not stepping into her shoes—the peephole was too damn high. "Who is it?" she asked through the door.

"Room service."

If this were a movie, this was where the bad guys charged inside because she was stupid enough to believe room service had been sent without her ordering anything.

Yes, because logically, you'd be a huge target.

It was official. She needed more caffeine—clearly her brain wasn't functioning at maximum capacity. Or even minimum capacity. Obviously thinking about unattainable guys zapped too many brain cells, on top of leaving you slightly depressed.

Finally she opened the door, a crack at first, and then wider when she saw the man with the silver tray and matching pitcher on the other side. The scent of dark roasted beans filled the air, and if she was going to go down over anything, caffeinated seemed like a good way to go.

"Mr. Quaid called and asked us to deliver coffee and pastries. He also insisted we run to the store for this." He tapped the large bottle of Southern butter pecan creamer.

Her heart went all squishy on her. He remembered her special creamer and paid who knew how much to ensure they'd deliver it with the coffee—amazing, blessed coffee. "Do I need to sign or...?"

The guy swiped a hand through the air. "Mr. Quaid already took care of it."

Charlotte thanked him and closed the door behind him. Since she had her priorities in order, she doctored a cup, sighing when the coffee hit her tongue. No surprise, this fancy resort had the good stuff. Good enough she probably didn't even need her special creamer, but after going without it, she could fully attest that it was so much better with it.

For a couple of seconds, she debated waiting to thank

Lance until after he returned. But sometimes it was easier to thank someone over the phone, where his big, oxygen-stealing presence couldn't twist up her thoughts and her tongue.

She took an Instagram-worthy picture of the mug, the pretty silver pitcher, and the creamer. She typed out *THANK YOU!!!!* in screaming caps with an inordinate amount of exclamation points. She added a heart. Deleted the heart. Added the two smaller pink hearts. Deleted them. Settled on a smiley face.

When her phone rang instead of chimed, she nearly dropped it. Of course he'd call—he was forever on the phone, so maybe he had something against texts.

"Hey," she said. "Seriously, thank you so much."

"Really it's selfish on my part," he said in that rich voice that caressed her skin and settled deep in her bones. "I've gotta keep you going."

She didn't buy it, but she smiled all the same. The cherry Danish was calling her name, so she plucked it off the tray and took a bite. It was so delicious she had to suppress a groan.

"I also need to warn you about something," he said, and she tensed. "My mother has your phone number. I tried to tell her I could pass on a message, but she insisted and gave me the Mom Glare, and I'm not proud to admit it, but I totally caved." She could picture him grinning and pacing, the phone held against his ear. "This is why I needed you here as a shield—she's relentless, and I end up agreeing to crazy things. God only knows how many horrible dates I would've been forced to endure."

Now she was glad she was here, too, only she was more worried the dates would've been good, and what was wrong with her? The guy had coffee, creamer, and pastries delivered, and suddenly she was ready to claim him as her own?

"Anyway, you can expect a call or text from her shortly. We just wrapped up the photo shoot, if you can believe it, but we ended up way down the beach so we could get a picture in the historic gazebo, and traffic's horrible because of some parade." Okay, so maybe he wasn't pacing but sitting in the back of a car. "The boys are upset they can't get out to watch, but Taylor's afraid they'll ruin their tuxes, and it's a whole thing, so now we're eating chicken nuggets in the car in our undershirts."

That was quite the picture, and not a sentence she ever imagined him uttering. Before coming here and seeing him with his family, it wouldn't have computed at all, and she liked that she got to see this other side of him. Even if it also put her weak-willed heart in danger.

"Hopefully I'll be back within the hour," he said.

"I'll keep guzzling the coffee, then."

"If you need anything else, just order it and tell them to charge the room." Voices sounded in the background, growing louder and louder. "Apparently someone's trying to use ketchup, and my tackling skills are required. Heaven help us all."

She was still giggling over the idea of a bunch of grown-ups attempting to wrestle ketchup packets from toddlers in the back of a car when her phone pinged. Sure enough, Maribelle had her number and wasn't afraid to use it. She invited Charlotte to go with the girls for manis and pedis tomorrow and added that Stacy was hoping she'd also attend the bachelorette party with her and her friends tomorrow night.

Longing rose up, even as her pulse hitched. She wanted to go—whenever she'd seen movies where the characters took part in those sorts of girly outings, she'd thought about how fun they looked and how much she'd like to take part in them if she ever got the chance. But was she getting too tangled up in these people she'd most likely never see again?

On the other hand, it'd give her some time away from

Lance, which meant less chance of her accidentally getting more attached to him.

On the other *other* hand, spending time with his family also made her quickly growing feelings for him that much stronger. This entire trip was acting as a catalyst, making everything bigger and faster, and she told herself it would calm down once they were back in the real world.

Besides, she might never get another chance to take part in all the pre-wedding fun, and she was already here. She didn't want to let her worries stop her from enjoying herself.

With the girls.

Lance was a whole different story, because even after this week ended, they'd still have to be around each other in the office.

Charlotte: *Of course I'll go, as long as my boss okays it. LOL*

Maribelle: *He will or else :)*

Charlotte sat back with a happy sigh, thinking today was a good day.

A loud *ping* sounded, her inbox letting her know it had a new message. A closer look revealed it was marked urgent.

The former coach had compiled a list of reasons to support his belief that he was wrongfully terminated and was asking for an outlandish amount of severance pay. The team's lawyer had added a note, asking her to disprove or verify the items. Naturally, she wanted her to find ways to disprove them.

Just like that, the afternoon went downhill at a rapid pace, and Charlotte was the one with her phone permanently glued to her ear.

By the time Lance arrived, Charlotte had drained every last drop of coffee. She'd burned through the caffeine boost way too quickly, and her limbs were dragging, along with her thoughts.

"Just got off the phone with our lawyer," Lance said, ditching his tuxedo coat. "She brought me up to speed on the situation with Coach Hurst. You said things were bigger in Texas, and he definitely gets the award for biggest baby."

In the office she might point out that those kinds of comments would only exacerbate the situation, but since they were in a more casual setting and he obviously needed to vent, she decided to let it go. "I was afraid he'd be bitter enough to do something like this." She was pretty sure the guy had convinced himself Mr. Price might leave at least part of the team to him because they'd worked together for so long, and his disappointment had been palpable after the funeral.

"She said you were already compiling information to help with the counterclaim. Any progress?"

"I printed out his contract and tabbed and highlighted places we can cite where he didn't completely fulfill his end." She pointed at the twenty-eight-page document. "Since he never had an official warning about them, it's going to make it that much harder to prove. I've also gone over all the forms and documents I've kept, including what few complaints I did receive about him—now might be a good time to thank me for being so thorough."

"Thank you," he said, sitting on the couch next to her. "I mean it. Does that mean there's good news?"

She wobbled her head back and forth. "Some of his claims are outrageous, and we can easily dispute them. Others… Well, it gets tricky. He asserts that he and your grandfather had a plan, and that Mr. Price gave him his word his position was safe for at least two more years while he put it into effect, which is ludicrous—no one gets that kind of a guarantee in this industry. And I have notes from several meetings that show how many times I insisted Mr. Price draw up addendums for every agreement; regardless of his opinion, his word was his bond, and everyone else's should be, too. It might be enough to fight it, but it'll be a messy, drawn-out process and might cost more than paying him off."

"Can we afford it? Either way?"

"That's a question for the CFO."

"We don't currently have one of those."

"I realize." Charlotte bit her lip. She'd gone back and forth on bringing up this subject, but in theory he appreciated how she always spoke her mind. He might change his stance on that here in a second, because he wasn't going to like this. "John was a really good CFO. The other guys never listened to his advice and put him in situations he'd have to dig us out of, but he did always manage to dig us out. I think it was…a bit hasty to lump him in with the rest and fire him."

A muscle flexed in his jaw, offense simmering under the surface. "You think it was a mistake."

She expelled a breath and lifted her chin, no backing down now that it was out there. Honestly, it'd bothered her since that meeting where the shit hit the fan. "I do. Like I said, I could see the others had gotten sloppy and weren't willing to change. But we could really use John right now."

"What do you want me to do? Call him up and beg him to come back?" Lance shook his head. "I don't know if I can do that. It's not my style."

"Just apologize and see what he says. Are you really going to let your pride get in the way of a decision that'd benefit the team?"

He growled.

She tilted her head. "Growl all you want. Doesn't change the facts." She gestured to her computer screen. "I've gathered everything I can, but I'm not sure it'll be enough.

You're asking me to do the job of two people—two huge jobs that usually require assistants. It's...too much."

The cushion dipped as he scooted to the edge of the couch. She thought he was going to stand and storm away or go to pacing like he did when he talked on the phone. Instead he raked his hands through his hair and cast her a sidelong glance. "I'll think about it."

"Sooner would be better than later."

"Yeah, yeah, yeah." He scrubbed a hand over his face and reached for the empty pot of coffee.

"It's gone, but I can order more."

"No, I'm already too hyped now anyway. It'd probably make it worse." He undid the bow tie, slipped it out of the collar, and flung it aside. "Did you get a hold of Galen Michaels?"

It'd been before the coffee delivery and the email with the bad news, and so much had happened it almost seemed like it was days ago. "Yeah. He's running a football camp back in his hometown—something about an old mentor who died and left it to him and his friends. He said it was complicated, but that even if he didn't have that going on, he wasn't interested. The NFL lifestyle never was his thing."

"Too bad."

It was. The world could use more guys like him, but so could the low-income kids he and his buddies would be doing the camp for.

Lance unfastened his cufflinks, tossed them on the coffee table with a *clink*, and then rolled up his sleeves. "How'd sorting through the résumés go? Any potentials there?"

"Good. I scribbled notes all over them, and there were a couple that sounded promising." She reached for the pile on the other side of her and handed him the ones she'd gone through.

He began flipping through them, and she sank farther

into the cushions, fighting off a yawn. Her head felt too heavy for her neck, too. Was it always so freaking heavy?

That's better, she thought when her head hit the top of the couch. Just a minute or two to rest and she'd finish up the last of the résumés.

The next thing she knew, she was diagonal, her cheek braced against something solid yet surprisingly comfortable. The scent of Lance's cologne invaded her senses as her sloggy mind tried to work out where she was. Her eyelids didn't want to open, but they fluttered enough to see that yes, yes she was leaning on Lance's shoulder.

"Sorry, I didn't realize," she said, starting to push herself up.

He curled up his arm, placed his hand on the side of her face, and guided her cheek back to his shoulder. "Relax. You've been working nonstop all day, and I need you here in case I have any questions about your notes. It's not against the rules to use me as a pillow."

"Pretty sure it is," she mumbled, but with that firm, warm shoulder underneath her, she was having trouble convincing her head to lift. The drag of his fingers across her cheekbone and jaw made it even more difficult to fight the tug of sleep.

And suddenly she couldn't recall why she was fighting it in the first place.

• • •

Lance skimmed to the end of the final résumé and finished reading the last of Charlotte's notes. Her stats, her comments—they were all spot-on. Just as he was wondering about something, she had a note about it, as if she were in his brain, already aware of exactly what he wanted.

Her silky hair brushed his jaw as he glanced down at her, so calm now that she'd drifted to sleep. It often felt like she was holding back, only occasionally letting her walls slip. Usually that was when she fled.

This evening she'd been too exhausted, and while he felt bad about that and knew it was partly on him, he couldn't help taking a second to enjoy the moment.

Affection stitched its way through his chest, a thread tethering him to her, and he wanted to place a kiss on her forehead. Unfortunately, that'd be against the rules, and not something he'd do unless she was awake enough to consent to it. For now, he'd simply enjoy her soft breaths and the scent of her shampoo or perfume or whatever she used that made her smell so damn good.

Gradually his eyelids began to droop as well, his mind and body hitting the wall. Today had been a blur of calls and so, so many photos. Then the mess with the crybaby coach. If only another team would snatch him up and help pay off the rest of a contract he never deserved. Unfortunately, the crap timing meant most coaches had been swapped or secured about three months ago.

Lance relaxed into the comfort of the couch, wrapping his arm around Charlotte's shoulders and tucking her closer without thinking. Her hand slipped down, falling high on his thigh, and desire coursed through his veins, bringing the reality of the situation to the surface.

He forced himself to jerk awake and lift his arm from her shoulders to the back of the couch. If they slept here they'd both be sore, and she'd be sore at him, too.

"Charlotte." He gently squeezed her knee. "Let's get you to your room."

Her eyes fluttered open, and she gave him a smile that he felt deep in his gut. Then dawning crossed her features, her eyes going wide. She moved to sit up, but her hand drifted higher on his thigh and then pressed right into his crotch.

He grunted, automatically curling in on himself.

"Oh shit," she said, and he'd point out she was the one swearing now if she didn't look so distraught.

"It's okay."

"No, it's not! My hand just violated section three of the handbook!"

"Accidental brushes happen."

Her cheeks flushed deeper as she shook her head. "It was embarrassing enough to fall asleep on you. Now I'm grabbing your crotch."

He doubted replying that he was okay with her grabbing his crotch would make her feel any better. He'd rather she be gentler next time, but— *Yeah, don't go there.*

"We should fill out a form." She stood and glanced around, as if she expected one to appear out of thin air. "I'll print one out tomorrow and we can get it on the record, and… yeah."

Like he wanted that on the record.

Charlotte snatched her purse off the floor and straightened. "Okay, so goodbye."

"Wait," he said, pushing to his feet. "It's late. As soon as I get my sixty seconds recovery from the crotch shot, I'll walk you to your room." He'd hoped it'd lighten the situation; instead he got a scowl. A really cute one that made him want to cup her face and kiss it off her.

"You don't need to walk me there. You wouldn't walk me back if I was a dude, or one of your other employees, would you?"

"Sure I would."

Skepticism pinched her features.

"I'm serious! Those three hundred-pound defensemen are big babies—they're scared of everything."

Her head tilted another half inch, but her mouth trembled against a smile. He gestured her ahead of him, snagging his hotel key off the coffee table as he walked past. He held the door open for her, and as they walked down the hall, he placed a palm against her lower back.

"Before you call me on it, this is how I walked the guys home, too."

"Shows what you know." A smile that managed to be both haughty and flirty flitted across her lips. "I was going to let it slide."

In that case... He splayed his hand and walked a little closer.

She slowed in front of her door and turned to face him, and his heart thundered in his chest. This woman had gotten under his skin, ridiculously fast at that.

He figured they'd already skipped a few bases, what with the hand on her butt to boost her over the balcony the other night and her accidental crotch grab moments ago. Even though he was a football guy, he hated to skip bases.

He braced his palm on the door by her head, and her throat worked a swallow, turning him on and pushing him to go ahead and voice his thoughts. "I have to confess something."

"To your HR rep?"

"No, just to you, James."

He leaned closer, his gaze locked on her tempting lips. "I really want to kiss you right now." He felt every inch between them. The only thing keeping him from giving in to the urge to flatten his body to hers was the knowledge that moving too fast would scare her off and screw everything up. "To be honest, I've been thinking about it since you made your first touchdown and jumped into my arms. Now I'm looking at you, and all I can think about is how much I want to kiss you."

She licked her lips, and he suppressed a groan. His body reacted, and it was a good thing the hallway was empty, because they were about to put on quite a show. Her hand came up on his chest, her fingers curving as if she was going to grip his shirt.

He could see the battle going on in that amazing brain of hers, whether or not she should fight the pull.

Don't fight it, he wanted to say but realized that wouldn't make her feel less conflicted about the situation, so he searched for the right words to reassure her. "I want you to know that whatever you say or do next has no bearing on your employment. I'd never do that, and you're way too valuable to the team for me to ever let you go. But if it'll make you feel better, I'll sign any paperwork you want."

"I appreciate that. It's not that I'm not tempted, or that I don't feel a certain pull…" A couple of blinks and a different expression descended upon her features, her hand flattening and holding him at bay instead of grabbing and pulling him closer. He froze in place, waiting for her to make the move, silently urging her to even though he'd felt the shift. "But it's still a bad idea. There's no way it won't upset the power balance, and it'd look bad to the rest of the employees and to all the people out there watching you so closely. And with you coming in and firing so much of the staff and the wrongful termination lawsuit hanging in the balance, we don't need any more bad PR. In fact, you should be playing up the eligible bachelor thing for extra publicity."

"I don't give a damn about PR," he said. "Once we rebuild the team and they start winning, the rest won't matter, either."

"But that'll take time and money, and that means we need some good PR anyway."

He grunted, and she sucked in a breath, her chest rising and falling. Not fear. No, that was desire. But it didn't change the fact that she had to say the word. He nodded and slowly dropped his hand, even though everything in him balked at the idea of stepping away from this. "Think about it. And I guess since I'm the one in the so-called power position— although I'd argue that you've been in charge since the moment you stormed into my office—you'll have to initiate any kissing."

"Sure, if you want it to be awkward," she murmured.

He lowered his voice, his gaze returning to the lips he so badly wanted to taste. "I don't care. I just want it. Whenever you're ready, know I'm all for it. Forms, blood samples— whatever you decide is needed—I'm game."

She sucked her bottom lip between her teeth, and he groaned again. He took the key from her hand and opened the door for her, a gentleman with very ungentlemanly thoughts.

For a few torturous yet amazing seconds, she stared at him, the chemistry snapping and sparking between them.

She reached out and squeezed his hand, a silent thank-you and good night. Or maybe an apology that she couldn't cross lines.

Then she slipped inside, and all he could do was retreat to his room and hope that sometime before they returned to San Antonio, where his life would only get crazier and more hectic, she'd take him up on his offer.

Chapter Fourteen

Charlotte knocked on the door to Lance's suite revoltingly early, hoping she wasn't waking him before he wanted to be up and going. When he didn't answer, she took out the key he'd given her and tapped it against her thigh, debating whether to use it or retreat to her hotel room.

Where she'd just had a worrisome call that made her want to throw herself into work. If she hadn't been so tired yesterday evening that she'd left her laptop in their "office," she could easily put in a few hours in the lobby or find a corner table in the resort restaurant to occupy.

I'll just sneak in and grab it, along with a few folders...

Right now she needed to lose herself in stats and football players and résumés and basically anything that'd take the edge off her panic. All that money and time, and he...

Not going there right now. Decision made, she slid in the card as quietly as possible and eased open the door. Lance wasn't in the living room area, but the door to the bedroom was cracked open.

On her way to the coffee table, she caught a glimpse of

the king-sized bed through the open bedroom door, sheets and covers rumpled and thrown back.

She paused, listening for the sounds of a shower. The bathroom door was also open, no sound coming out. "Lance?"

After a few seconds of ringing silence, she called again, louder this time.

No answer. A quick look around confirmed he wasn't there.

Maybe last night after he dropped me off, he found a woman who was willing to kiss him. To do more... Her stomach pitched at the thought, a toxic burning coming along for the rocky ride. It couldn't be jealousy.

More like it *shouldn't* be jealousy. But there it was anyway, the bite and the sting.

It wasn't like she hadn't wanted to kiss him—she'd nearly come unraveled when he'd told her he wanted to kiss her, and that he'd been thinking about it since she made her first touchdown. Her lips and body had been shouting that they were definitely ready and willing, her common sense was just stronger. Although right now she was cursing her stupid brain for not letting her give in to her racing hormones. How often did insanely hot, wickedly smart men want to kiss her?

Wasn't the beach like Vegas? What happened there stayed there?

Only idiots truly believe that—of Vegas and *the beach.*

The other woman would be beautiful and have one of those bodies made for string bikinis, no need for a skirt. Was she currently snuggled up next to Lance? Running her hand over his scruff?

That line of thinking is nearly as toxic as the one that sent me running here in the first place. Stats. Paperwork. Rules. They'd save her, the way they always had.

What the company needed from her right now was a solid football team. They had a whole crew who analyzed players before the draft—correction: they'd *had*. The reports were kept in a big Google doc, so she grabbed her laptop and began poring through them. She read through report after report, comparing what they'd said and the stats in her head, trying to get a fuller picture.

On the screen it was hard to do, though, so she dug through her bag and found the stack of index cards she used on the corkboard in her office whenever she needed to write herself reminders and memos and such.

Luckily she had a roll of tape as well, in a shoe-shaped dispenser, no less—and to think she'd wondered if it was silly to have packed it, just in case.

The project took over, pushing other thoughts far from her mind, and she began furiously scribbling on the cards. The whiteboard Lance had brought in their first day was covered in his handwriting. Since she wasn't sure if he still needed the information, she flipped it to the other side and taped the cards there, connecting lines and writing extra notes in marker.

When she'd filled every inch of that, she taped the index cards to the wall around it. Marking up the walls wasn't an option, so she simply numbered each note to correspond to the ones on the board.

Within thirty minutes, she'd transformed the area into her very own war room. Sure, it was much smaller scale than the massive one back at Mustangs' headquarters, where the staff compiled lists for the draft, but impressive all the same.

The *beep* of the door sounded, and Charlotte braced herself to see Lance in his walk-of-shame clothes and pretend she didn't care.

He stepped inside shirtless, mesh shorts slung low on his hips, sneakers on his feet, and a sheen of sweat covering his entire body. It highlighted every muscle and made it impossible not to gape at him. The scent of beach and cedar and him filled the air, and desire hijacked her system.

Clearly, she hadn't prepared herself for the right image.

Not that she believed there was any way any heterosexual woman could fully prepare herself for the sight of Lance Quaid after what'd clearly been a strenuous workout.

• • •

Lance hadn't expected Charlotte this early, and as she stared at him, all the deep breaths he'd taken to calm his rapid pulse had now been done in vain.

His heart hammered against his rib cage at the sight of her standing in his hotel room, her eyes wide and—if he wasn't mistaken—flooding with lust.

It made him want to stalk across the room, watch those endlessly green eyes widen even more, and claim her mouth with the predatory flare she awoke in him.

His feet took him a couple of steps before he recalled telling her that she'd have to initiate. Why the hell had he gone and done that?

Because that's what she needs.

If he kept staring at her, though, it'd be that much harder to keep the grip on his control, so he glanced away.

At the madness on the whiteboard and the wall. "Whoa. It's like *A Beautiful Mind* erupted in here." His gaze flicked back to her. "Is there an imaginary friend in the room I should know about?"

That seemed to break the spell, and she cocked her head, that admonitory pinch to her lips. "Very funny. I just woke up early, and I felt restless, so I came to the"—she made air quotes—"'office' and dug in." There was a hint of sorrow in there. Something that didn't quite ring true, although obviously she'd done a lot of work. "How was your...run? Along the beach, I'm guessing?"

"It was good. I was feeling a bit restless myself." With all the wedding events, he'd have even less time over these next few days, and there were still so many positions to fill, not to mention the draft. The only benefit to having a shut-out season was getting top pick, and he needed to find the right piece to help complete the puzzle, which would be a lot easier if the bulk of the pieces weren't currently in a messy pile.

But that wasn't the only reason he'd tossed and turned so much last night.

He'd kept thinking about Charlotte's head against his shoulder as she slept. About her laugh and her smile and how much fun he'd had with her the past four days. It'd been a long time since he'd let anyone in besides his immediate family, yet he could feel himself opening up to her, and something about that both calmed him and scared the shit out of him.

Mostly he'd thought of that moment in the hallway and how much he'd wanted to kiss her.

Since she didn't say anything else, he added, "I figured I should take the chance to run along the beach, especially before it got too warm."

"How's your knee?"

"Fine." He ran a hand through his hair, realized how sweaty he was, and gestured toward the bedroom area. "I'll jump through the shower and then you can explain the crazy wall to me."

"Calling it the crazy wall doesn't exactly make me eager to comply."

"When are you *ever* eager to comply?" he teased, and a knot he hadn't realized had formed in his chest loosened when she cracked a smile.

They were okay.

Although her smile wasn't as bright, and she had to work for it. Something had upset her. And if it was someone, he'd make sure they regretted it.

Stifling his urge to seek and destroy, he focused on her. He moved closer and brushed his fingers down her arm. "What's up?"

"Nothing. I'm totally fine. I just need coffee. I bet you could use some, too." She reached for the phone on the desk. "I'll put in an order."

Evidently, it was going to take some extra digging. He'd get to the bottom of it, but he'd let her order her coffee and explain what she'd done before trying again. Since his mom informed him Charlotte was going to need a few hours off in the middle of the day for spa time, and tonight was his brother's bachelor party, they'd need to get as much work done as possible in the limited time they had.

He also wanted to get as much Charlotte time as he could before then. Another thing that caused a strange mix of trepidation and calm.

Yep. Pretty sure I'm losing my mind over this girl.

Was it bad the thought that immediately followed was that if it meant a few days to explore and enjoy this connection between them, he'd happily slip into madness for a little bit?

· · ·

Torture.

This was torture, sitting here listening to the *whoosh* of fabric, knowing that behind that bathroom door, Lance was getting undressed.

Charlotte's attempt to swallow was thwarted by her sandpaper-dry throat. She stared at the closed door, her mind replaying what he'd said last night about how she'd have to initiate any kissing. She still could hardly believe he'd laid it all out like that—that he even wanted her in the first place. Her eyes narrowed, and for a delirious second or two, she wished for X-ray vision.

The spray of water sounded, and she wondered what Lance would do if she snuck into the bathroom, yanked back the shower curtain, and told him she was going to join him.

Heat streaked through her body, growing faster and hotter until her entire body was aflame.

It'd be so satisfying to see the shock on his face. To be that brazen and bold.

It'd break every rule. Of the team's and of mine and...

For once that didn't seem as big a deal as it should.

He has those big hands and long fingers...those muscular thighs, that ripped torso. She could picture the way the water would pour over them, and while she was picturing stuff, she figured she might as well reach out in her daydream and run her hand over those pecs and abs.

She imagined his eyes darkening, the way they did last night when he'd had her almost pinned against the door, the inches between them proper yet not and still way too much.

The knock on the door brought the real world screeching back.

Fanning her face in a futile attempt to cool herself down, she rushed to the door and accepted the large pitcher of room service coffee, along with the two breakfasts she'd ordered.

"Do you feel all right?" the guy asked, concern filling the creases of his forehead. "You look flushed. If the A/C unit's not functioning properly, I can call and—"

"It's fine, thank you!" She scribbled her name and closed the door. Hazards of staying at a place where the staff were so friendly, she supposed, but had he not ever delivered food to someone who'd been flushed from sex?

Not that she'd had sex. Unfortunately. Or good on her, cheers to being strong! Or... Shit, she was a mess. Not just a conflicted mess, but one who was suddenly using British phrases she'd never used before. No wonder the room service guy was concerned. She walked over to the thermostat and made the room a couple of degrees cooler for good measure, then focused on doctoring her coffee with the creamer in the mini-fridge.

A few minutes later Lance emerged, freshly showered, hair wet, smelling all soapy fresh. Like with her earlier attempt to steel herself, the cooler temperature didn't much matter.

"Breakfast is here," she said, her voice way too high. To keep herself from saying anything else that might reveal her traitorous preoccupation, she quickly shoved a piece of bacon in her mouth.

His eyebrows lifted slightly, but she ignored them and settled on the couch with her plate.

They ate in silence for a while before he pointed his fork at the wall. "You think we should pick Darius Fox first?"

"Defense wins championships. He has a record number of sacks, along with interceptions, and for such a big dude, he's remarkably fast." She set her plate aside, stood, and walked over to the wall. She explained the names along the top, the connecting lines, and how her system worked, along with how she'd come to those conclusions. "A star means the names lined up with the reports our former GM, coaches, and the rest of the staff made. I put an X on the ones they picked that I disagree the most with, although I'm not saying they're wrong, for the record."

Lance walked up behind her, and she wished she weren't so acutely aware of how close he was. Of his height and the arms that'd hugged her after she'd scored her first touchdown and how amazing he smelled. "We need a quarterback."

"I know," she said.

"Everyone likes Richards."

"Another thing I know."

"And? I want to hear your thoughts."

"He's a three-quarter quarterback. We need one who

can go four, plus overtime. Rookie quarterbacks also take a while to train, and often they're on the skittish side, especially when the going gets rough. They rarely make the playoffs—and have a .355 winning percentage of those games when they do—and so far none have made it to the Super Bowl. I'm just not sure he's the player to pull us out of our losing streak and get us our best chance at playoffs."

When Lance didn't say anything, she glanced over her shoulder at him. "What? You disagree?"

"No. I'm just…" He swallowed, his Adam's apple bobbing up and down. "I'm so turned on right now."

Heat streaked through her again, more savage than before, and apparently she should've set the damn thermostat to sixty degrees. "I… I'm right there with you." She should take it back, but she couldn't, not with her gaze trapped by the intensity in his. "But we're drifting toward dangerous territory."

He stepped closer, not touching, yet she could feel every inch of his tall body. Every ounce of oxygen whooshed out of her lungs and she was afraid to move or to speak, and even more afraid not to say what she should.

"What if I just *think* about violating a rule?" He asked it lightly, but the question was heavy with flirtation. His voice dipped lower, and goose bumps skated across her skin when he added a husky, "Maybe picture it in my mind."

Now she was imagining tipping her head back a bit more so his mouth could descend on hers, how his scruff would scrape lightly across her skin. "The problem with that is thoughts lead to actions," she said, her voice way too breathy.

"But there are no punishments for thoughts, correct? No reprimands?"

Lifting her chin in a facsimile of firmness, she spun to face him and attempted some fake it till she made it sternness. "I'll, uh, see that you're thinking about it and reprimand you anyway."

Instead of looking repentant, a smirk twisted his lips. "Now I'm picturing that."

"Lance, this is... We shouldn't..." She started past him, needing space to keep herself in check, but he gently placed his hand on her elbow, halting her steps.

"I'm sorry. I slipped there for a second, but I'll try to behave." He crossed his arms tightly across his chest and gripped his elbows, as if that'd be enough to keep him on his best behavior. Amusement flickered through the eyes that met hers. "Please finish explaining your crazy wall."

He was so damn impossible. And sexy. And *holy shit I'm in trouble*. She turned back around and rattled off her last few thoughts.

He reached over her and flipped the board to the other side, where he'd written a long list of names. "And your top pick for GM?"

She hesitated before pointing at the second name from the top. "He was in the middle of transforming the last team he worked for, but the owner, who's made nothing but stupid decisions, fired him before his plans could come to fruition. It's sad because they'll probably benefit from what he did anyway, but then they'll go downhill again."

Lance made a noncommittal *hmm*. His fingers wrapped around her shoulders, and she tried to stifle her earlier thoughts about his hands. "Now, tell me what upset you so early in the morning. Why were you so bothered that you came in here and did weeks' worth of analysis in a matter of an hour?"

"Thirty minutes," she said, and his fingers dug in a bit deeper.

"Spill."

Chapter Fifteen

Subconsciously, part of the reason she'd shown up at Lance's room so early might be because she'd wanted to talk to someone. Needed to, really. But she still wasn't sure it was a good idea. It was so personal and possibly TMI when it came to subjects that were okay to talk about with your boss.

But tidbits about her dad had spilled out here and there already. Shannon wasn't a good option—she'd point out that she was enabling him again, or maybe tell her that she'd warned her not to get her hopes up that he'd change, and Charlotte didn't want to hear what boiled down to "I told you so."

"My dad called this morning."

Lance didn't push. He simply waited, those long fingers still curled around her shoulders.

"He's in rehab." There it was. The secret she'd kept buried deep. There was a difference between telling people he was a gambler and admitting he was lost to the addiction that'd cost him hundreds of thousands of dollars, his reputation, and any chance at ever coaching again.

She slowly turned to face Lance, the desire to watch his response stronger than her instinct to hide the way it ripped her apart inside.

"Gambling?" he asked, and she nodded.

"In my attempt to win his affection, I accidentally enabled him enough to turn him from a frequent gambler to one who lost everything." If she hadn't been wrong about that game, the other dominos wouldn't have fallen, not so fast and not so hard.

"That's bullshit. You're not responsible for any of that."

"I don't know. Yes, he makes his own decisions, and I think he would've continued to gamble no matter what, but once he saw what I could do with stats and numbers... That's when his gambling took on a new life, one that scared me, but I didn't stop." A tight band formed around her chest. She'd never confessed this much to anyone. "We were finally spending time together, and it was nice. I also justified it by telling myself that when I wasn't with him, he lost more often. But maybe losing more frequently would've forced him to slow down."

"I doubt it. There aren't hundreds of casinos out there because people slow down once they get a taste for doubling and tripling their money. Those are the stories everyone tells, of course. How they paid for their entire trip with their winnings."

She'd heard that one from Dad and from several of his friends. "We had a good run. But I'm sure you know better than anyone that all the facts and figures in the world don't account for everything."

"You mentioned the illusion of the perfect game before," he said, reminding her that she had. To apply to love. At least *that* was metaphorical.

"Well, his luck ran out during the worst possible time. I could blame the refs and the fact that there were a lot of injuries and that it was the first game the quarterback performed so poorly, but it doesn't matter why." She reached up and twisted a strand of hair around her finger. "He got into trouble with some people who were determined to get their money back, and he ended up losing everything."

Lance continued to watch her face, not talking, not judging—from what she could tell. She debated telling him about how, in order to pay them, her dad bet against his own team and then made moves to ensure they lost, but his lawyer had settled a lot of lawsuits in the name of reasonable doubt. It also seemed unfair to bring up Dad's past mistakes when he claimed he was working hard to overcome them.

Maybe he is. Maybe I'm just paranoid and jaded.

She stuck to the recent development, about how he'd come to her to ask for help. After a long, emotionally exhausting talk, she'd convinced him to go into a facility, something she was also paying for. "This morning he calls and tells me that between the treatments and the new medication he's on to help with his impulse control, he's all better. He wants to leave early and get a job because he says he's ready to start his new life, and he can't stop worrying about how he can do that if he doesn't even have a job."

"And you have your doubts he's better?"

"It makes me feel bad to say it, but I highly doubt it. Years of addiction that spiraled out of control, and he claims a month is enough to cure him? When I dropped him off, they suggested two to three. Why not finish just to be sure? It was also expensive enough that I want to demand I get my money's worth." She rubbed at the twinge in her chest, not that it helped. "That probably makes me a bad person, too."

Lance placed his hand on the side of her neck and gently tipped up her chin with his thumb. "The fact that you're paying for it in the first place proves you're not a bad person."

"The question is, am I just an enabler? Or am I truly

helping?"

"I think this is one of those instances that intent matters."

"Like murder," she said.

Lance chuckled, but the humor quickly faded, a serious expression replacing it. "It's normal to want to help out your family. Especially when he's your only family."

"But?"

"No buts," he said. "Do you need more money?"

She simply gaped at him for several seconds, shocked at the...offer? She was pretty sure that's what it was, and the whirl of affection it caused beat out her bruised pride. Not that she could or would ever take it. "No. The consulting fee will help. I'm just not sure if I should assure him I can help him financially while he gets on his feet, because what if that makes him more determined to leave instead of stay?"

"I get that."

The way he'd listened while remaining so nonjudgmental was what she'd truly needed. She placed her hand on the center of his chest, focusing on the steady beat of his heart—a heart that clearly had more gold than ice, no matter what he claimed. "Thank you for letting me talk it out."

He covered her hand with his, holding it against the firm pecs she'd gotten an eyeful of this morning. "Anytime."

"Now I want to throw myself back into work so I don't have to worry about it again until tonight, when I can't fall asleep because of it."

"Well, if you can't fall asleep, you should come over and not sleep with me."

She bit back a smile.

"I'm serious. I'm too stressed with everything to sleep anyway."

"I'll keep that in mind," she said, even though she shouldn't. "Right now, though, give me a work challenge. Something that'll keep my mind nice and occupied until I'm supposed to meet up with the girls for manis and pedis."

"Figure out how to get us our defenseman and a quarterback who can go the distance without breaking the salary cap."

It was more than a challenge—more like an impossible mission that'd require so much math that she'd see figures for weeks—and it was exactly what she needed.

Chapter Sixteen

Bachelor party time. Lance wondered if something was wrong with him, because the thought of the party only exhausted him.

He also wasn't in that big of a hurry to hang out with a bunch of dudes, not when there was a certain woman taking up all his brain space.

But he'd do anything to make his brother happy, so he put on his game face and climbed into the limo.

There was another black limo ahead of them, and through the windshield, he watched as Stacy, her bridesmaids, and the woman he couldn't stop thinking about walked toward it. The women were laughing, and he was glad to see that Charlotte was part of the group.

Since he wouldn't be around her and a lot of horny guys most likely would be, he was less glad about the fitted purple dress that showed off her hourglass figure, along with a few inches of thigh. She'd put on fishnet stockings that immediately made his mind dive into the gutter, and if she could see him now and read the thoughts written across his face, she'd definitely reprimand him.

"Where are they going?" he asked, and his brother shot him a smug expression.

"Why?"

He grunted.

"Jealous of your girl going somewhere without you?" Hunter asked.

Yes, yes he was. His gut clenched and burned, and he curled his hands into fists. But what he said was, "She's not my girl."

"Why not?"

"She works for the Mustangs, and there are rules against it."

"So can I—?"

"No," Lance said, with enough bite that Hunter lifted his hands in the classic backing-down signal.

Mitch's smugness moved into punch-it-off-him territory. "I knew it. Mom's going to be thrilled."

"Like I said, it can't happen, and it would be better not to crush Mom's dreams, so I'd rather you not mention it."

"Fine." Mitch reached inside the stocked minibar and dug out the booze as the limo pulled away from the hotel. "But it's not like we can't all see it, Mom included. You should've heard her when they got back from the nail salon. It was Charlotte this and Charlotte that, and 'I'm so glad Lance finally found a nice girl.'"

When he'd suggested bringing her along to his brother's wedding, he thought it'd keep his mom off his case. While she'd dropped the blind date requests and hadn't given his number to any women so they could randomly call him, she was going to end up disappointed.

Something to worry about later. He only had so much room in his brain for worries. Right now, every ounce of his focus was on rebuilding the team.

Or it should be.

If he was being honest with himself—which he was really trying not to be—it was on the other limo and how it and Charlotte were going in the opposite direction.

Three stops and countless drinks later, half the guys in the wedding party were one more shot away from belligerence. Lance had stuck to mostly beer and a tumbler of inordinately expensive whiskey, and now he was beyond ready to go back to the resort and put the night behind him. He'd been over the party scene long ago, and clubs had never been his thing.

Mitch looked at his phone, his face illuminated by the bright screen. He shifted forward in his seat and told the driver, "One more stop."

Lance bit back a groan as Mitch rattled off the name of what sounded like a pretentious club. "I'm not sure that's a good idea. Pretty soon these guys are going to be stupid enough to end up in the tabloids. You, too."

"Oh, and you don't want me stealing your most-eligible-bachelor-status thunder?"

Lance whacked the back of his brother's head, earning a laugh from him and most everyone in the car. "You can have all the thunder, jackass. I just want to go back to the hotel and live out my bachelor status by going to bed."

"If you want, you can ask the driver to take you to the resort after he drops us off, and I'll just have him come back for us afterward."

Thank God. Lance didn't want to sit in a club and watch the guys drink, and he didn't want to brush off women's advances, the way he had at the last place. It was hard to explain that he was taken when he wasn't.

Although he was.

Dammit, it was complicated, and he hated when people said stupid shit like that about their relationship status. Either you were in one or not. He didn't want to be in one. Didn't have time.

But...

"Okay, you guys have fun," he said when the limo pulled up to the curb. The smile Mitch gave him sent foreboding prickling across his skin. He was about to be the brunt of a joke, he could sense it.

"I should probably mention that the reason we're coming to this particular club is because the girls are here. Which means that Charlotte is here, too." His brother's grin widened. "Still want to go back to the hotel, old man?"

Lance lifted his middle finger.

But then he climbed out of the limo, and at the thought of seeing Charlotte, every ounce of tiredness that'd crept into his body melted away.

• • •

Charlotte laughed as their group danced around the center of the floor, their moves exaggerated and extra sloppy thanks to the alcohol they'd consumed.

They'd done a pub crawl of sorts, hitting bars up and down the outer banks. Somewhere in the middle they'd also stopped at a luxury lingerie and beauty boutique where the employees had taken their spree in stride. Then they'd ended up in this club, where they'd had another round of drinks. Thanks to all the dancing, Charlotte's buzz was already fading, which meant other thoughts were creeping in.

I probably should've called Dad back. What if I'm not being supportive enough, and that makes it harder for him to succeed?

No, it's okay to take a day to figure out how I feel, and I'm not thinking about that for another hour. Or two?

It's not like she could have an intense conversation like that at a noisy nightclub, and the girls didn't seem as if they'd be stopping anytime soon.

Stacy's *Bride-to-Be* sash slipped down her shoulders, stopping around her waist.

Charlotte stepped toward her and readjusted it. "Those moves are too awesome to be constrained. Not to mention I'd never forgive myself if you tripped and sprained your ankle or something."

Stacy giggled and grabbed Charlotte's hands, swaying and spinning her before pulling her in for a hug. "I'm so glad you came. It's been a long time since I've seen Lance so happy, too. He's usually sorta grumpy."

"Oh, he's plenty grumpy still. I drive him crazy."

"Yes, you do, but in a good way."

"I'm not sure that's a thing," Charlotte said with a laugh, but Stacy nodded, her mini-veil bobbing with the movement.

"It is. And you can't disagree with a bride before her wedding—it's a rule."

"Well, I am a rule follower."

Stacy gave her a sloppy grin. "Good. You know, ever since Lance's last girlfriend cheated on him, he hasn't dated at all. That and the injury turned him into a hermit, and Maribelle's been so worried about him. I told her that when the right girl came along, he'd get it together."

Charlotte didn't know what to say. Everyone was getting the wrong idea—hell, even she was. Earlier today he'd listened to her, and they'd had a great afternoon, getting a ton of work done and culling down their list to their top picks for several positions.

"I'm not disagreeing with the bride-to-be, per se," Charlotte started, "but you should know that Lance and I aren't a couple. We just work together."

"Okay, but then why is he striding over here like he's coming to claim you?"

Charlotte whipped around. She thought Stacy would laugh about how she'd proved her point by pretending Lance was at the club, and how fast Charlotte had turned to check.

But there he was, striding toward her exactly like she'd said, and even as she told herself it wasn't a big deal and the rest of the guys were heading their way as well, a thrill shivered up her core.

His gaze was predatory, and her flight instinct should really be kicking in about now.

But if she was in fact his prey, she couldn't even pretend that she didn't want to be caught.

Chapter Seventeen

Lance glared at the vultures who'd been circling, adding an extra glower at the dude who'd been ogling Charlotte's legs.

Not that he could blame him, but those were *his* legs to ogle.

Rational thought had fled the instant he'd seen her on the floor, dancing and laughing, and he didn't even care if his brother gave him shit.

Finally he reached her, and his hand automatically went to her hip. "Fancy seeing you here."

"I was thinking the same about you," she said, her voice slightly breathless from the dancing. Her cheeks were flushed, too, and holy shit she was beautiful.

He glanced around at the gyrating bodies and felt completely out of place. This was what he got for charging without thinking. He jerked his chin in the direction of the bar. "Wanna grab a drink?"

Before Charlotte could answer, Stacy gave her a firm shove, hard enough Charlotte wobbled and gripped on to his arms for support.

"Have fun, you two," she said with a grin. He'd have to thank her later.

Still, he waited to make sure Charlotte was on board with the plan to grab a drink with him instead of tossing her over his shoulder like the caveman she'd turned him into. He raised an eyebrow, and the tiny groove in her cheek came out as she nodded. "A drink sounds good."

He took hold of her hand so he wouldn't lose her in the push and pull of the moving crowd, and an electric current twisted up his arm as she laced her fingers with his.

Once they reached the bar, he ordered a whiskey neat and turned to get her order.

"The same for me," she said to the bartender.

He couldn't keep the surprise off his face.

"When in Rome," she said with a shrug. "Also, whiskey was what my dad always kept in the house, and sometimes when friends came over, we'd break into his stash, so it's my go-to when I want something with a kick."

"Underage drinking?" He gasped. "You broke some rules?"

"Back in the day." She reached for the tumbler the bartender slid across the bar and tipped it back in one big gulp. "Speaking of the rules"—she lowered her voice into flirtatious territory as she batted her dark eyelashes at him— "your hand is in danger of breaking section three of the handbook, Mr. Quaid."

He hadn't realized he'd hooked it over her hip, but now tantalizing heat was replacing the blood in his body, compelling him to tighten his grip. He tipped back his own drink and tugged her closer so her body was flush with his. "I'm still a bit fuzzy on the rules."

"Sounds like I'd better give you a lesson."

Usually he'd groan and prepare for a lecture, but she hadn't moved away, and her voice had a sultry edge, as did the curve of her lips.

"This is the line…" She put her hand over his and moved it higher on her side. Then she moved it down, sliding it along her hip and leaving it on the curve of her ass. "This would be breaking it." She moved it up again. "Fine." Back down to her ass, and his fingers twitched of their own accord. She *tsked*. "Definitely breaking it."

Desire inundated his system and his thoughts grew fuzzy—and not from the whiskey.

"Also, this…" She pressed the front of her body against his. "Too close, lots of improper touching—it'd definitely make other coworkers uncomfortable, too."

His throat went dry, and he rasped out, "Good thing none of our coworkers are here."

"Yeah. Guess that's the positive spin to you firing them all." Her smile turned haughty, and no amount of thinking of plays or drills could keep him from hardening against her stomach.

The pulse beating at the base of her throat fluttered, and he reached his other hand up and cupped her neck, his thumb resting against that rush of blood.

"See, I'm used to football rules. Whenever I'd put my finger on those laces…" He moved his hand to her lower back, spreading his fingers and holding her flush against him. "Protect the ball at all costs. Don't get sacked. Because when you get sacked, a lot of times things get dirty."

"Ooh," she said, and he gave her a look.

"Head out of the gutter, James. I mean that players might take advantage of the fact that refs can't see very well. They might rough the passer a bit." He gently jostled her. Then he lowered his mouth to her ear. "There's even been some biting."

He sank his teeth into the shell of her ear, and she arched against him, as if she couldn't help herself. Which made it that much harder to control himself.

He didn't even care if they were creating a spectacle. All he cared about was that she wasn't pulling away.

"With the helmets," she breathed, "ear biting seems highly unlikely."

His lips brushed her temple as he said, "Did you want me to bite somewhere else?"

Her fingers dug into his biceps, and her breasts bumped against his chest as she inhaled and exhaled. "Lance," she whispered, and the want flooding his insides turned to need. He needed this woman.

But a deal was a deal. Or a decree or whatever the hell it was. *She* had to make the move. He stayed perfectly still, silently urging her to rise onto her toes and kiss him. "Mm-hmm," he finally said.

She peered up at him, suddenly shy. "I..." She glanced around. "There are all these other women here, undoubtedly wanting a shot at dancing with you. There's a chance someone might snap a few pics to send out to the gossip rags, and it'd be free PR, the NFL's newest eligible bachelor out on the town for a night."

Talk about whiplash. He was thinking of kissing her breathless and whisking her out of the club, and she was worried about PR?

"Didn't I tell you I didn't care about PR?"

"You can't just not care about it," she said.

"Fine. If I leave your side, other guys will hit on you, and that'll piss me off and then I'll get into a fight, which would be *bad* PR." Since he wanted a reason to keep touching her, keep this night going where he wanted it to, he took a few breaths to calm himself down the best he could and tugged her toward the floor. "This bachelor only wants to dance with you. And, Charlotte, that's coming from a guy who would usually run the other way at the mention of the word *dance*."

Chapter Eighteen

This was the most pathetic attempt at putting up a fight *ever*. No, she didn't fight, didn't drag her feet, simply let Lance tug her into the crowd of swaying bodies on the dance floor.

As if Fate—or the Master Temptress—was in charge, the music changed to a slow song. Lance drew her close and wound his arms around her waist. She tipped onto her toes and linked her fingers behind his neck.

Every inch of her body was plastered against him, and since she had to reach—even in her heels—it meant she was also leaning heavily on him.

"I like this dress you're wearing," Lance said, his gaze dipping to take her in. Passion flared in the blue depths, and his pupils nearly swallowed them up. That same passion transferred to her, rolling through her body in a molten wave. "And those fucking tights. The mix of siren and sweet shoes with bows on them made me crazy the instant I saw them."

She swallowed and worked to keep her voice even. "Usually I wear more proper ones, but I decided the club and this purple bandage dress called for fishnets, so I picked some up on my way back from the nail salon."

"Proper," he said with a *pft*. "Those other tights with the black line are just as sexy. Every time I see them my fingers twitch with the need to trace that line up the back of your calves, thighs…all the way up your skirt."

Her attempt to swallow again went nowhere, her throat too tight. "They're classic. And vintage."

"They're naughty."

She shook her head but couldn't help the smile. "I stand by my classic claim. I do see what you mean about the combo, though. Yours is also doing strange things to my insides." She ran one finger down the buttons on his shirt. "Part business, with top buttons casually undone. Sleeves rolled up, showing off your muscled forearms…"

With a smile, he lifted his arm and let her get up close and personal with one of her favorites of his features. She traced the large vein across the top, her mouth going dry.

"Then there's the beard…" As soon as she shifted to touch his jaw, his hand returned to the curve of her ass, an inch or so lower than proper. She dragged her fingertips across the stubble, up to the scruff above his lip. She flattened her hand and smoothed her palm down the side of his face, enjoying the scrape of whiskers against sensitive skin.

They barely swayed, their eyes locked on each other. The rest of the people faded away, her world narrowing to the feel of his body against hers. His blue eyes. The soulful musician singing about love. The flickering lights highlighting each one of Lance's rugged features.

Her attention narrowed in on those lips, so inviting, so close. "Prepare for the awkward," she whispered, and he held her tighter as a slow smile spread across his face.

He inclined his head, his mouth a breath away. "Okay. I'm prepared."

"I don't think you are." She moved her hands to his

shoulders and tipped as far on to her toes as she could. Seconds ground out in the air, and her rapid pulse thundered through her head. Self-consciousness set in, and she really should've popped a mint or something. Without thinking, she lowered herself back onto her heels.

"You're right," he said. "This *is* awkward."

She gave him a dirty look. "I just need…" Her tongue struggled to form the right words, which were never going to come to her anyway.

"What do you need, Charlotte? Name it."

Okay. Try two. She could do this. "Don't move…"

"Your wish is my…wish."

Her stomach rose up, up, up, and she mimicked the movement with her whole body, tipping onto her toes again. One last sip of oxygen and she pressed her lips against his. A jolt whipped through her body, zapping every organ at once.

But he didn't move. Didn't deepen the kiss. She pulled back an inch and scrunched up her eyebrows. "I thought… I thought you'd help a little more."

His low laugh echoed against the hands she'd braced on his chest. "You told me not to move. Trust me, it wasn't easy, either."

"I didn't mean like forever. Just as I was—"

His lips crashed down on hers, insistent yet soft, and her body went pliant. If he hadn't held her up as he parted her lips with his tongue and delved inside, she would've melted to the floor. She clung on to him as the world around them spun, lights flickering faster, the music drowned out by the rush of her heated blood.

His thigh slipped between both of hers, and she moaned as he pressed against the ache forming between her legs. Her body arched of its own accord, and she gasped at his hard length.

She fisted his shirt in her hands and moved her mouth

against his, wanting more—needing more.

He gave it, too. Friction, hands roving, tongue stroking. A groan that ripped from his throat and sent her desire into the intoxicating range.

Holy shit, holy shit. She thought she'd been kissed before, but this kiss… It blew those kisses out of the water so far that they couldn't even be categorized as kisses anymore.

They broke apart, and satisfaction zinged through her veins when he was breathing as heavily as she was.

He lowered his forehead to hers, brushing his lips across hers before giving them a gentle kiss. "That was worth the awkward. Worth the wait."

"We're going to have to add an addendum to our Wedding Deal agreement."

He closed his eyes and shook his head. "There's the ego check I guess I needed."

"What? Oh. No." She placed both hands on the sides of his face and kissed him. "That kiss was…fucking amazing."

His eyes darkened again. His fingers dug into her ass, not even close to the proper range now.

"I just meant that I'm thinking…" More like she wasn't thinking, not properly. But after that kiss, with the want in her body screeching toward need… Everything inside her screamed to give in to her baser instincts, throw caution to the wind, and have sex with Lance Quaid while she had the chance. After that kiss, her stance on what she might regret had flipped, and she was almost sure she'd regret it if she *didn't*. "I want to take you up on your offer. To come to your room tonight and not-sleep with you."

Since he'd told her she needed to initiate, she ran her hand down his torso, watching the muscles in his jaw flex and tighten. She swiped her finger back and forth over the top of his waistband. Her eyes homed in on the bulge behind his zipper, and wetness pooled between her thighs. "No, I don't think we're going to get much sleep tonight."

He caught her wrist and folded it against his chest. "I just need a moment or two of you not touching me and then we'll get out of here."

• • •

Getting himself under control wasn't easy with Charlotte so close, especially with the taste of her still on his lips, her scent overwhelming his senses.

Admittedly he'd previously judged people for grinding against each other in a club with other people watching. Now he got it and then some. It'd been so easy to get carried away.

And if you think about that, you're never going to calm down enough to leave.

Just as he was ready and had grabbed her hand to pull her off the floor, Stacy and Grace showed up.

"Bridget just texted to say she got sick in the bathroom," Stacy said with a grimace, swiveling her phone screen toward them as if they would need proof. She also turned it back to herself before he could read it, and he was glad, since he was pretty sure there was a picture. "I guess it's not a party until someone tells a stranger she loves them before running to the bathroom to puke. Anyway, I need help getting her out of the bathroom and into the car. Charlotte, I hope you're stronger than you look."

Charlotte glanced at him, and he wanted to shout *no, forget the drunken bridesmaid*, but her apologetic expression made it clear she felt the need to go help.

After a couple of seconds to process and switch gears from spending the night touching and kissing Charlotte to the emergency bridesmaid-down situation, he couldn't just leave Stacy and Grace to deal with it themselves, either. "Once you girls get her out of the bathroom," he said, "I'll help you get her into the car."

Mitch rushed over before they could take so much as a step. "Small problem." His words came out clipped as he worked to catch his breath. "Jack's all riled up about some girl who apparently has a boyfriend. Hunter's holding him back, but it's going to get ugly fast, and I need your help." He glanced at his fiancée. "Sorry, babe. I was having fun dancing with you. Gonna have blue balls till Saturday night from it, but still."

She leaned forward and gave him a sloppy kiss. She wobbled back on her heels, clamped on to Charlotte's hand, and tugged her in the direction of the bathrooms.

"I'll call you later," Lance mouthed, but he wasn't sure if Charlotte saw, and he was worried she was going to talk herself out of the moment they'd had. Of course he wouldn't want her to regret anything later, so he told himself it was for the best, in spite of how much it sucked for her to get ripped away.

Then he went with his brother to go break up a fight, cursing testosterone on two different levels.

Chapter Nineteen

Being the "sober one" had its ups and downs. Charlotte's alcohol buzz had worn off, leaving her in charge of cramming the girls in the limo and ensuring they were all safely tucked into their beds.

It'd taken twenty minutes and three upturned purses before the girls had found the key to the two-bedroom suite they were sharing. The entire time they kept telling Charlotte how glad they were they'd met and how she was such a good friend. They also doled out the kind of compliments about her outfit, hair, and makeup that inebriated girls were famous for.

Honestly, it was nice, albeit exhausting.

After helping Bridget wash up and change into clean clothes, Charlotte wrestled her into bed.

The other two she simply removed shoes and helped arrange sheets and covers.

Partway through tucking Stacy in, the bride-to-be reached up and patted Charlotte's cheek. "I'm so glad you're here. You're so pretty and nice, and I'm so glad you're here."

Charlotte didn't bother telling her she'd said that glad part twice. Or that she'd already told her she was pretty. "Thank you for inviting me. It was the best bachelorette party I've ever been to." And it was, something she was sure would hold up even if she'd been to more than one.

"Sorry we got so drunk. Usually I'm the responsible one, and it was nice to take a night off from it. Sometimes you just have to let go and blow off some steam, you know?"

Charlotte didn't know, but she was considering finding out. Especially since her Lance buzz was still in full effect, every part of her tingling whenever she thought about him. About that kiss and their dance.

Once she'd placed ibuprofen and bottles of water on nightstands, Charlotte went the extra mile by plugging phones into chargers and putting them on do-not-disturb mode.

With everyone settled, she crept out of their room and dug her phone out of her clutch. It'd taken much longer to get the girls situated than she'd thought it would.

She wondered how Lance and the guys had fared at the club after she and the rest of the bridal party had left. He hadn't called or texted.

After debating her next move for a couple of seconds, she went to her hotel room.

Paced across the space a few times.

Then she decided she'd regret not at least checking if things were still as steamy between them as they had been in the club. It was more than just her body craving his; earlier today he'd been there for her in a way no one else really had.

He'd listened. He was kind. He cared if she played football with him, and more than that, if she caught a pass.

If she went to his room tonight, she was sure he would take care of her in more than one way, and that thought sealed the deal.

No more hesitation.

Except to rush into the bathroom, brush her teeth, and add an extra swipe of deodorant and spritz of perfume. She pulled her dress from her body, double-checking she had on her sexiest bra. The panties matched, too. Might as well take advantage of that, because it didn't happen all that often.

"Taking a night off from being responsible," she muttered as she exited her room. "Blowing off some steam. I deserve that."

I deserve a night of amazing sex, too.

It felt a bit naughty to be sneaking down the hallway so late, and that amped her up even more.

Once she reached Lance's room, she lifted her fist to knock.

But before she could follow through, the door swung open, and Lance nearly bumped into her as he stepped into the hallway. He caught her shoulders, double-checking she was steady, but with his hands on her, she was anything but. "I was just coming to see you," he said.

"You were going to walk all the way down the hallway and everything?"

A devastating smile spread across his ridiculously handsome face. "For the right woman, I might walk down *two* hallways."

"But then you'd miss my room, because I'm not that far, and—"

He tugged her through the open doorway, into his room. "You can never just take a compliment, can you?"

"It's my curse to bear. That and, you know, rule-following."

"And how are you feeling about that last one right now? If you've changed your mind, all you have to do is say the word. We can just sit and talk. Order room service..." His gaze ran down the length of her body, and his throat worked a swallow. "But to be clear, I really want to kiss you again. I just need to know if it's what you want."

"I can say with 100 percent certainty that I want you to kiss me again." Her exhale came out shaky, equal parts nerves and excitement. "That I want to finish what we started on the dance floor."

Lance flipped the second lock and flattened a palm by the side of her head. "Then brace yourself." He lowered himself onto her, his large body pinning her to the door. "I'm about to violate every section of the handbook."

For one torturous eternity he froze like that, and then his lips descended on hers. Unlike in the club, he kissed her slower this time, as if he were memorizing and savoring every nip and lick.

His hand slid up her side, grazing her hip, her breast. He plunged his other hand into her hair, fisting it and jerking her head to the side so he could kiss the column of her neck.

A whimper escaped as she arched against him, needing that friction that'd set her on fire at the club. He reached down, hooked his hand under her knee, and brought it up and over his hip. It lined her core up with his erection, and a groan rumbled deep in his throat as she rolled her hips. He peppered kisses along her collarbone, up to her jaw, across to that spot right under her ear that made her moan. Back to her lips

She threw herself fully into the kiss, tangling her tongue with his. He growled into her mouth, sending her spiraling that much higher.

His hand skimmed up the thigh of the leg she had around him, his thumb snagging the fabric and yanking her skirt higher. She bucked against him as he skated the pad over the spot where her inner thigh met her panties.

The next stroke was over her center and tipped her toward frantic madness. She looped her arms around his neck and climbed his massive frame, wrapping both legs around his waist. He moved both hands to her butt, hefting her fully into his arms before spinning them around and carrying her toward the bedroom.

He lowered her to her feet, and when she made a noise of protest, he said, "Patience."

"I don't have any of that." Proper, filtered responses had fled her brain after he'd so thoroughly kissed and groped her. The only thing left was pure unadulterated need, the kind that consumed and conquered.

"Me neither," Lance said, his voice rough. "But I'm going to do my best to find some, because I want to take my time with you."

Fire licked at her, twisted up her core.

"Now spin around."

She wanted to protest again, but her tongue was too tied and there was something hot about his demand, and *holy shit* she was in trouble in the best possible way.

As soon as she did as instructed, he wrapped an arm around her and pulled her back against his chest, his erection lined up with her ass. Since he was having his fun, she pushed against it, grinning when he groaned.

Cool air swept over her as he slowly undid the zipper of her dress, closely followed by his warm breath skating across her shoulders. The combination of soft lips and rough scruff hit her skin as he tugged off one strap and then the other. His hands glided across her back as he pushed down her dress. The fabric caught on her hips and butt for a moment before he gave another jerk that sent it pooling to her still-heeled feet.

Her insecurities began to drift to the surface with so much of her on display, but they were shoved right back down when Lance swore and dragged his fingers across the waistband of her thong. Those strong fingers dug into her hips and turned her around to face him. His eyes drank her in, his pupils dilating and promising an exhilarating mix of danger and fun, and a shiver of desire racked her body.

"You. Drive me." He kissed her again, his tongue stroking hers as his hands roved over her curves, squeezing and exploring. "Completely crazy." Unlike the other time he'd told her as much, the words were filled with a different kind of passion, one that echoed through her.

She brushed her fingers across his jaw, finding it hard to get enough of touching his beard after thinking about it so much. "Right back at you, big guy."

He backed her onto the edge of the bed, easing her into a sitting position, then dropped to his knees. As he slid off her shoes, all she could do was watch, completely mesmerized.

It suddenly struck her that she was now only wearing underwear while he was still sporting way too many clothes. So when he reached for the top of her tights, she playfully smacked his hand. "If I'm going to be this naked, you've got to shed some of your clothes before I lose what little of mine I have left."

She scooted to the edge of the bed, her legs on either side of him, and began undoing the buttons on his shirt. Her fingers trembled a bit, her entire body so keyed up she wasn't sure she'd ever come down again.

After the last button was undone, she pushed his shirt off his shoulders, exposing that glorious torso. He watched every movement, those blue eyes so steady on hers.

"Is this really happening?" she whispered.

He nodded. "Hell yeah."

Him on his knees, staring at her in a way that made her feel more beautiful and sexier than she'd ever felt before? "Hell yeah," she echoed. As she leaned forward to unbutton his pants, she kissed him again—it wasn't something she ever thought she'd get used to.

I probably won't have the chance, she thought and

immediately batted away. Tonight was about letting loose. Later she'd worry about, well, later.

The low noise he made in the back of his throat as he sprang free spurred her on, and she cupped him over his underwear, exploring his impressive length before giving it a squeeze.

His eyes rolled back. Then he gripped her wrist, his voice coming out gruff. "My turn. I want to see how those sexy tights look piled on the floor next to my bed."

She'd expected him to rip them off, but he moved his hands over her legs, torturously slowly like he'd done when he'd removed her dress. He kissed between the diamond strings, his lips and tongue wetting her bare skin.

"See. Naughty." Up and up he went, and her breath lodged in her throat when he placed a hot, open-mouth kiss on her hip bone. His fingers curled into the elastic top, and she lifted her hips as he peeled off the fishnets and tossed them next to her shoes and dress.

His palms ran up the inside of her legs as he climbed over her. His lips recaptured hers, and the next thing she knew, her bra was loose. A quick tug in the center and it was all the way off, her exposed nipples peaking under the combination of cool air and his lust-filled gaze.

Under other circumstances, she might have been embarrassed about the needy noises she made as he licked and sucked her breasts, but she was too far gone to her desires to care.

Charlotte hummed as his lips moved lower, first to the top of her stomach, her navel. Lower...

Her panties joined the pile of clothes on the floor, and then his mouth was over her, his tongue circling and stroking and making her lose her grip on any thoughts besides *more, there,* and *omigosh yes.*

Right as she teetered on the blissful edge, so close she

stopped breathing altogether, he added a finger, curling it deep inside her. She shattered apart, freefalling into oblivion.

And he was there to catch her, pulling her so tightly in his arms that she went ahead and let herself fall even deeper.

· · ·

Watching Charlotte come apart, no walls in sight, flooded him with affection and desire and a dozen other emotions he couldn't name.

"Amazing" didn't quite cover it, but it was the closest word he had.

He lowered her back to the bed, satisfaction going through him at her swollen lips and hooded lids.

One of her hands drifted up his arms as she made an *mmm* noise. Her hand slid up a few more inches, cupping his neck and bringing him down on top of her.

The feel of her soft skin made him that much harder, and a second ago he would've said that was impossible. He reached over to the nightstand, fumbling for his wallet. First he came up with the notepad and then his hotel key.

Finally, his fingers found the leather square. He took out a condom, disposed of the wrapper, and rolled it on.

"Hurry," she said, rubbing her thighs together. "I need you inside me now."

If his craving for her hadn't turned all-consuming, he might've told her to be patient, the way he had earlier when he was teasing her and drawing it out. But he couldn't wait to sink himself between her legs and get even more lost in the feel of her.

Bracing himself on his elbows, he nudged her slick entrance. He covered her mouth with his, kissing her as he thrust inside.

He did his best to draw it out, but it'd been a while, and

part of him still couldn't believe he was having sex with this incredible, beautiful woman. He managed to hold on until he felt her clench around him. She cried out his name, and the second her release had finished having its way with her body, he let go and followed after her.

As soon as his breathing returned to semi-normal, he drew her to him. He kissed her bare shoulder and skimmed his fingers down her side. He knew how quickly things could change, how life could give you a great moment and take it away, so he wanted to hold on to this one as long as he could. "Stay the night with me?"

She twisted enough to look at him, those green eyes peering deep into his soul and grabbing hold of it. "Okay," she said.

As he drifted off with her warm body against his, he took a few seconds to memorize everything about her, from her scent to her mussed hair to how perfectly she fit against him and the happy sigh sound she made when he hugged her tighter.

That way, when the bulldozer called life inevitably came calling, he could relive this moment, this night, again and again.

Chapter Twenty

To help ensure Charlotte didn't wake up and immediately regret everything, Lance ordered coffee and asked them to bring more of the creamer she liked, since he'd noticed it was running low. He'd also added bacon, because bacon.

She rolled over in bed as he finished up the call, her head coming to rest on his shoulder.

"I ordered breakfast," he said after he'd done a contortionist-worthy twist to get the phone back in its cradle without risking Charlotte slipping off him.

"I heard."

He swiped the hair off her face and dragged his thumb over her cheekbone. "How are you feeling this morning?"

A contented sigh came out, punctuated by a brilliant smile.

"Good," he said. "I was afraid you might regret crossing lines."

She sat up, the sheet tucked across her breasts. "No. But that does remind me, I need to work up a new addendum and—"

He groaned. "I should've never said anything. And that can wait. Right now, we're enjoying the chance to lay in bed for a few more minutes." He tugged her back to him, wrapping an arm around her and planting a kiss on her lips. It'd been a long time since he'd woken up next to anyone, and he found that he liked it. He knew he couldn't get used to it—not when his life and the team was in such upheaval—but none of the panic that'd accompanied some of his previous relationships came along for the ride.

Probably because she knew where he stood and he knew where she did, and that helped alleviate some of that pressure.

"They said the food would arrive in about thirty minutes," he said. "Think that gives us enough time to take a shower?"

"Well, it'd certainly save time if we showered together, and we do have all that work to do."

He brushed his lips across hers. "Have I mentioned I like the way your mind works?"

She surprised him by climbing over his body to straddle him and take control of the kiss. He happily let her have her way with him for a minute or two. Then he pushed himself up with her in his arms and carried her into the bathroom, where under the spray of water, they managed to amp up the steam even more.

• • •

After shower sex and breakfast, Charlotte had barely had time to rush to her room and change into fresh clothes before hurrying back to the "office" for the phone call with a prospective quarterback. His agent had contacted Lance yesterday while she was at the spa. His client was currently a restricted free agent who'd been wanting to play for someone different for a while.

As the thirty-minute call was winding down, Lance

thanked him for taking the time to talk with them and for his interest in the Mustangs.

Charlotte was so lost in thought that Lance had to nudge her knee. "Oh. Yeah. Goodbye. It was nice chatting with you."

"We'll be in touch." Lance disconnected the call and twisted on the couch to face her. "What is it?"

"You tell me your thoughts first."

He looked like he was going to object, but then he braced his forearms on his knees. "He's our top prospect so far. He's willing to play for us, for one, and he's got a hell of an arm. He has a few seasons under his belt, so he doesn't have some of the issues a rookie would, but he hasn't played for long enough that he's so set in his ways it's impossible to get him to change it up. I think we can make it work."

She nodded. Then nodded some more.

Lance curled his hand around her calf. He picked up her leg and settled her foot in his lap. His fingers dug in, and she nearly moaned at how good it felt. Dancing all night in heels wasn't for the faint of heart. "You have your reservations. Why?"

"I hesitate to voice them because I haven't dug deep enough to know if the numbers will back me up." She should've done a better job studying up on the guy before the call so she'd have more than the surface stats her brain automatically retained, but she'd chosen sex, and while she hated feeling unprepared, she didn't regret it one bit.

"Tell me your gut instinct."

Her lungs constricted, too many memories of her father getting upset about her failed hunches bobbing to the surface and increasing the pressure. "Gut instincts are sometimes wrong. Maybe my gut is just saying I've had too much coffee."

"Charlotte. Spill."

The dang guy could read her like a book, so she went

ahead and let the thoughts bouncing through her brain pour out. "He's been playing with some of the best, most seasoned receivers in the league, and when I mentioned that, he didn't say one nice thing about them—just that he was ready to come up with some of his own plays and set his own records. He's so entitled, and I could tell he thinks of us as either a stepping stone or his way to get famous quick."

"There are plenty of entitled, self-centered players. Several who win championships."

"He doesn't play by the rules."

"Ah. I can see how that's a big strike in your book."

She searched for the words to explain why everything in her was screaming *wrong, wrong, wrong.* "Right, but that combined with the other things… He got into a bit of trouble with the law back in college and was also under investigation for seeking improper benefits while being recruited. Not that it seemed to matter to his other team when they drafted him, but the last thing we need is a Deflategate on our hands."

Lance sighed and ran his hand over his face, and she worried he was getting upset with the opinion she'd voiced.

"I could be wrong. I'm only a consultant. In the end, it's your choice. The coach's and general manager's as well, if we have those in place before the draft in two weeks. But we could also think we have him secured, and he could be playing the field, promising several teams he'll play with them to drive up his salary. Then if we do get him, we pay a lot *and* lose one of our draft picks."

"Hey." He gestured for the other foot, and she swung it up so he could give it the same treatment. "The reason I'm sighing isn't because I disagree. It's because my gut says no, too. I wanted you to talk me into him, since he's the best prospect we have."

"I can find a way to try to do that if you really need me to."

He stared at her for a few beats before using his grip on her foot to tug her closer. He leaned over and kissed her. "You are smart and beautiful, and I'm so damn lucky that my grandpa hired you. I value your opinion and like that you're so willing to help me however I need you to. I need your gut more than I need you to bullshit me."

"Good," she muttered against his lips. "Because I'm no good at bullshitting. And that guy just isn't the one."

"I thought you didn't believe in the one."

"In football I do," she said, although she was feeling more optimistic about the possibility of it in other areas after last night and this morning.

He smiled and rested his forehead against hers. "How are we ever going to pull this team together in time?"

"We'll find a way. That's the thing about not having a choice."

"Maybe just an ounce of bullshit would be good about now."

She laughed and slanted her lips over his, leaving her hand on the side of his face. "I promise we'll get a team hammered together. It might be a bumpy ride, but we only have to win one game to be doing better than last year— That's not even bullshit. Just a little sunshiney truth for you."

He squeezed her foot. "Thank you."

"Anytime. Also, see how good we're doing since signing the addendum for the l—dating contract?" She'd almost called it the love contract, which was the nickname she usually used for the Consensual Romance in the Workplace Agreement. Saying *love*—even as a nickname—seemed too serious and would probably scare both of them, and calling it a *sex contract* made it sound too *Fifty Shades of Grey*.

For now the Wedding Deal had been updated with the paragraphs she'd taken out before, putting their semi-undefined relationship in print to cover both of their asses.

His as the boss and hers as the human resources manager.

"Yep," Lance said. "Bonus, none of our nonexistent coworkers are uncomfortable with our PDA."

Charlotte giggled and even held her hand up for a high five. "Killing it." The loud *smack* of their palms filled the air.

"Hey, another reason not to hire anyone else. Silver lining right there."

"Sure. You play quarterback, I'll be your tight end." She waggled her eyebrows. "Then you can also coach while I do the GM thing. And human resources. And...I might need a raise. But now that we're in a personal entanglement, you can't give that to me, so..." She tapped her finger to her lip. "I'm starting to see a few flaws."

"Hey, babe," he said, and her heart skipped at the pet name. "Maybe just rest the brain and logic for a bit."

"It's not something I can just shut off."

"Well then let me do the honors," he said, lowering his lips to hers and making her forget what they'd been talking about and why she'd thought it'd been important in the first place.

Chapter Twenty-One

As tempting as it was to get lost in Charlotte again and again, Lance's phone refused to stop ringing. If he didn't answer, it'd only ring more. Dropping off the grid would also worry people or possibly lose him the chance to snag a player he might need, and as he lifted the phone, despising it the tiniest bit, he had to work to keep a snarl out of his greeting.

Charlotte started to slide off his lap, their lunch/make-out break over, but he put his hand on her knee, holding her in place.

"Say that again." He needed to know he'd heard what he'd thought he'd heard correctly. Because it sounded like the agent on the other end of the phone had said the Pythons were willing to part with their second-string quarterback.

Gavin Frost was a great player who rarely got game time — hazards of being backup for one of the top quarterbacks in the NFL.

Lance swiveled the mouthpiece and gave Charlotte the name. Her eyes widened. He loved how she automatically understood.

She slipped off his lap and began pacing the room, which struck him as funny since they'd reversed their usual positions for whenever he was on a call.

Excitement rose up, growing stronger with each second, despite his best attempts to tell himself not to get too carried away. Not to let his desperation show. "What's it going to take to get him to play for the Mustangs?"

"Look, I'll just lay it out there. He's gotten a lot of interest. Money's important, but it's not what's most important to him. We were both impressed when we heard the kind of changes you're making, and he'd like to be part of rebuilding a team. What we both want is to find a place that'd make him a franchise quarterback, one synonymous with turning around the team. He's scrappy and determined, and he won't stop until he wins a championship, either."

"That's exactly what we're looking for," Lance said.

"So, make us an offer."

"I'm definitely interested, but I need some time to crunch numbers and see what we can do. I'll get back to you."

"The sooner the better."

"I hear you. I'll be in touch." He hit the end button, waiting a few extra seconds to make sure the call was disconnected. He was almost afraid to say anything or even hope this could work. He'd admired Gavin Frost's college career and wondered why no one had snatched him up until the third round of the draft. He was a damn good quarterback who'd sat the bench unless he was saving the Pythons' praised golden boy from injury or fatigue. That would've irritated the shit out of him back in the day, so he could only imagine how frustrated Gavin had been the past three years.

"You haven't said anything," he said, glancing up at Charlotte. She'd stopped her pacing, but she was biting her thumbnail, anxiousness radiating off her. His gut sank. Maybe he was wrong about Frost. If she told him she didn't think he was the one, either, they might have their first huge disagreement about the actual team, and he wasn't sure what that'd do. To them or to his head—it'd give him more doubts than he wanted to have about a decision this big, that was for sure.

Her eyes met his. "I was waiting for you."

"I want him on the team." Everything inside of him yelled *yes* all over again. There wasn't a better option; he felt it in his bones.

She nodded. "He's exactly what we've been looking for. And we can afford to lose a third-round pick if we get a decent quarterback with a few seasons under his belt. I'm afraid to say it because I don't want to jinx us, but that thing I said earlier about the other guy not being...you know. Well, Gavin Frost, he's...you know."

Half the time he couldn't follow her rambling or her references, but he perfectly understood what she was saying in this instance. The fact that she agreed and clearly felt so strongly about it sent reassurance rushing through him. "How do we figure out how much to offer so we won't break the salary cap, lose him, or go completely broke?"

"That's a question for the CFO. I know I said that before when we were talking about the lawsuit, but this is a decision like that times twenty. You need to call John."

Lance could feel himself bristling, his shoulders crawling way up to his ears. It went against everything in him. Once he made a decision, he'd made it, and he dealt with the consequences, good or bad. "I told you I'd consider it."

"The time for considering is over, Lance. You need to call him, apologize, and beg him to come back so that we have that information ASAP."

Beg? Like hell he'd beg. His pride wouldn't allow it. Not only was he shit at apologizing, his pride was one of the few things he'd kept all through his injury and even when his ex tried to break him in other ways. He'd be damned if he lost it now. "Just do what you can. I trust you."

Charlotte slowly walked around the coffee table, perched on the edge of it directly in front of him, and grabbed his hand. She smoothed his fingers out from the fist he hadn't even realized he'd formed. "I'm good with numbers, but I don't have access to those records. Even if I did, I don't know the ins and outs, and I can't take on another job."

She slipped her fingers between his, her calming influence breaking through his aggravation. "Even if it would mean not having anyone else to make uncomfortable at the office with all our PDA. Not that we'll still be... I know we're just taking it a day at a time, so I'm not saying..."

"I know what you mean." He almost added *of course we're still going to be doing this when we return to the office*, because now that he'd had his hands and lips on her, he couldn't imagine going back to not kissing her. Not touching her. But there was what he wanted and what he could realistically do. No promises or guarantees, not right now. And if he couldn't get a reliable quarterback, that wasn't going to change for a long time.

"It's too much pressure, and it's unfair to ask that of me. It'd be setting me up for failure." She was right. He hated that she was, but it was also why she was good for him.

"Fine. I'll...call John." He eyed his phone but didn't pick it up. "I'm not good at swallowing my pride. Not good at apologizing."

"Well, now you need to turn your team around. That's part of being a leader, and I remember watching you on the field. You were one of the best at rallying your team. At leading them."

She'd watched him play. She'd said as much when they were on speaker phone with Foster, and when he'd made a comment about it, she'd called him Mr. Ego. It seemed like a lifetime ago in some ways, but this time, instead of saying she followed football, not him, she was purposely stroking his ego. There was genuine admiration in her voice, too, and it went a long way toward helping him prepare for the hit his pride was about to take.

"One question before I make this call," he said, dragging his thumb over her knuckles. "Back in the day, when you were watching me play, did you cheer for or against me?"

"Depended on who you were playing that game," she said in that sassy way of hers that turned him on. Her eyes locked onto his, a whole heap of passion swimming the green of her pupils. "But I'm cheering for you now. So stop stalling and make the call."

"Okay, but I just realized I don't have his number, so I guess you'll have to get your computer and pull up the personnel files. While you're doing that, I'm just going to—"

"No need." She lifted her cell, and he watched as she input her passcode.

"One-two-three-two? You deal with stats and numbers every day, and that's the best you can come up with to secure your phone?"

She rolled her eyes. "I deal with stats and forms, and there's only so much information I can cram into my brain, so I don't want my phone to take extra effort. Also, I'm not falling for another stalling tactic—we should be in Texas right now because *that's how big of a staller you are.*"

"I don't think staller is a word. I do have another big thing you might be interested in, though…" He leaned closer and waggled his eyebrows.

The loud sigh wasn't exactly the reaction he'd been hoping for. She pulled up John's information and swiveled the screen toward him. He wrapped his hand around the phone but couldn't seem to force his fingers to move.

Before he could protest or come up with another way to

drag out the minutes, Charlotte hit the call button. "There. I even did the hard part for you."

"That's not the hard part. The hard part is—"

"Hello?" a voice said on the other line.

Charlotte moved next to him on the couch and gave his hand an encouraging squeeze.

Lance identified himself and then pushed through the skin-tightening sensation and forced words that didn't want to come out. He told John he might've made a mistake by firing him with the rest of the staff. He revised it to "it was a mistake" when Charlotte mouthed it at him.

This call was akin to walking over hot coals, and he tugged on his collar and cleared his throat an inordinate amount of times.

"Is Charlotte with you?" John asked.

He glanced at her, the steady rock at his side. "Yes."

"Can I talk to her?"

Lance passed the phone.

"Hey, John," she said, the smile on her face flooding her words with sunshine. She asked him a few questions and laughed at one point, and all Lance could do was hold his breath and wait. "Okay. Putting you on speaker now."

"We're gonna build an amazing team," Lance promised. "And again, I'm sorry that I fired you without realizing how badly we needed you on it. Charlotte informed me that you tried to rein in the other two."

"That was my mistake, not being firmer. But my hands were tied. I've got a few conditions if I come back…"

Lance winced, sure it'd be a higher salary that he couldn't afford to pay him. All the demands were reasonable, though. A five-year contract and better health insurance for his family. "I'm a die-hard fan," he added. "Always have been."

"Is that you saying you're in?" Lance asked, needing the clarification.

"I'm in."

The tension in the room eased, and judging from Charlotte's grin and the loosening of her shoulders, she felt it, too. "Okay, what we need is—"

"Wait," Charlotte said. "Paperwork first. I'll email you a new contract, as well as an updated NDA. You can virtually sign it, and we'll do the same on our end."

Lance hit the mute button. "Do we have time for that?"

"The question is do we have the time to risk not having it. Spoiler alert: the answer is no. We're talking about insider information, and while I know John and don't think he'd ever do anything like that, you did recently piss him off, and I'm a forms girl. I want documentation and that extra protection for the team's sake and for yours."

Lance nodded, glad she had his back. For once, the forms did seem like a good idea.

Charlotte unmuted the call. "Hey, I'm sending it all now. I need you to turn it around as soon as you get it, and then we'll need to hit the ground running, and I mean tonight."

"You got it," John said.

Within a few minutes, Charlotte had pulled up the necessary forms, made changes, and sent them off.

Another slew of calls came in, and Lance kept watching the clock, pacing the floor, and silently chanting for John to hurry up.

"Got it," Charlotte said as he was wrapping up another call. "I'm dialing him up now..." The second John picked up, she launched right into everything they needed, starting with a decent salary for Gavin Frost. "And, John? Please talk fast. Lance and I have a rehearsal dinner to attend in an hour..."

Chapter Twenty-Two

If Stacy and Maribelle hadn't both texted her during the day to say they couldn't wait to see her at the dinner, Charlotte would consider skipping the rehearsal. It was nice to know she'd be missed, though, and with her time here ticking down, she wanted to see the people she'd quickly grown attached to a few more times before she lost the chance.

So it didn't matter if she was exhausted or if she'd just gotten a call from her roommate saying that Dad had shown up at their apartment.

"He asked where you were," Shannon had said, and Charlotte's stomach had dropped down to her toes. "I told him out of town, but since I didn't know if you wanted him to be able to find you, I said I wasn't exactly sure where you were."

"He probably just wants money." Wasn't it like him to show up and ask for something right when she'd started to feel like her life was taking a turn for the better? She'd hoped that in time they could heal, but that healing was supposed to start once he finished the program. Not after checking himself out early, which was clearly what he'd done if he was showing up on her doorstep.

Guess this was what she got for burying her complicated feelings about how to best help him without resenting him underneath the nonstop work emergencies that kept popping up. If he would've just stayed in rehab, he'd be in the facility until after the draft, and she'd be more equipped to deal.

In theory.

Maybe if I'd called him back earlier today like I should've, I could've worked out a bargain. Her plan had been to tell him that if he would finish the entire program, she'd help him get back on his feet financially.

Now she worried she'd end up being an enabler who got walked over and hurt again.

"How did he seem?" she'd asked Shannon, even though she wasn't sure how a man who was truly done with gambling would seem. It was one of the hardest addictions to see, and one of the easiest to hide until someone poked around your bank accounts or your credit cards were declined when you went to pay for dinner.

"Sober. Clear-headed."

At least there was that. A glimmer of hope had risen up and called to her. Maybe he really was better.

After she'd thanked Shannon, she'd let loose a squeak at the time and rushed to get dressed. Now she was staring at her phone, considering whether or not she had time to call Dad and hash out everything they needed to. Or at least a portion of what they needed to.

The knock on the door made up her mind for her. Later. Not only did she not want to be late for the rehearsal dinner, she also wanted to enjoy a few hours of being around a more traditional family before she figured out where her messed-up one was, even though she also felt guilty for having that thought in the first place.

Shoving it down for a bit longer won't hurt anything. You've only got a little over twenty-four hours left to enjoy your time with the Quaids before everything gets more complicated.

A full-body flutter went through her after she swung open the door. Lance was in a crisp white collared shirt, all the buttons done up, wearing a simple black tie that matched his pants and jacket.

He was so tall and handsome, and her legs turned liquid as she took him in.

She got to arrive on his arm.

Got to kiss his lips.

Got to wrap her naked body around his.

Her cheeks heated at that thought, and Lance arched an eyebrow as if he could read her mind. "Do I need to come in for a few minutes?"

"Better not," she said, grabbing her bag and nudging him back into the hall. "But later tonight, you should definitely come in. For more than a few minutes."

He put his hand low on her back—low enough to break section three, had they not signed that contract—and his lips brushed her ear as he whispered, "Your wish is my wish."

• • •

"Interesting about how you two just work together," Mom said after Lance winked at Charlotte, who was over by Stacy and her bridesmaids. Somehow she'd been roped into helping out with the rehearsal.

Not somehow exactly. She was organized and on task, and man, she was so pretty it almost hurt to look at her.

Lance reluctantly pulled his gaze off her and her red dress and turned to his mom. Another wedding and unborn grandchildren were dancing in her eyes, and he wanted to shut it down before she got carried away.

Or maybe more accurately, he didn't want to shut it down as hard as he should, even though it was going to set them both up for failure. His mom and him, although he supposed it'd probably hurt Charlotte, too. That was the *last* thing he wanted to do.

"I thought I'd done a good job picking women who might catch your interest, but I'm not too proud to admit that they would've paled in comparison to Charlotte. It's not easy to find someone who's kind, beautiful, and smart. Even more impressive, she can keep up with you." Mom reached for a champagne flute the waiters were passing around. "Not just keep up with you but deal with your moods and give it right back."

Champagne wasn't his usual, but he grabbed a glass, too, just for something to do.

"You're not denying it," Mom said, and he sighed.

"How can I? She's all the things you've said and more." Hope he had no business entertaining bubbled up, and he worked to squash it. He lived in the real world. He wasn't some wide-eyed young buck anymore who believed things would work out if love was involved. "But the timing's off. My life… I wasn't kidding when I said I'd be married to my job for the foreseeable future. It has to be my priority."

"Understandable, I suppose. But that doesn't mean you and Charlotte can't continue to date and see where it goes."

Continue to date—considering he'd had his arm wrapped around her when they'd arrived and he couldn't stop staring and grinning at her like a lovesick loon, he could only blame himself that the jig was up. He hadn't missed the *I suppose* she'd added, either, which was *you're being an idiot* in Mom language.

"Just look at your brother and how happy he is to be getting married," she continued to push. "That doesn't mean he's not committed to his career or his team."

"And I'm happy for him. But it's different. He and Stacy met in college and have known each other for years. Plus, he only has himself and how he plays to worry about, not an entire franchise resting on his shoulders."

"Are you worried it'll get messy because of work, or are you scared of getting hurt again?" Mom placed her hand on his arm, and he had no choice but to look at her.

"I wouldn't say I got hurt."

She frowned. "Oh, come on, son. That last woman violated your trust. She talked to reporters and was more interested in attention than supporting you when you needed her most."

He didn't need to be reminded. Worse, when he'd told Sage his injury wasn't healing as quickly or as well as it should and that he was afraid the doctors were right about him having to retire or risk losing the use of his knee, she freaked out. She was furious after discovering he'd told his coach to find a permanent replacement, and after he'd announced his plans to retire early, she'd slept with his fullback out of spite. The fact that his teammate had done it hurt more than anything she'd done. They were a team. He'd trusted both of them, but especially the guy who'd kept him protected on the field.

"Charlotte's not like that woman," Mom said.

"No, she's not." He knew it, but there was still a part of him that held back, just in case.

Since this was the very sort of thing he'd wanted to avoid—well, that and being set up on blind dates—he sought out Charlotte, and once their eyes met, he silently conveyed he could use a save or a block or something.

Ever great at reading cues, she strode over and linked her elbow in his. "Mind if I steal him away for a few minutes? I need a strand of lights adjusted, and while I might be tall enough in these heels if I also stood on a chair, that sounds like a broken neck waiting to happen."

"Of course, dear," his mom said, and as they started away, his cell buzzed in his pocket. He was fielding calls, doing his best not to constantly check his phone, but he slipped it out, just in case it was important.

> Mom: *You might think you got out of discussing you and Charlotte, but all you did was prove how well you can read each other, and that she's there for you when you need her. Joke's on you ;)*

He didn't know whether to sigh and shake his head or laugh.

> Mom: *Also, you're not supposed to be checking your phone.*

He glanced over his shoulder, and Mom gave him a smug smile. Charlotte followed his gaze. "Do I even want to know?"

"My mom adores you. Not like she's made a secret of it."

"And she's pressuring you about us, and you needed an escape." Her smile tightened, and while she tried to hold it, he could see it took effort.

He curled her to him and cupped her cheek. "No. I mean yes. What I mean is… You realize my life is crazy right now."

"Of course." Her glittery earrings caught the light as she swept back the section of hair that'd fallen over one eye. "My life is pretty crazy, too, you know. I got a new boss who's brash and extra demanding, and he's had me putting in a ton of overtime."

He loved that she could make a joke about it, but he didn't want her to think he was taking advantage of her, even if he probably was. "Sorry to hear that. Is there anything good about your new boss?"

She ran her hand down his tie and playfully tugged on the end. "He looks pretty sexy in a suit. Not that I'd ever say that to him, because it'd be highly inappropriate."

"Ah. It just so happens one of my new employees is hot as hell. Sassy and feisty, and she's saved my ass so many times it's insane. I'm not sure if I've thanked her for that."

"Well, it is a nice ass— Funny story, when I first noticed how nice it was, I reread the interoffice dating section of the handbook."

He grinned and wrapped his arms around her. With the pretense of only being work associates officially blown, he didn't see any reason to hold back. "That day you stormed into my office and reprimanded me for my language, I knew I was in trouble. I could handle a bunch of lazy, pompous dudes, but you..." He nuzzled his nose into the curve of her neck and sucked in a big inhale before straightening and peering down at her. "I had no idea how to handle you."

"Don't act like you do now."

He touched his lips to hers. "I'm still going to do my damnedest."

Her lips parted, and he gave her a proper kiss, holding her tighter as she relaxed into his embrace. Earlier today she'd been amazing. When he'd needed to suck it up and swallow his pride, she'd given him a push. After she'd helped him reinstate John, she'd tasked herself with getting the necessary information to put together an offer for Gavin Frost.

They made one hell of a team. He didn't want to let her go, not tonight, not when they got back to San Antonio. He didn't want to pretend they weren't more, and he wondered if they committed to this thing between them, could they pull it off?

It'd be hectic, but she was good with hectic. She was the only reason he'd kept his cool all week. She calmed him and pushed him and made him better, and he'd be an idiot not to hold on to that.

"What if I wanted to try to make us work?" he asked before he could ruin it with overthinking.

"Like…revise our contract from dating to a full-blown relationship?"

He laughed—of course she wanted the correct documentation. "Yes. I don't want to lose this. I know it'll be tricky, but we're great together. You get my job and how busy it's going to keep me in a way most women wouldn't."

"You had me till that last part when you made me sound more like a convenience."

The panic that twisted through him obviously showed because she reached up and patted his cheek, slightly lighter than after he'd implied he was maintaining the scruff for her sake. "It's okay. I understand what you meant, but let me coach you closer to the right territory. Like maybe you want to say you've had so much fun with me it's unbelievable."

"It really is."

"And you could always mention my—"

"Amazing ass."

"Not where I was going, but I appreciate you noticing."

"In that dress, it'd be impossible not to." He craned his neck, giving it a longing glance. Then he pulled back to look her in the eye. "You're smart and funny and sexy, and I honestly have had more fun with you this week than I've had in a long time. I didn't even realize how empty my life had become until I saw what I've been missing out on."

She pointed to herself. "Me?"

"Yes, you. I want you to be more than my work associate. I want you to be my girlfriend." Putting it like that made him feel a bit like he was back in high school, but it was the most nervous he'd been talking to a girl since then, so it fit.

She'd come in and taken his life by storm. She'd crawled under his skin so quickly it made his head spin. Over the past week, she'd become his center of gravity, the person who kept him grounded while helping him achieve his dreams.

This woman could wreck him.

A different sort of panic climbed up and attached itself to his lungs, constricting his flow of air.

I can trust her. She's different.

Her smile lit up her face as she threw her arms around him. "I'm in. Honestly, I can't wait to call you my boyfriend. I'm gonna tell everyone my boyfriend is Lance Quaid."

He tensed the slightest bit, but she didn't mean it like that, in the attention-seeking way. Not like Sage.

She kissed his cheek, and his worries calmed. Gradually his heart returned to beating at a nice, steady level. Until she moved her lips next to his ear and added, "And Mr. Quaid, you're definitely going to score tonight."

A steady heart rate was overrated anyway.

Chapter Twenty-Three

The absurdly handsome man lying next to her in bed was sleeping like a rock, and Charlotte took advantage of the chance to unabashedly stare. Not that she'd ever held back very well when it came to Lance Quaid, but he was always on the go, always moving, forever on the phone.

Apparently all he needed to slow down was insanely hot sex several times in a twenty-four hour period.

If it weren't for his declaration about five of those hours ago, she'd be lamenting the fact that the wedding was tomorrow and their trip was almost over.

He wants to try to make us work. Even when we get back to San Antonio.

He asked me to be his girlfriend.

Since she was too keyed up to sleep, she sent off a quick text to Shannon letting her know about the new development.

Shannon: *Nice catch! I mean he sort of breaks your football rules on EVERY SINGLE LEVEL, but he's smoking hot and his net worth is through the roof.*

Shannon's sudden obsession with net worth came from her issues with her last freeloading boyfriend, which was why she now had a salary requirement for the guys she was willing to consider dating.

But Charlotte hardly cared about that. Of course, it was easy to say money didn't matter when you were sleeping on Egyptian cotton sheets in a five-star hotel room you'd arrived at by flying across the country in a private jet.

While her family had never been anywhere near the same wealth stratosphere as the Quaids, she'd experienced life with and—after Dad lost everything they had—without money. While it definitely made things easier in a lot of ways, it was far from the most important thing to her.

Especially when it came to guys—to her boyfriend.

Under Lance's all-business exterior beat a heart of gold. His brashness came from his desire to change the team and to do what was best for it. And in spite of how difficult it'd been for him to swallow his pride, he'd been a trouper about calling and apologizing to their old/new CFO.

At the end of the wedding rehearsal, he'd made sure they stopped to say goodbye to his nephews, his sister and her husband, and his parents. They'd been hand in hand when Lance told his mom she'd be happy to know he'd considered what she'd talked to him about, and that Charlotte was now his work associate *and* his girlfriend.

The woman had embraced her so tightly that Charlotte could still feel the residual hug, feel the acceptance and happiness that'd flowed through her veins.

It was like a damn fairy tale.

She was far from a princess, but she did love her shoes. Enough she wouldn't go losing one of them like Cinderella. She'd rather a guy see her in rags and talking to mice than leave one of her pretties behind.

The idea of a football princess hit her, and she smiled at

her silly, late-night thoughts.

This was going to work. She'd never truly believed she could have it all and had given up on fairy tales long ago, and yet… She looked at Lance again. She snuggled up next to him, and when he automatically reached out for her and pulled her closer, she kissed his cheek.

It wasn't until sleep had nearly sucked her under that she realized she'd never called her dad.

. . .

Charlotte lifted her satiny pink skirt and strode down the hall in her unbuckled silver heels as quickly as she dared, her suitcase trailing behind her. She'd been nearly done curling her hair when Lance had texted and said he needed her for a call—*the call*—ASAP.

She slid her key into the hotel room, swearing when it flashed red instead of green. Before she could try again, Lance swung open the door.

"Maybe we should increase the offer. I'm sure he could get a higher salary with…" His gaze ran down her, snagging at the slit that came halfway up her thigh. She'd wondered if she should pin it together to ensure it remained in the proper range, but as his eyes heated, she decided that from time to time, a little impropriety was in order. As long as she didn't show up the bride she was good, and she'd seen Stacy's dress right before they'd taken the photos of the female portion of the wedding party—that was hardly a risk.

"With who?"

"Huh?" Lance said, jerking his head back up. In his black slacks and open white shirt, he was quite the sight himself.

She smiled, a thrill going through her. Not only because he was all hers, but also because she'd managed to elicit such a strong reaction from him. Maybe breaking the rules now and then did have its advantages. "You were in the middle of a sentence."

"Right. I..." He leaned forward, bracketed her head in his hands, and kissed her. His mouth was urgent and demanding, and she happily acquiesced and let him devour her. By the time he broke the kiss, they were both breathless. He exhaled and rested his forehead against hers. "That was supposed to help put kissing you out of my head so I could focus. But now I'm getting other ideas, and I don't have time for ideas. Unless it's a genius plan on how to increase our budget without increasing it."

"That...would be impressive. Maybe not so much realistic, though." She wrapped her arms around his waist. "It'll be enough."

"But he could probably get more from another team."

"He doesn't want another team. He wants to play for the Mustangs and turn them into a championship-winning team. To do that, we still need to acquire several other players. He'll understand that, and we can negotiate a bit if we need to."

A bit meant about half a million to a million in this instance, which was mind-blowing when she thought about it, but even that would be tricky.

Lance's phone rang. "It's Gavin."

Charlotte smacked his ass like one of his fellow teammates would do on the field. "Go get us a quarterback."

. . .

Without ever taking her eyes off her laptop screen, Charlotte poured a couple of fingers of whiskey in a glass and pushed it toward him. "Drink that. I've got this part."

She was quite the sight, standing there in that pale pink dress, the rapid *tap tap tap* of her keyboard filling the air. He sipped from the glass as instructed, but what he was really drinking in was the way her hair was swept to the opposite side of her face, exposing her neck. The back of her dress dipped low, and he got lost in staring at all the creamy skin and thinking about how she clearly wasn't wearing a full bra.

Then he wondered if she was wearing one at all, and he could hardly believe his thoughts were so wrapped up in her instead of the huge deal he'd just made— Charlotte was typing up the official offer sheet now.

"Why are your shoes undone?" he asked.

The silver strappy things got a brief glance. "You said you needed me ASAP, and the buckles are tiny and complicated, and I have to twist up my leg to get the right angle, and I'll worry about it later."

He squatted and fumbled with the ankle strap, his big fingers adding an extra challenge to securing the tiny buckle, but he finally secured one and then the other. He might've also brushed the smooth skin of her calves a bit more than necessary.

The printer whirred to life, and she said, "There's the official offer sheet. You can read through it real quick and then I'll send it to Gavin's agent."

From there the Pythons would have first right of refusal, meaning they could still match the offer and retain him, and if they took five days to decide it'd feel like a wheel-spinning eternity.

Even though he had no doubt that Charlotte had been thorough, he wanted to hold the solid proof of the offer in his hands, so it could feel real. For the first time ever, he understood her obsession with paperwork.

"What would I do without you?" he asked as his eyes skimmed down the page. His nerves were frayed, his hands shaky—and they were *never* shaky. He'd prided himself on how steady he'd been during his career, even during the big games. No need to talk about the nights before, because he'd always pulled himself together come coin toss time. But he'd just offered a lot of money to a player, gambling he'd be the captain they needed to help turn the team around and make it to playoffs this upcoming season. He was sure it was the right call, but still…

"Probably insult people, ignore paperwork, and pay too much for a quarterback."

"Rhetorical questions are more supposed to go unanswered," he teased back. "You could just choose to feel flattered and say something like, 'I don't know what I'd do without you, either, you handsome, brilliant devil.'"

"Next time print me up a script, will ya?"

He shook his head, a smile breaking free. "Like you'd follow it."

"Depends on whether or not it played by the rules."

He lowered his lips to the neck he couldn't stop staring at. Her sharp intake of breath spurred him on, and he flicked out his tongue. "Not if I have anything to do with it."

"Clock's on," she said, her voice raspy.

He lightly dragged his teeth over her soft, heavenly scented skin. He blindly fumbled around for a pen on the desk, quickly signed the papers, and handed them back to her.

"And the electronic signature, too. Unless you want me to go old-school and scan it in."

The trackpad and his finger made for a sloppy approximation of his signature, and as she typed in an email address, he stood behind her and kissed the back of her neck, the top of her bare shoulder…

"Sent," she said, and then she turned to face him. Finally he could get his lips on hers. "How long do you have till you need to get over to the annex?"

As much as he hated to look, it was a valid question. He couldn't be late to his brother's wedding. "Twenty-five minutes." He returned his phone to his pocket and secured an arm around her waist, drawing her against him. "Just enough time for Part I of what I have planned for you."

"No way," she said, tipping her head to the side to give his lips better access to her neck. "This dress isn't easy to get into—and neither are the shoes, which thank you for your help with them—and I don't have time to get ready again."

He slid his hand up her thigh, parting the slit in her skirt wider. "Good thing your dress came equipped with easy access."

Her chest heaved against his, her lashes fluttering. "But my hair and my makeup, and…"

His fingers drifted higher, and he stroked her over the silky fabric of her blessedly tiny panties, a strangled groan coming out when he found them already damp. "What if I promise we can both get off without messing up your dress or your hair?"

Her lips skimmed up his jawline, up to his ear. "Then I'd say stop talking and start showing. We've already lost a few minutes with all this unnecessary chatting."

He didn't need to be told twice. He pushed her panties aside and stroked her again, smothering her moan with his mouth. She rolled her tongue over his, and he backed her up against the wall.

He wanted to free her breasts but decided that'd have to wait for Part II, later tonight. Right now it'd be fast and furious—just not so fast that she didn't finish, and to make sure, he pushed a finger inside her.

The strangled noise she made sent his erection into raging territory, and he undid the button and fly of his pants with his free hand as he continued to pump into her.

He added another finger, curling them and searching for that spot that—

"*Holy shit*, right there," she said, panting and arching her hips to take his fingers in deeper. He glanced from her face to his fingers inside of her, and he couldn't decide which he wanted to watch more.

At her whimper, he looked up into those bottomless green eyes. Decision made. He increased the tempo of his fingers, watching as pleasure flickered across her features in waves. Her muscles tightened, her release close, and he lowered his lips to hers. He stroked her tongue with his, mimicking the movement of his fingers, and her fingernails dug into his arms as her orgasm took hold.

He slowly brought her back down, pride going through him at the sated expression on her face. There was something else in the mix, something that felt more serious. His chest tightened as that adoration and awe echoed through him, and he searched for the right words but came up empty.

Maybe later tonight he'd find them. Right now they didn't have enough time for messy emotions anyway.

He was about to take her right there against the wall, but then he remembered the condoms were in the bedroom. "Hold on to me," he said, and she wrapped her arms around his neck.

He maneuvered them through the hall and around the large bed. He grabbed a foil square out of the nightstand drawer and made quick work of the wrapper. He rolled the condom in place, not bothering to take the time to fully shed his clothes.

Any minute his phone would start ringing, his family members wondering where he was.

Just a few minutes of getting lost in Charlotte and then I'll be ready for the rest of the long evening.

He pushed everything out of his mind besides the sexy woman in front of him. It was a struggle not to thread his hands through her hair, but he'd promised not to mess it up. After the wedding when they returned to his room, he'd make sure she looked as ravaged as possible. For now, he'd happily focus on pinning her to the wall and making himself at home between her thighs.

He kept thinking he'd get used to having sex with her—or not get used to, because he no longer thought that was a possibility with Charlotte—but more like not be on the verge of explosion at the first thrust.

Luckily this time, speed was the name of the game, and within a few thrusts she was crying his name as they roared over the edge together.

He wrapped his arm around her waist and half-carried, half-walked her into the bathroom to clean up. As he redid his pants and tucked in his shirt, she smoothed down her skirt.

His phone began to ring and time was up. He slipped his bow tie underneath the collar and answered.

"On my way," he said to his mom as he tied the ridiculous thing at his throat. "Just finishing up a…" He gave Charlotte a wink. "Business transaction."

"Thanks for making me sound like a hooker," Charlotte said as soon as he hung up.

"Oh, did you want me to tell my mother we were just finishing up a hot sex session? I worried that'd be TMI, but I'll clear it up when I see her in a few minutes."

Charlotte smacked his arm. "Don't you dare." She reached up and wiped lipstick off his mouth and jaw.

He grabbed his jacket off the chair in the corner, too hot to put it on just yet. "See you out there. Will you be okay?"

"I'll find a way to occupy myself." She pivoted toward the mirror, using her thumb to swipe at the lipstick that'd also been smeared on his lips and skin moments ago. "I'm going to need to touch up my makeup since *someone* decided to make a mess of it."

Mere minutes after he was buried inside her, and he grew

hard again, his body already ready for round two. Since she was going to redo her lipstick anyway, he kissed her again. "Save a dance for me, okay?"

"I'll see if I can fit you in," she said with a self-assured smugness that he liked seeing her own. Then she shoved him toward the door. "Go before your mom calls me— I'm not nearly as good at making up stuff on the fly, and I'll end up confessing everything."

He pushed open the door, casting one last glance at her because he was going to miss her—which was crazy. Missing her when she'd be only a few feet away and he'd be able to talk to her in an hour or so?

"And don't worry," she said. "I'll keep an eye out for a counteroffer and text you the second I hear any news from Gavin or from the Pythons."

What was even crazier was that he'd managed to forget there was an offer hanging in the balance. She was so perfect, having his back now, just like she'd had through this entire process.

He muttered a "thank you" and rushed toward the annex where the wedding party would be gathered. He tried to clear his head so he could focus on the ceremony and not offers or trades or Charlotte. But what became crystal clear was that in spite of all the other madness going on in his life, he'd managed to completely lose his mind over the woman.

Chapter Twenty-Four

There was nothing like a wedding to make you long for a relationship, long for a person who'd look at you like his world revolved around you and who would always be there for you.

For the past several months, Charlotte had congratulated herself on realizing that she didn't need anyone. Patted herself on the back for giving up on the idea of being a part of a duo, because when it came down to it, she'd been mostly alone a large chunk of her life, and she was best that way. She got to choose when she did things and how, and no one hurt her feelings, and...

It was all bullshit. As much as she'd tried to convince herself she'd be perfectly happy as a me, myself, and I, she'd seen the Quaids and how they were all there for each other. She wanted that. To be part of something more. To have a group that'd be more supportive than draining.

The damn love bug was in full force this evening, and she'd caught it bad.

Honestly, even if she weren't in a decorated reception center, surrounded by dressed-up people who'd been telling stories about the couple even before they'd walked down the aisle, the longing would still be there.

Because that guy standing up front next to his brother had made it rise up and take hold. Not only was he devastatingly sexy and smart, he listened to her and valued her opinion. The way he held her and kissed her... It made her feel things she thought she'd never feel.

He caught her eye and gave her a devilish smile that sent her stomach somersaulting.

I'm falling so hard.

Panic roiled inside her, but on its heels came the reminder of how things had changed. They'd lowered their walls and let each other in. He'd called her his Sam, told her he didn't know what he'd do without her, and said he wanted to be with her. That made it okay to embrace the fall.

Right?

Her phone chimed, and her eyes flew wide.

Shit, shit, shit. She'd been sure she silenced it.

This dress didn't exactly have pockets, either, so she'd shoved it into her cleavage and now...well, now if she didn't go digging—witnesses be damned—it might chime again.

Or worse, ring.

The people around her gave her stern, reproachful glares as she unearthed her phone.

Her thumb quickly flicked the switch to silence it, and her gaze snagged on Lance's— He was looking at her, fighting a laugh.

She tried to silently convey with her expression it wasn't funny. Not to mention it was basically his fault. After all, she'd only turned it on again so that if someone texted back about...

O-M-G! Excitement zipped through her as she read the words on her phone screen, one strong blast after another, and she fought the urge to dance-bounce in her seat.

Since she didn't want to disturb the wedding any more than she accidentally had, she dropped her phone in her lap and concentrated on the ceremony. The bride and groom were about to exchange vows.

They said beautiful things about each other and to each other, and promised a lifetime of love and laughter, and Charlotte let the romance of it all sweep her away.

As soon as the groom kissed the bride, Charlotte again sought out Lance.

Their gazes locked, and desire and affection melded together and streaked through her body. Right then and there, she decided she was going to stop holding back and second-guessing everything and just let herself enjoy being a girl who was dangerously close to being in love.

She filed out along with her row, showing great restraint by not pushing through the crowd like a running back determined to reach the goal line.

Finally, a hole opened up. She quickened her pace and dodged and weaved. The crowd parted, and she searched for that dark head of hair and the blue eyes.

There.

Since there were still too many people between them, Charlotte pointed at her phone and then surreptitiously held up her thumb, keeping it against her sternum.

It took him a second, and then his eyes flew wide, his smile widening to dazzling range.

He understood. The Mustangs had just acquired their quarterback.

A woman tried to catch his attention, her intent to flirt clear, but he politely brushed her off, his eyes still on Charlotte. He started her way, the crowd parting more easily for him than they had for her.

As fast as her heels would take her, Charlotte strode toward him, her pulse steadily increasing as his long, muscular legs ate up the distance.

Then he was pulling her into his arms, her feet no longer touching the ground. "The Pythons didn't match? I need to hear you say it before I get too carried away."

"Nope. They want the draft pick and even agreed to keep it under wraps until you can make an official announcement— Gavin and his agent are on board as well." A squeal slipped out. "We have our quarterback. Gavin Frost is going to be a Mustang."

"Part of me didn't think we'd really get him," he whispered into her ear with a laugh.

"You did, though. You did it."

"It's a good start, one that takes off at least an ounce or two of pressure as we're racing toward Draft Day." He pulled back and met her gaze. "And *we* did it— I couldn't have done it without you and your crazy wall and amazing brain and gut instincts. Or without you pushing me to rehire John. Or without you here. You really are my Sam. But a much, much hotter Sam." His lips crashed down over hers as his fingers fitted into her rib cage and held her tightly against him. "Have I mentioned I'm crazy about you?"

Crazy was an accurate word for how she felt whenever she thought about him, and it went double when she was in his arms. "Right back at you. I'd call you Frodo, but I'm not sure—"

"As long as you're mine, I don't really care what you call me."

"I'm yours," she whispered, and then she placed her hand on the side of his face and added, "Lance Quaid."

He kissed her again, not seeming to care about their audience as he delved his tongue inside her mouth and branded himself upon her very soul.

Okay, so that part about being dangerously close to falling in love?

Yeah, that ship had sailed.

She was already there.

. . .

In theory, taking the groomsman and bridesmaid pictures days before the wedding was supposed to make it so there'd be fewer pictures today.

In reality, if he was posed or told to smile one more time, Lance might flip off the camera.

As soon as he was released—"for now"—he circled the reception area, his eyes peeled for a beautiful brunette in a pale pink dress.

Everything inside him froze when he spotted her. She was talking to Martin Simms, one of the most annoying sports reporters in the biz. Not the one he'd gotten in trouble for verbally threatening, but Simms had poked him about the story plenty back when it was just a rumor. One Lance had denied because he'd been a blind idiot.

The media had been carefully controlled for the wedding, so he'd probably been invited to the reception. Mitch was nicer than he was, not to mention better at walking the line and schmoozing the right people.

The sight of Simms so close to Charlotte rubbed a raw nerve, and when she laughed at something he said, irritation ate away the lining of Lance's gut.

They're just talking, he tried to tell himself, but he couldn't help thinking of another woman who'd "just talked" to reporters, time after time. Now he was wondering if his instincts were wrong again.

After all, he'd only known Charlotte for a couple of weeks.

He strode over, jaw clenched, and placed his hand on Charlotte's back. "Hey," he said, and he knew it'd come out too sharp. The way her eyebrows ticked up in the middle confirmed it. He still aimed his next comment toward Simms. "I didn't know my brother had invited bottom-feeders to the wedding."

Charlotte elbowed him in the gut. "Excuse him. He gets grumpy when he hasn't eaten in a while. Do I need to find you a Snickers to shove into your mouth?" She lowered her voice even more. "Think you can be nice for the rest of the night then, huh?"

"I think you're confusing me with a different quarterback."

Simms backed up a couple of paces. "I'll leave you to feed the beast. I remember how cranky he can get, and this mug is too pretty to be rearranged."

Lance growled—he couldn't help it. He hadn't even realized he'd taken a step toward Simms until Charlotte's hand came up on his chest.

Simms gave an obnoxious chuckle before shooting Charlotte a smile. "I'll be in touch."

"Looking forward to it." Charlotte kept the smile plastered on her face until she turned to him, and then she gave him a scowl he hadn't seen since early this week, before he'd thought everything had changed between them.

"What were you two talking about?" he demanded.

"The happy couple, the lovely weather, the upcoming season."

"Me?"

"Someone's a little self-centered," Charlotte said, reaching for one of the mixed entrée plates and shoving it toward him. "There aren't any candy bars, so this'll have to do."

"I notice you didn't answer."

She gave a long-suffering sigh. "If you're wondering if he asked about the Mustangs and what our plans are and what I think about you as an owner, of course he did."

Lance's hand clenched into a fist, and she covered it with her hand.

"Do you honestly think I don't know how to handle that? I've had reporters approach me in the grocery store to ask about the team, thinking I won't recognize who they are. I've had men corner me after work."

His temper flared for a different reason, but it all went to the same place in his brain, his rage ebbing and flowing along with his doubts.

"I kept my answers super vague and said 'you'll just have to see' a lot, including when the topics of our coaching staff and the draft came up. But if we're lucky, he'll write something that'll stir up curiosity and give us some free PR."

"Oh, and you're trained in PR now?"

Her hand slipped off his, and he hated the absence of it— his pride restrained him from doing anything about it, though. "I could recite a whole section from the handbook about it, so I know as much as I need to for my job." She slammed the plate back down on the table. "Eat or don't. I'm not going to force-feed you, even if you're acting like a toddler."

She took a step away, and he caught her elbow. He didn't want her to leave. Didn't want to be in a fight. "I'm sorry." The words scraped on the way out of his mouth, but at least he'd managed to spit them out. "I...overreacted."

"Yeah, you did," she said, never one to let him off easy.

He gave a gentle tug, slowly spinning her to face him again. "Trust...doesn't come easily for me. You yourself mentioned that I'm not great with reporters."

"It's one thing to not be great with reporters or to lose your cool when they corner you after your personal life's blown up. It's another to take your issues out on me when I was only trying to help." Her lip quivered, her strong facade crumbling, and he felt like shit.

He cupped her cheek. "You're right. Can we go back to

before I screwed up? When we were hugging and celebrating and it was you and me against the world?"

She pressed her lips together, considering, and then slowly moved closer. "I realize you're stressed, but all you've got to do is talk to me." Another step, the toes of her heels bumping into his shiny black shoes. "I do like the idea of us against the world."

Relief washed through him, and he tugged her closer. "Me, too. I'm going to need you on my team more than ever over the next few weeks."

"Then maybe try harder not to piss me off."

He dipped his head and dragged his lips across hers. "Will do. Now, ready to go sit through dinner with my family? And all the toasts?"

"Yes. But can I ask you a favor?"

"Anything," he said, back to being completely under her spell.

"Well, I was going to ask if you'd hold on to my phone, but now that you've gone and said *anything*, I'm thinking I should ask for something bigger. Maybe a yacht? A raise— wait, that'd be against the contract. How about a desert island to escape to with you?"

"Final answer?"

She handed over her cell, and he slipped it inside his interior suit coat pocket. She smoothed her hand down the lapel on his jacket. "Just tell me if the desert island thing is possible."

"Too late. You already gave me your phone to hold."

"Damn it," she said, snapping her fingers. Her giggle filled the air, chasing away the last of the remaining tension.

He put his hand on her back and guided her over to the table where the rest of his family was already seated. As he pulled out her chair, he moved his lips next to her ear. "I'll look into that desert island thing. Maybe once we win a Super

Bowl, I can make it happen."

"Sounds like a plan."

. . .

The waiters cleared away their dinner plates, and Charlotte relaxed farther into her seat and observed the Quaids as they continued their lighthearted laughing and talking. As she soaked in the happy buzz of it, she reached over and rubbed Lance's back. He had a toast to give in a few minutes, and she'd seen him glancing through note cards under the table.

"You'll do great," she whispered, and he curled his hand around her knee.

When he'd first confronted her about the reporter, she'd wanted to slam that plate of food over his head. But then he'd apologized and told her he needed her, and while she knew he'd been joking about the desert island, he'd said maybe once *we* win a Super Bowl. He'd included her in that long-term goal, which made her think they were on the same page—that he was falling for her, too, even if it wasn't quite as fast.

As long as he's working and trying, it's okay if it takes him a while to love me.

This trip had gone so differently than she'd imagined.

For one, she never would've dared to imagine a guy like Lance could ever fall for a girl like her. Maybe she should pinch herself to make sure it was real, but if it was a dream, it was one she never wanted to wake up from.

"Here goes nothing," Lance said, and before he stood, he dropped a quick kiss on her lips.

Then he stepped up to the microphone stand that'd been set up to the right of Mitch and Stacy's table.

Charlotte held her breath while trying not to let show she was nervous for him.

His speech started with memories of playing football

with his brother and how Mitch had always been the best at knowing which plays to make. Which risks were worth it.

"Some people might say marriage is the biggest risk of all," Lance said into the microphone, his words echoing across the space.

Careful. No one wants a best man toast that's anti-marriage. Especially the woman dating the best man.

"But Mitch has never been scared of taking a risk. And while asking out Stacy might've been a risk—because look at her, she's clearly out of his league…"

Sniggers went around the room.

"—Marrying her, though, was a sure bet. These two scored big when they fell in love, and I'm so happy for my brother, and happy to have Stacy joining our family. We're loud and opinionated and get all worked up over football, even if it's a friendly game on the beach, but she fits right in. More than that, you two have shown me the beauty of having someone who balances and calms you and makes your life better." Lance lifted his champagne flute. "To your life together."

Everyone raised their glass and drank.

Good job, babe.

Maribelle clasped her hands over her heart. "I've never seen him so happy."

"He does look really happy," Charlotte said. "Stacy, too. They're a lovely couple."

"They are, but I wasn't talking about Mitch." Maribelle leaned closer. "I was talking about Lance. That speech wasn't just fancy words. He meant it, and the reason he meant it is because of you. Trust me"—she reached out and took Charlotte's hand—"a mother can see it."

Everyone at the table was beaming at her, from Maribelle to Chuck to Taylor to… Well, Aaron and Austin had saved their table knives and were sword fighting. The Quaids had accepted her so easily, and a deeper yearning went through her as Maribelle squeezed her hand.

"Uh-oh," Lance said, surveying them as he returned to the table. "This looks like trouble."

"Don't worry," Maribelle said, giving him a big grin. "We were only talking about you."

Lance settled back into the open chair on Charlotte's right. "I repeat my 'uh-oh.'"

"I've decided Charlotte is a good luck charm," Chuck said, busting into the conversation because he clearly didn't realize there'd been a different one sorta going on. "Now that you two are dating, it's changed up the bad juju to good juju, and the Mustangs are going to start winning games. Mark my words."

"Do we need to seal that prediction with a secret handshake or something?" Charlotte asked. "Because I'll do just about anything." She leaned over Maribelle to address Chuck. "We should gather up all the candles after the reception and do some kind of cleansing ritual just to be safe."

"You two." Maribelle *tsked*. "Charlotte, really, you're supposed to be on my side. I've told him that superstitious stuff is nothing more than mumbo jumbo for years."

"Now she's said that, we're gonna *have* to do a cleansing," Lance added, and the three of them laughed while Maribelle shook her head and gave them exasperated yet affectionate looks.

"I'm not sure who taught you manners. Lord knows I tried, but clearly they didn't take very well."

"Not true," Charlotte said. "When Lance kept opening my doors for me, even though I insisted he didn't need to because we were colleagues and he wouldn't do the same if I was a man, he informed me his Southern mother would skin him alive if he didn't."

Pride radiated from Maribelle. "Good to hear that some of what I taught him stuck. If he ever acts like a knucklehead, you just call me, and I'll set him straight."

"Oh, I'm afraid if I did that, I'd never stop calling you," Charlotte joked, bumping her shoulder into Lance's.

Lance took a sip of champagne, frowned at the bubbly drink as if it'd personally offended him, and passed it to her. "I should've known that if I left you alone with my family for even five minutes, they'd fall for your charms and choose your side over mine."

She tipped back the last of the champagne, happy to help him finish it off so he could do what he wanted to and go order *a real drink*. "Yeah, big mistake on your part. I'm ridiculously charming."

He moved his mouth next to her ear and whispered, "Just wait till I get you back to the hotel room. I'll show you exactly how charming I can be."

She turned her face so their lips were a mere breath apart. "Can't wait," she said aloud as she silently challenged him to *bring it on. Bring it all.*

He kissed her and curled her to him as they listened to the rest of the toasts. Maribelle kept smiling at her, and she was laughing and talking with the family, and all the while she gripped on to the moment, on to Lance.

As the clock ticked down on the evening, their time in North Carolina moving to the only-hours-left range, worries rose up one by one. About how it'd be when they got back to Texas, and how they were going to balance their relationship at the office, and all of the things she'd forgotten to worry about during the past few days.

Lance had said he wanted to make them work, and they'd even signed a quarterback today, leaving the team well on its way to becoming something bigger and better.

So why did she feel like she needed to hold tighter to the moment? As if it might slip right through her fingers if she dared to loosen her grip.

Chapter Twenty-Five

The party was winding down, and Lance was counting the minutes until the reception would come to a close.

He'd walked up to the bar to grab another round of drinks for Charlotte and himself when he felt the prickling presence of someone approaching.

After the bartender handed him his order, Lance slowly turned.

Simms stood behind him, too close, his gaze too sharp.

"I'm not giving a statement of any kind right now— It's my brother's wedding, and he was kind enough to invite you for some strange reason. Tomorrow you can go back to being a pain in my ass."

The guy simply cocked his head, and something about the gesture sent foreboding across Lance's skin.

It's just because of my past with reporters and everything that happened with Sage. Because I have a beef with him for the story he ran afterward, about how I was as blind in love as I'd been on the field.

As if that weren't enough, Simms had added, *I called this*

one from the beginning. His temper got the best of him again and again, and his stats were never going to be strong enough to keep him from a future as a washed-up has-been, injury or not.

The washed-up part was a bit too accurate until now, but he was in the process of changing that.

"Just one question," Simms said as Lance went to step around him, clearly as bad at listening now as he'd been a few years ago. "Charlotte James works for you?"

Lance blew out a careful, measured breath. He wanted to tell him not to approach her without his say-so, but then the guy would undoubtedly tell her he'd threatened him. "Yes."

If Simms thought he could work the angle of Lance sleeping with one of his employees, he'd meet the brick wall of Charlotte's ironclad consensual romance agreement, and for the first time, he was glad she'd insisted on it. Mostly to keep her name from being dragged through the mud as Simms worked on grinding his personal ax.

Just the idea of anyone talking shit about her ignited his anger and made his teeth clench. *I can't control what people think, I can't control what people think.* "Now, if you'll excuse me."

"I'm just surprised."

A threatening noise slipped out as Lance leered at him, and the idiot at least had the good sense to back up a step. "She knows more about football than you do. She's smart, and she cares about the team, and I'd expect better than sexist drivel from you, Simms. Actually, that's a lie. I don't expect anything but a cheap ploy to sell a story, no matter who it hurts."

Simms held up his hands as if he was surrendering, and Lance hoped that was what he was doing. It'd be bad PR for him to punch the guy, and he wouldn't even care all that much if it didn't mean that Charlotte would be pissed and it might mess with their last night before they had to return to the real world.

Heading back to the office in San Antonio would make it easier to do their jobs, but complications would also arise— He wasn't foolish enough to think they wouldn't simply because he didn't want them to.

"You do realize who she is, don't you?" Simms asked. "Who her dad is?"

Of course he did. She was the human resources manager who drove him crazy as she also drove him wild with desire. He also knew it bothered her that her dad was a gambler, although he racked his brain, trying to remember if she'd ever said his name.

"You don't know," Simms said, glee creeping into his expression. "Her last name sounded so familiar, but it's common enough that it took me a bit of Googling to figure out why."

"Just say what you're going to say. I'm busy." He wanted to claim it didn't matter and walk past him, but his worries about trusting her fully rushed to the surface, desperately wanting to be reassured.

"Pete James."

It did sound familiar, but he couldn't place it.

"The coach from UTSA who was fired for gambling— against his own team."

• • •

"Goodbye," Charlotte said, hugging Stacy as she was getting ready to leave with her new husband. They were so crazy cute, and with things going so well with her and Lance, she didn't experience even a tinge of jealousy. Just happiness that she'd gotten to meet her and the rest of Lance's family at such a happy time.

"I'm so glad we got to meet you. There I go, using 'we' now, but, like, we are a we." A cute twitterpated squeal followed Stacy's words, and she pulled back to look Charlotte in the eye. "I know I've been a bit airheaded, but next time we see you and Lance, we'll have more time to hang out."

Charlotte nodded, liking the sound of that.

Mitch neared, automatically stretching his hand out for Stacy's. As soon as they linked fingers, he gave Charlotte the nod. "Later, Charlotte. Tell my brother he owes me a rematch on the field."

Mere seconds later, Lance approached their group, so Mitch saved her the trouble and went ahead and repeated it himself.

Lance barely cracked a smile, which was rare whenever he and his brother messed with each other. Clearly he was preoccupied.

Charlotte nudged him and muttered, "This is where you return the trash talk. Tell him that you have me as your official tight end now, and I can sort of catch and everything, so we're totally going to kick their asses."

He peered down at her with a perplexed expression, the same one he wore whenever he was brainstorming or processing. It only lasted a second or two and then he snapped out of it, smiling at his brother as he congratulated him and Stacy yet again and told them to enjoy their honeymoon.

It seemed a smidge forced, though. Not the well wishes, but-more like Lance's mind was still spinning on something else— Perhaps he'd learned something new about one of their current or prospective players.

"Is everything okay?" she asked. "Is it work? Because we've got a plan in place, and your dad declared we have our good juju back, so nothing to worry about there."

Before he had the chance to answer, Maribelle rushed over and handed them long sparklers, asking Lance to help light the ends so the couple could run through the archway they were going to make with them.

The next few minutes were a blur of sparklers and the happy couple rushing toward a decked-out limo with streamers and "just married" hearts. Then Aaron nearly set Austin's hair on fire, so all of the sparklers were dashed out with nearby glasses of water.

Charlotte began gathering trash and carried everything she could fit in her arms to the closest trash can.

"I appreciate that, dear," Maribelle said, "but you don't need to do that. The hotel has a whole crew that'll clean up."

Of course they did. In so many ways the Quaids seemed like everyone else, but there were those little reminders that everything they did was on a much grander scale.

Maribelle took both of her hands in hers. "I'm sure I've probably made it clear already, but I like to say things to people I care about, so they don't have to wonder. I'm so glad my son brought you along. Even if I suspect it was originally to thwart my setup attempts."

Charlotte bit back a smile. "I can neither confirm nor deny."

"Well, as I told him last night, you far surpass the women I was originally trying to introduce him to, so joke's on him. Or is it on me?" She shook her head. "Either way, I'm happy. I'm also going to take full credit for being the push that got you two together."

Charlotte didn't really care who got credit, only that she was incredibly happy things had worked out the way they had. "I'm so glad I got to meet you all. The wedding was beautiful, too. Thank you for including me in the activities and making me feel so welcome."

"You are welcome. Anytime. I'm guessing you two will be taking off early tomorrow morning?"

Charlotte nodded. "Yeah, we have a lot to do in the next

couple weeks. There are players and staff to acquire and big announcements to be made. It'll be a whirlwind till Draft Day. Then there will be training and pre-season and..." It all hit her at once, an exhausted sort of excitement— It'd probably slammed into Lance a few minutes ago, and now she understood why he'd felt further away. "Let's just say the foreseeable future is going to be very, very busy."

Maribelle used her grip on her hands to pull Charlotte into a hug. "Take care of him for me, will you? I've been worried about him for a while, even *before* he inherited the team. Sure, he's younger than most owners, but pressure is rough on people, emotionally and physically. That concern for your kids never stops, you know, in spite of how often they insist they're fully grown and you don't need to worry anymore. As if that's all it takes."

Charlotte couldn't help but laugh a little at that. Although a pang followed as she wondered if her dad ever truly worried about her. She'd always felt like it was the other way around. But they were working on it, and she couldn't let herself give up hope yet. Not until she at least saw for herself if the treatment had helped, and if things went any differently from here on out.

"You have no idea how much it comforts me that Lance has you," Maribelle said as she dropped her arms and gave her a big smile.

Warmth wound through her, and she set a mental note to ensure Lance's parents were invited to the first big game. Then they could see how much Lance had accomplished.

She'd tell herself not to count her chicks before they hatched, but she felt it in her bones— This season was going to surprise people, even if it took a couple years to fully turn the franchise around.

Lance walked up to them, and Maribelle threw her arms around him. He hugged her right back, and another swirl of affection twisted through Charlotte at seeing such a big dude with an obvious soft spot for his mom.

They exchanged another round of goodbyes, and then Charlotte slipped her hand into Lance's.

Once they hit the sand, she bent and removed her high heels, the way she had on that first night he'd walked her to the hotel from the restaurant. Luckily they were far easier to get off than on.

A hint of residual embarrassment crawled through her as she recalled that night, at how she'd freaked out and had him catapult her over the balcony. At least that version of her might be consoled by the fact that she'd ended up here, holding hands with Lance, fully committed to making this relationship work.

Even more comforting, they'd completed the necessary paperwork, although they were breaking the rule about supervisors not dating their direct reports the tiniest bit.

A thread of worry still remained about what others would think, but she did her best to bat it away. What mattered was they worked as a couple and made each other better. Best of all, there wasn't a strange power balance—had never been. And if anyone thought she only kept her job because she was sleeping with the boss, she'd rattle off a boatload of stats and tell them to shove it.

Well, she'd say it in a nicer way because she was the human resources person, after all.

Feel free to fill out a form, and we'll review all concerns.

Then promptly throw them away, you jerks.

Now she was irritated by the *possibility* of people having a problem with them. What was Lance's mantra, the one that got him through the constant speculation about his life?

Oh, yeah. You can't control what other people think. Might be time to adopt it as her motto as well.

Thanks to the absence of her heels, she felt even shorter

than usual, especially as she glanced up, up, up at her sexy boyfriend. "You're quiet."

"I'm exhausted. Although my brain's decided to ignore that fact and kick into high gear, in spite of doing my best to tell it to shut up."

"Want to bounce any of those thoughts off me? It might help."

He sighed, the weariness he'd admitted to coming through. "Let's get to our room first."

"Okay." With the sun gone from the sky, the sand had cooled off considerably, but if she dragged her toes, she still felt some of the warmth. "Where does one even go on their honeymoon when they've already been staying at a beautiful beach resort for a week?"

"I think they're doing a quick tour of Europe before he has to be back to start the offseason workout program with the rest of the team."

"What's going to happen when the Mustangs play against his team?"

Lance shrugged. "We used to play for different teams, and while they were always hard games, we managed to work it out."

Something was off. He seemed to be holding her at bay a bit, his words coming out shorter and more emotionless than usual. She tried not to take it personally. Clearly the stress and pressure of the upcoming week were hitting him now that the wedding was over, the same way they were tugging at her. He was probably also sad to be leaving his family but trying to do the macho thing and not talk about it or let it show that he actually had feelings. *Men.*

Charlotte had promised his mom she'd take care of him, and she planned on doing just that. They'd definitely have a conversation about whatever was weighing on his mind—along with his moods, because she wasn't going to let him push her away. But since she desperately needed to get off her feet and out of her dress, she'd honor his request and wait till they arrived at the room.

Our room, he'd called it.

When they reached the resort's main entrance, she stepped into her shoes, grimacing at the gritty sand and how it acted like, well, sandpaper against her feet. On the upside, her feet should be super smooth. On the downside, ouch.

She didn't bother fastening the buckles on the ankle straps, since she only had to make it down the hall and into the room. She hooked her hand on the crook of Lance's elbow, leaning heavily on him as they walked down the hallway. Exhaustion was seeping into her body, and she rested her head against his shoulder.

It'd only been a few days ago that it'd drifted there of its own accord. She smiled at the memory of him guiding her head back down after the embarrassing realization she'd been using him as a pillow. How awesome was it that she could now freely indulge in resting her head on his shoulder? On his chest…

Not only was she eager to crawl into bed, but also to curl up next to him.

Of course he had promised her a Part II, and that woke up certain areas of her body, which in turn, chased off most of her fatigue.

Lance fished the key out of his pocket, unlocked the door, and flipped on the lights as they stepped inside. Between last-minute contracts and the wedding prep, the place was a disaster, papers and computers and clothes strewn everywhere.

Fortunately her suitcase sat in the mix. She grabbed hold of the handle and rolled it toward the bathroom. "I'm going to rinse the sand off my feet and change into something more comfortable. And that *is* a pick-up line, in case you were wondering."

He was turned away, so she couldn't tell if it was one that'd landed.

Well, sex would help with the stress, too. First they could blow off some steam that way and then they'd talk, and she'd find other ways to keep his worries at bay.

Charlotte sighed as she kicked off her shoes. She walked over to the tub and began filling it with warm water. Then she opened her suitcase and found the very sheer nightie the girls had talked her into buying at the lingerie shop stop during the bachelorette party.

• • •

He was going to have to say something. He couldn't have sex with her and *then* ask about her dad. Yes, she'd told him the guy was a gambler, but he needed to know if she'd purposely left out his name, along with the other exact details.

Even if he'd rather forget about it and get lost in her. He wanted to go back to before that asshole threw who her dad was in his face. Simms had stood there waiting, too, wanting to record his reaction.

I know her. Maybe he hadn't known her for long, but he'd always considered himself a good judge of character.

Yeah, like with Sage. And your fullback. You did a great job putting your trust in them.

But Charlotte was different.

His phone buzzed, and he dug it out of his inside pocket.

Only it wasn't his phone—he still had Charlotte's cell and she'd just received a text. From *Dad*.

Only the beginning of the message showed: *I hear you, but I just need to get a leg up…*

Lance's heart pounded hard in his chest. The thunder of it echoed through his head, so loud he was sure that Charlotte would be able to hear it, even through the closed door of the bathroom. That she'd sense he was dangerously close to crossing a line.

But wasn't it his job to keep his company safe? To ensure he could give their new quarterback and coach everything he'd promised? There was so much money at play, and he couldn't have anyone working for him whom he couldn't fully trust.

He'd seen her enter her code. Had made that joke about how simple it was.

It'd be so simple to type it in real quick. To just take a peek.

Back and forth he debated.

It was a violation.

Then again, so was telling people outside the organization about the team's plans, especially if it involved a man who would use the information to gamble. To cheat.

It almost seemed like someone else was in charge of his body as he punched in the code, telling himself he'd only look at that one text. Just to ensure he wasn't making a mistake putting so much on the line by trusting Charlotte so fully. He could even understand helping out someone you loved, but he couldn't stand for it, and he had to know.

Dad: *I hear you, but I just need to get a leg up. Thanks for the tip.*

What tip? Lance scrolled up, but the text above it didn't go along with the conversation.

Dad: *Give me a call. I need a check in.*

Check in on who the Mustangs were talking to? On contract negotiations?

The next message down was from Shannon, and he

tapped on it, too—he was already in, after all.

> Charlotte: *Guess what? Lance asked me to be his girlfriend! Eep!*

> Shannon: *Nice catch! I mean he sort of breaks your football rules on EVERY SINGLE LEVEL, but he's smoking hot and his net worth is through the roof.*

Football rules? Did she usually only go for players? Of course now he was going to be making more than the players, so maybe that's why she made an exception. Charlotte hadn't struck him as a gold digger, but she'd mentioned how fancy the hotel was more than once. She'd also been working in the NFL long enough that she'd know how to play the innocent, struck girl.

She hadn't responded to that text, either. Hadn't said she didn't care, or that wasn't what was important to her.

Sage had acted like she didn't care, but when it looked like his career was going down in flames, she'd sure jumped into another man's bed quickly—one who was going to continue to make millions of dollars.

His phone rang and he jumped, his guilt getting the best of him. He scrambled to answer.

The guy rattled off his name and something about being from some paper? Lance had been distracted by noises coming from the bathroom and wondering if Charlotte was about to step out and didn't catch everything. "I just heard that you guys signed Gavin Frost as your new quarterback. I'm going to be running it in tomorrow's paper and on the blog. Care to comment?"

The tip. She'd given her dad a tip. Lance wondered how much that primo information had gone for. She'd worked so hard to ensure no one had told the press before he could announce it—or that's what she'd made it sound like when she convinced Gavin and his agent to keep it on the down low until Monday.

"No comment," he gritted out and hung up the phone. Betrayal sliced open his veins, a familiar stabbing pain he'd sworn to guard against so he'd never have to experience it again. Yet here he was, and this time, it ached with a ferocity so strong his previous hurts felt like child's play.

This flayed him, down to the quick. Every ounce of his faith leaked out the gaping wound, and he knew he'd never trust another woman again.

Then the door to the bathroom swung open, and he steeled himself for an ugly confrontation that was going to sting like a motherfucker.

Chapter Twenty-Six

Immediately Charlotte knew something was wrong, her instincts screaming at her, although her brain struggled to comprehend the what and why.

Suddenly she felt supremely underdressed, so many inches of her so exposed, but it wasn't like she could simply duck back into the bathroom when Lance had that look on his face. Raw hurt and shock, and something bad must've happened.

"Is your family okay?" she asked.

"Funny you mention families," he said, his words sharp and slicing.

A sense of vulnerability slithered through her, even as she told herself that he couldn't be mad at her.

Right?

Her mind spun, and she wondered if she'd stepped into some alternate dimension because this didn't seem like the guy she'd spent the past few days with. "I'm sorry, but I'm totally lost on what's going on. Tell me and we'll find a way to fix it."

"This isn't a situation that can be magically fixed—especially by you. You and I are supposed to be the only two people who know we successfully acquired Gavin Frost, so why don't you tell me how a reporter found out?"

Offense pinched her gut. "I told you at the reception that I would never give out information about the team to a reporter. I was simply trying to be nice to Martin Simms, something you evidently need more lessons in."

"This was a different reporter. Equally as slimy, I'm sure. You know what he just told me?"

"I'm guessing something about how we were going to acquire Gavin Frost. He was probably fishing— People know we need a quarterback and that he's been looking for a new position. It's not exactly rocket science."

"You want me to believe that, don't you?"

She crossed her arms over her chest, too aware of her nipples brushing the gauzy fabric and how this night was going vastly differently than she'd thought it would. "What I want is for you to stop being an asshole so we can have a calm conversation about this."

"Oh, we're far past calm. Simms told me who your dad is."

In spite of her best efforts to fight it, she felt her face pale, and she forced her chin to remain steady. "I told you he was a gambler. Pardon me for not wanting to dive into the whole messy story— When your grandpa hired me, he told me that he didn't judge people by their parents. I always appreciated that, and apparently it's not something you inherited from him."

She turned to gather her clothes, furious he'd make such a big deal about who her dad was. That he was going to make her feel like shit because Dad had made a mistake, and while yes, it was a big one, he'd done his penance and was working to overcome his addiction.

It hurt even more after opening up to Lance about how rocky her relationship with Dad was. He knew, and he didn't care— He still threw it in her face.

"My grandpa obviously didn't know you fed your dad information to ensure he won more than he lost. Does he at least give you a cut?"

Her spine went stick straight, and she whipped around. "Are you serious right now?"

Lance strode toward her, every line of his body tense. "I've never been more serious. I was such an idiot, playing right into it. Telling you everything."

Tears stung her eyes. "Everything? Are you forgetting who made that draft wall over there? Who dived in and helped you every step of the way while doing the job of three people—people you fired because you're a hothead who apparently loses his mind on a regular basis?"

"Right, like when I trusted you. Clearly a decision I made when I wasn't in my right mind."

The tears were going to spill, no matter how much she blinked against them.

"I saw the text. You don't have to keep denying it." Lance pulled her phone out of his suit pocket and shoved it at her. "Your dad thanked you for the tip."

She lowered her eyebrows, trying to put it together. Somehow she managed to reach for the phone. She saw the text, the one Dad must've sent after listening to her voicemail message about how one of the local construction companies was hiring. She'd added that it should keep him busy enough that he wouldn't be tempted by his phone or his computer as much, since he'd said he had to be careful about ending up on gambling websites.

The sides of her cell dug into her palm as she squeezed it, her lungs flattening as betrayal burned up what little oxygen she had left. "You went through my phone?"

"Don't turn this back on me," he said. "It was in my pocket. I felt it buzz and pulled it out, thinking it was mine. But when I saw that text, knowing what I now know about your father, you're damn right I read it. I have an obligation to my team."

"You didn't think you had an obligation to talk to me instead of jumping to conclusions?"

"I don't have the luxury of trusting someone, especially when proof that I can't lands in my lap. And when I saw your roommate congratulating you on my net worth, I figured that made it pretty clear our relationship was never about just you and me anyway."

Her throat tightened to the painful point while her heart formed a knot she wasn't sure it'd ever come undone from. Every organ was working at self-preservation, and they were all too late. "How can you think so little of me? *She* cares about your net worth. I cared about who I thought you were, but clearly I was wrong about that."

Charlotte stormed into the bathroom, shoved everything she owned into her suitcase, and grabbed the bathrobe off the hook on the door. Once she'd secured it over her nightie, the belt tied tight, she forced herself to walk out of the bathroom instead of lock herself inside it to cry.

Lance was still just standing there, anger wafting from him, his expression shuttered off and his walls up.

"I told you I was raised by a dad who gambled a lot and how often I ended up hurt because of it," she said. "I figured that was enough information, especially since he's been working hard to change. Not to mention there was a big complicated legal battle and his lawyer warned me not to talk about it. Most of all, I wanted to hold on to that hope that the program he was enrolled in—the one I also told you about—was going to help him get better.

"But if you want the ugly truth, he's called me several

times through the years, asking what I know. Asking about the draft, asking who's starting or injured before the reports go out. Wanting me to rattle off stats and give him percentages. I haven't given him anything since I was a naive teenager. Since I realized that I was enabling him and making it worse—that his calls didn't mean he loved me, but that he loved using me— I became a vault when it came to information he might use for gambling."

It hurt to admit it aloud. To feel that same shame and pain she'd experienced when the truth had hit her hard. "After that I clung to the rules, determined never to dabble in any gray areas that'd send me down the path I'd seen him go so far down. Every time he called to ask me for information, I'd tell him he had a problem and that he needed professional help. It took eight long years and an offer to pay for it to get him in that program.

"You can't control what people think— That's your thing, right? But you can control what *you* think, and you've chosen to go with the worst." How could she have been so wrong? About him, about stupid fairy tales—about any of it. "If you would've simply asked instead of jumping to conclusions, I would've told you my dad checked himself out of rehab early, and while that scares the shit out of me, he seems to be doing well and wanted help finding a job. I put out a few feelers and found a company that was hiring, so his *thanks for the tip* was in response to that."

"You expect me to believe that? If you didn't tell your dad about Gavin Frost, and you didn't tell Simms at the reception, how exactly did the press find out, Charlotte?"

"I don't know! I would *never* disclose any of what we've been working on. Not to my dad, not to reporters, and not even to my best friend, who's currently obsessed with guys' salaries because she had a freeloader boyfriend who bled her dry. Not only because it's not who I am, but I signed a nondisclosure agreement. Don't you remember what a stickler I am for the rules?"

"And yet you still slept with me."

Everything inside of her shattered apart. The only thing that kept her knees from buckling was sheer force of will. She wouldn't let him see how easily he'd destroyed her. "You asshole," she said, her voice shakier than she would've liked, but at least she'd managed to force out the words.

Each step was a challenge, but she made it to the door. She didn't allow herself to look back, doing her best to ignore the fact that the distance she was putting between them made her physically ache—how stupid for her body to hurt so much when he clearly didn't care about her.

By the time she made it down the hall, her heart was nothing more than a mangled mass that bled misery. But she made it inside the safety of her room before she dropped to the floor and allowed the tears to overtake her.

As she cried out every ounce of saltwater she had in her, she told herself that it wouldn't hurt this badly forever.

Even as a tiny part of her whispered it'd be impossible to fully get over the loss of what she thought she'd had.

Chapter Twenty-Seven

That had to be the worst night of sleep Lance had ever had, and he'd had plenty of bad nights in his day. Nights in physical pain and hours spent tossing and turning before a big game. Lumpy mattresses and bumpy flights and countless other things had kept him awake and miserable.

But this…?

Every inch of him ached, and it felt like someone had punched a hole clean through his chest. Rolling over only reminded him Charlotte wasn't next to him, regardless of it being something he'd already known.

Over and over her hurt expression flickered through his mind on a torturous loop.

The news about who her dad was had sent him spiraling, stirring up his trust issues and making him doubt everything, and that damn text had pushed him over the edge.

The fight spun out of control so quickly, words spewing from his mouth before he could check himself. A pounding headache loomed as he recalled that retort he'd made about how she'd slept with him despite the rules.

He *was* an asshole.

He groaned and shoved a pillow over his head, not wanting to face the day or the plane ride home. Was it bad that a small part of him didn't care if she had told her dad and he'd leaked it?

Yes, yes it was. He couldn't afford not to care. Couldn't afford to get so wrapped up in a woman who hadn't been 100 percent honest with him. He was already so tangled in her web that every ounce of happiness had drained from him the instant she'd stormed out the door. Much longer and he'd be sucked dry and unable to break free.

After a few minutes of wallowing, he sat up and reached for his phone.

His stomach sank. There were several missed calls from Gavin Frost and his agent in the mix of dozens of others. The news must've broken, and Gavin was probably upset he hadn't gotten to announce it the way he'd hoped—hell, the way any of them hoped.

As much as he wanted to put it off, it wouldn't change anything, so he dialed up Gavin, preferring to talk to him over his agent. He'd been in the guy's shoes and was always better with players anyway.

"Gavin, I'm so sorry."

"No, I'm sorry," he said, and Lance focused on the way he'd said the words. Not sarcastic. Genuine, with a hint of remorse. "I told my mom not to answer the phone, but when I wouldn't talk to the reporters, they called her, and she has this thing about lying. I tried to tell her it wasn't lying, but you know how pushy those reporters are. She cracked. My family was just so excited about me playing for the Mustangs, and…"

The rest of his words faded as Lance put together what he was saying. "Your mom talked to a reporter."

"Like I said, I'm sorry."

It wasn't Charlotte. *Of course* it wasn't her.

It'd never seemed quite right, and he hadn't wanted to believe it. But he'd let himself believe it anyway, and he'd accused her of tipping off her dad and *shit, shit, shit.*

"If your people want to put together a statement for me to release or read," Gavin said, "I'm happy to do it. I'll do whatever I can to make this right."

Lance pinched the bridge of his nose. Pre-Charlotte, he would've let his frustrations spill out of his mouth without thinking, but he was slowly learning to take a second before he spoke—with the exception of last night, damn it. She'd made him better, and for all her efforts, he'd accused her of being a liar. He cleared his throat and concentrated on staying on good terms with his newly acquired quarterback. "Don't worry about it, it happens. Let me get back to you on the statement."

He didn't have people quite yet. Technically, he had one person, and he'd screwed up so badly he wasn't sure she'd ever speak to him again.

Every thought turned to going to find Charlotte so he could apologize and beg for forgiveness. He hung up, flung off the covers, and tugged on jeans and a T-shirt— Even a shower would take too long. He finger-combed his hair and stepped into his shoes as he made his way to the door.

As his horrible luck would have it, the halls were full of people checking out.

Not that it mattered. He knocked on the door to her hotel room. When she didn't answer, he pounded on it. "Charlotte? Charlotte, please talk to me. I was an asshole, and I'm sorry, and I..."

Everyone in the vicinity was staring now, but he didn't give a shit. "Charlotte, please. Please let me in so I can tell you what an idiot I am. Not that you don't already know."

Nothing.

He strode to the front desk, impatiently tapping his fingers against his thigh as he waited in line.

Finally a desk clerk waved him over, and he asked about getting a key to Charlotte's room— He'd paid for it, after all, and desperate times called for desperate measures.

"Oh, Miss James checked out early this morning."

It was early *now*. "What time?"

"Four thirty."

Two hours ago. "Did she say where she was going?"

The desk clerk hesitated.

"We work together, and I'm sure you can see that my name is on the room. I just... My phone's not charged," he lied.

"We called her a cab to take her to the airport."

His tattletale phone rang in his pocket, and when the desk clerk frowned at him, he gave him a sheepish look.

The second he answered it, Gavin's agent added his apologies about the leak. "We know you wanted to make a big announcement, and that's what we wanted, too."

"It's fine. Let me call you back." Lance disconnected the call and tapped Charlotte's number. As the phone rang and rang, he paced the lobby like a madman. Considering he'd completely lost his mind, it was accurate.

He swore when it reached her voicemail, earning him dirty glares from a few of the people in the lobby. With no other choice but to go on with the day he'd planned before his life fell apart, he went back to his hotel room, shoved everything in suitcases, and called for a car to take him to the private airfield where a plane would be waiting for him.

On the drive over, he wrote up two press releases using the examples of others he'd found online—one from the team and one for Gavin. Then he fired them off to the sports reporters he had a good rapport with and told Gavin and his agent they were free to shout the news from the rooftop.

He called Charlotte again as he was boarding, leaving her a voicemail that begged her to call him back.

Just before the plane landed in San Antonio, he called again and left another voicemail.

Lance's phone rang nonstop the rest of the day, long after his flight had landed and he'd arrived back at his empty penthouse that seemed even emptier than when he'd left it.

But none of the calls were from Charlotte, and as he fell into bed at the end of the day, completely exhausted, he worried that she'd never talk to him again.

Chapter Twenty-Eight

Charlotte's heels clacked a happy-sounding rhythm against the hardwood floor Tuesday morning, so at odds with how she felt inside.

Those sucky emotions were going to stay under a rock-hard facade of okayness, because she was nothing if not professional. Over the last couple of days, she'd seriously thought about quitting. Enough so she'd called in a personal day yesterday so she'd have another twenty-four hours to decide. But to let go of everything she'd worked for because her boss turned out to be an asshole?

Nope. She wouldn't let Lance take that from her.

She settled behind her desk, opened her inbox, and winced, and then she got to work.

After two hours, she'd filled out and emailed enough forms to make her head swim.

At the heavy footsteps that neared her door, she tensed and steeled herself.

But it was just Sean Bryant, their new head coach. Official as of yesterday, and the news had hit the interwebs first thing this morning.

"Hello," she said, standing halfway and extending a hand. "So nice to meet you in person."

"You, too." He gave her hand a firm shake and settled into the chair across from her. His blond hair was thick and had a hint of strawberry to it. His simple T-shirt and jeans style paired with the beard, chiseled facial features, and all the muscles gave him a sort of *All-American Dude meets Viking* vibe. His knees went to bouncing, the frantic energy she'd heard a hint of over the phone fully on display now. "The receptionist said you were the person who could help get me started."

"I am. Let me just get some information and a few signatures and then I'll grab you an employee handbook, and you'll be good to go."

A lot of the paperwork had been done thanks to one of the many emails Lance had sent her—some business and some personal—but she inputted the few missing items into her computer, printed off the forms, and had Sean sign.

"Is Quaid in yet?" he asked, his knees bouncing again.

"I haven't seen him," she said, since she didn't know and she didn't *want* to know, and holy hell she was going to have to see him and his name was enough to cause her internal organs to deflate.

"Here's the handbook." She twisted in her chair to snag one off her shelves and slid it across her desk to Sean. "I know you've got a ton to study and write up as you're whipping the team into shape, but please make sure to read through the policies, and if you have any questions, feel free to come to me."

He nodded and slowly stood, looking unsure what to do next.

"Did you have the grand tour yesterday?" she asked.

"Yeah." He glanced around before conspiratorially

leaning in, as if someone might be spying on them. "Confession time? I was so excited to be here yesterday, and then I got the official offer, and it was all kind of a blur." He scratched his neck. "I, uh, don't exactly remember which office is mine."

Charlotte laughed. It surprised her to hear the happy sound come out after days of gloom and doom, but it gave her a sliver of hope maybe she wouldn't be sad forever. "I'll show you where it is, and if you'd like, we can grab coffee on the way."

"That's right. You said something about dessert coffee."

"If you don't like it, I'm afraid we can't be friends." As she stood, she realized how tall he was. Sure, everyone was tall compared to her, but he had to have even a few inches on Lance. So an extra point to the Viking comparison, but the baby blues swung him back to All-American.

No doubt he'd be joining Lance on the eligible bachelor list soon, and she really needed to stop thinking about him because the gloom was settling in like a fog again, smothering everything happy.

Sean ran a hand over his beard. "Wow, and I thought the most pressure I'd feel today was when I meet up with the players this afternoon."

It took her a second to realize he was referencing her comment about the coffee, and she laughed again. Not quite as hard, but there was a flicker of happiness that lasted a good five seconds before fading.

They made a quick stop in the kitchen, and after tasting the creamer—although he'd used significantly less than she had—he announced he liked it. "Ooh, crackers shaped like Texas! How cool are those?"

"Help yourself," she said, and damn it, now she was thinking of Lance and that morning he'd complained all their budget must be going to crackers.

As she and Sean talked, though, she was glad she'd

pushed for him. If he was even half as enthusiastic on the field as in the office, the Mustangs were in good hands.

They continued down the hall to his office, her stupidly happy *clack, clack, clack* mixing with Sean's heavier footsteps. Her stomach crawled way up to her throat as they neared Lance's office, only returning to where it belonged when he wasn't inside.

Thank goodness. Their first interaction was going to be hard enough without someone else looking on, and she wasn't ready. She wasn't sure if she'd *ever* be ready. "Here you go. Right side, fourth door down from the kitchen, just to help you remember."

"Ah, you're assuming I can count to four," Sean said, and she smiled. He really was charming. Not for her—and not just because she'd learned her lesson about dating coworkers and was going back to her no-football-guys decree—but she hoped they could be friends.

"If you need office supplies, let the receptionist know, and she'll put in an order."

"Thanks."

"Charlotte." It came from her right, his voice caressing her skin even as it scraped her raw.

Her heart beat too shallow and fast, and dizziness set in. She'd been better prepared for the inevitability of seeing him while seated in her office, where she would've had the desk between them. Since there wasn't anything to shield herself with or create space, she made do with her arms, crossing them in front of her chest and hoping they'd hold her together.

Looking directly at him would be too painful, so she merely glanced in his direction. "Oh, good, you're here. Coach Bryant was just getting settled in. I'll leave you two to talk."

Lance caught her arm instead of letting her stride by, the bastard. All her walls, and all the tape and glue she'd used to put herself together—mostly ice cream and tirades against men—all of it crumbled under his steady blue eyes.

"You haven't returned any of my calls," he said. "We need to talk."

"Business?"

The line of his jaw tightened. "Damn it, Charlotte—"

She tugged her arm free and aimed a smile at Sean. "If you want to go into your office, Mr. Quaid will be in shortly. We just need to iron out a few details."

"You'll be okay?" he asked, his expression conflicted as he glanced from her to Lance. She appreciated how he was ready to step in if she needed him, even if it meant causing trouble with his new boss.

"I'm fine, I promise."

Sean slowly backed into his office, but he left the door open, and she was suddenly aware of how many people were around, of all the windows and hallways, and all the eyes on them.

It was good. She would need to avoid places where they'd be alone for a while—forever if the vise squeezing her heart and lungs into a pancake of despair was any indicator. "Coach Bryant's signed all the necessary paperwork and is ready to get started. I've emailed you anything I felt was urgent, so just email me back when you've read my messages and I'll take it from there."

Lance's gaze bored into hers. "I don't want the robot. I need you. The woman from the beach who wasn't afraid to tell me when I was a jerk. And I was a jerk—more than that, I was every inch the asshole you accused me of being. I'm sorry that I jumped to all the wrong conclusions. Gavin told me that the press contacted his mom and she was the one who spilled the information. I should've never accused you, should've never gone through your phone, and I regret the way we left things."

Breathe in, breathe out. She took a step away from him, working to rebuild the wall around her emotions, although the pulverized remains no longer fit into place very well. "I'm glad you got to the bottom of it. Now, if you'll excuse me, I have a lot of work to do."

"That's it? You're just going to walk away like nothing happened?" His voice echoed through the area.

She spun back to him. "You probably didn't read the consensual romance in the workplace contract as thoroughly as you should've. It states that we'll act professionally toward each other at all times, even if the relationship has ended." To her dismay, her voice broke, and she worked to steady it. "Furthermore, we'll respect the other person's decision and agree not to engage in unprofessional or inappropriate efforts to resume the relationship or participate in other conduct toward the person that could violate section three of the handbook."

"Trying to explain my side—trying to apologize—is inappropriate?"

"It is in the middle of the hallway with our coworkers looking on," she gritted out, hoping that to everyone else they simply appeared to be having a business dispute. *Yeah, fat chance.*

"Fine. Have dinner with me tonight."

"No, thank you."

"Tomorrow."

"My week is all filled up." *Be strong, be strong, be strong.* "But let me just save us both the trouble of an uncomfortable meal that'd only waste our time. I'm a rules girl. I went against my instincts and broke a few, and I paid for it. It's not the first time I've lost someone I cared about to football, but this time, I'm going to learn my lesson and cut my losses. My heart can only get stomped on so many times before it stops working. From now on, all our interactions will be professional and business driven, and I'd prefer most of them be over email."

He blinked at her, hurt swimming in those blue eyes, and she did her best to tamp down her rising empathy. She had learned her lesson. Had lost enough to guys who gambled on football. She was sick of being the girl who got used up and tossed away. Maybe it was good that she'd found out sooner rather than later, although *good* was the last thing she felt.

"Your wish is…" He swallowed, hard. "Charlotte, it's not what I want."

A deep bruising ache radiated through her chest, and tears stung her eyes. She clenched her jaw against the sob in her throat.

"But if it's what you want…"

She managed to give one sharp nod, words no longer an option. And still her heart rebelled at the lie, throwing itself against the walls of her chest like it meant to break out of its cage and offer itself up to him.

Silly, stupid heart.

"Okay." He lifted his hand as if to touch her cheek, and when she flinched, he limply lowered it to his side. "Okay," he repeated.

From now on, her brain was in charge. No more foolishly believing a guy would change, or that she meant more to someone than she did. As she walked away, even it turned redcoat on her, though, whispering that she'd never care for anyone else as strongly as she cared for Lance Quaid.

• • •

It wasn't fucking okay.

All day he'd pretended he was fine with Charlotte's decree. For one, he hadn't known their relationship had officially ended, and he hardly agreed about respecting the other person's decision, regardless of the fact he'd signed the stupid contract.

Guess that was what he got for signing something without thoroughly reading it.

He paused in the open doorway of her office, bracing himself for the onslaught of misery that would flood him when he peered into her pretty face and saw a mixture of hurt and disdain. It'd nearly killed him this morning. All day it'd played on a loop, merging with the memory of the night when everything went to shit.

Now you're the one who needs to find his balls. You're running a billion-dollar organization, and you need an employee you pay to consult to do her job.

He stepped inside, and when she continued to type away at her computer, lost in whatever was on the screen, he cleared his throat.

She jumped, and he bit back a smile. Remorse for how he treated her immediately followed, so strong it threatened to take him to his knees.

If he thought his dropping to them and begging her to take him back would do any good, he'd throw his pride out the window and attempt it. "After talking to Coach Bryant, we're looking more seriously at the GM position. Your top pick wasn't interested— He got an offer from a championship team who's willing to pay him a lot more than we can."

"Too bad," she said.

"What about Brett Williams? I know he wasn't on our original list because—"

"He had a job elsewhere up until two days ago. I like him." She picked up the pen on her desk and clicked the end a couple of times. "He's done good things, and his draft picks have always been solid. Most of them go on to be MVPs and Super Bowl champs, but thanks to the fact that the owner refuses to pay players what they're worth, they're always on different teams when they win those accolades."

As he'd flown back from North Carolina, he'd worried Charlotte would never talk to him, but this was almost worse. Having her talk to him like a robot. Like they hadn't shared something. Not just something, but the realest, most amazing connection he'd ever had.

"So you think the problem was the ownership, not Williams?" he asked.

She sat back in her chair and adjusted her glasses, but it obviously wasn't so she could see him more clearly because she was staring more in his general direction than at him. "That and deciding to keep coaching in the family. It's hard to overcome a bad head coach. I guess that's why it's better to have a cold-hearted owner. The Mama Bear McCaskey type who'll fire her own son if that's what it takes."

Lance wasn't sure if that was a remark on his cold heart or simply a fact. It'd happened often enough, trying to keep a team and several of its positions in the family, only to realize some members weren't competent or equipped to handle the pressure, followed by making a hard decision that would benefit the organization.

"Williams has some family stuff going on, so instead of flying him here, I'm going to go to California to meet with him." Now he was wishing he'd grabbed a pen to spin through his fingers. Or something else to fiddle with it. Since he didn't want to add stealing a pen to his list of crimes against Charlotte, he jammed both hands in his pockets. "I'd like you to go with me. Coach Bryant will be going as well."

He noticed the hurt that flickered across her features. The rise and fall of her chest. The way her eyebrows pitched up in the middle as she fought to keep her emotions off her face. "I'm sure you guys will make the right decision. I have a lot of work to catch up on here."

A helpless, hopeless sensation gripped his body. He'd actually lost her. "If you need me, I'll be on my cell. Feel free to call it day or night."

She turned back to her computer, and he knew she wouldn't call. He opened his mouth—to say what, he wasn't sure, but his phone rang for the billionth time, give or take a few.

Over the past couple of days, his life had gone from hectic to whatever was beyond that. Turbulent? Chaotic? Complete pandemonium?

All of the above.

Even if she gave him another chance, he wasn't sure how he'd fit in dates or find the time to be in a relationship. To console himself, he told himself they'd been doomed from the start. That it was for the best.

But as he answered the phone and walked away from her, he felt every inch of distance, and each one of them felt so damn wrong.

It was the worst kind of torture to realize he'd have to constantly see her and deal with the knowledge he no longer could hold her hand or kiss her. That she'd never be curled up next to him in bed, her head on his shoulder.

That she'd never be his again.

Chapter Twenty-Nine

It'd been easy enough to stay busy. Over the past week and a half, he'd had countless meetings and phone calls. He'd traveled in zigzag patterns across the US and had several potential employees flown to headquarters. A new offensive and defensive coordinator were in place, every last vacant position was filled, and suddenly Draft Day was here.

The team was coming together, slowly but surely, and if the Mustangs got even 50 percent of the players they wanted today, they'd be well on their way. Thanks to a trade late last season that his grandpa had made—one he wouldn't have, but that was neither here nor there, and after securing Frost it might just work out in their favor—they had the number four pick, too.

Most of the staff was gathered in the war room, including Charlotte, who'd set up in the farthest corner from him, way up top on the back row of the tiered seats. Lance had glanced at her a few times, always finding her looking down at her laptop. Or super focused on her coffee and the jug of creamer she'd brought into the room with her.

Definitely not at him. Never at him.

"Ooh, cracker me," Coach Bryant said, holding his hand out for some of her Texas-shaped crackers as he walked past her. Somehow she managed to pour a few into his palm without lifting her head enough to possibly catch sight of him in even her peripheral vision.

The two of them seemed close already, not in a way that made him romantically jealous, but every time she laughed at the coach's jokes—or hell, just the fact that she talked to him—Lance understood the phrase "green with envy" all too well. It made him sick to his stomach, and yet he also experienced a clashing surge of relief that she could laugh and talk with someone.

He certainly couldn't.

He was avoiding calls with his family, except for one misguided conversation he'd had with Mitch that hadn't ended up being as safe or as comforting as he'd expected.

Just look at me, dammit. I'll… I don't know. Wave?

Solid plan. That'll win her over for sure.

Of course he wanted to be the one Charlotte was laughing and talking with, but as he'd told himself again and again, he'd lost that right. Had no one to blame but himself.

The clock up front showed they had seven minutes until the start of the draft.

Coach Bryant finished his descent to the front of the room, slapping his hands together to wipe off cracker bits before clapping Lance on the back. "Nervous, Quaid?"

"Not at all. You?"

"Nope." Bryant crossed his arms and cast him a sidelong glance. "A team that lies together stays together, right?"

A chuckle slipped out. Dang guy *was* funny. "Let's hope so. I don't want to ever have to build this team from the ground up again." His gaze slipped to Charlotte, and he couldn't help thinking that if he did have to, she'd never agree to come along for the ride. An internal shudder went through him at the thought of having to go about it without her. When he dragged his attention back to Coach Bryant, it was clear he'd been caught staring.

"Ever gonna tell me what that's all about?"

Lance shoved his hands in his pockets and focused on the timer. For some reason it seemed like it was ticking away more minutes of his life without Charlotte rather than heading toward exciting possibilities. "I'm not contractually allowed."

"Girl does love her paperwork and contracts," Bryant said with a laugh. The humor faded from his features, and he widened his stance, planting his hands on his hips in a classic coaching position that made Lance feel like he was about to get told which play to make. At this point, he'd consider anything he thought might actually work. "She's also pretty tight-lipped about it, but even the new guys can tell that there's some unresolved shit between you two."

"That's rich, you calling them *the new guys*."

"Hey, I was here for a good three days before our GM arrived, and a whole week before the rest. I'm old hat compared to these babies."

Lance managed a smile, one he hoped said *very clever, but Charlotte's off-limits* at the same time.

"Me, I'm a never-say-die kind of guy. If your usual play isn't working, it's time to change it up. Go bigger. I've always been a fan of the flea flicker. Or there's the hitch and go." Bryant raised an eyebrow. "Fake spike? I'm kind of hoping that's what you're doing. Pretending to give up, but then you pop up and throw that amazing Hail Mary pass and clinch the girl."

Was this guy for real?

"Big risks, big rewards," Bryant said with a shrug.

"Funny enough, that's why she encouraged me to hire

you."

"Yeah, a woman like that doesn't come along every day."

Why did everyone insist on telling him what he already knew? But they also kept forgetting to factor in that she wouldn't so much as look at him. Wouldn't allow him to say anything that didn't fall in the "business only" category.

The flat screen television up front announced the draft had started right as their clock ticked down to zero. Around the world, millions of football fans from every team were watching, the Mustang fans in the mix hoping and pleading that this would be the season their team turned it around.

All their hopes and dreams for the team, along with the players' and every single other person in this room.

No pressure.

The clock had been reset to count down the ten minutes they had to select their pick, and it was go time.

Lance nodded to Brett Williams, their brand-new GM, who picked up the phone and called in. They sent in the ticket for Darius Fox, the linebacker he and Charlotte had decided on the day she'd put up her wall of craziness. Luckily, the rest of the team was on board, and part of that was because Lance had asked Charlotte to stand up in their meeting the other day and help explain why they wanted him as their first pick.

A few of the guys raised questions, but she'd done her stats wizardry thing, drawing across the white board at the front of the war room like she'd done to the one in the hotel. She added the stats about rookie quarterbacks and pointed out the percentages of division champions and Super Bowl champions who'd won mostly because of their defense.

It'd been a long time since he'd seen a roomful of guys stunned silent.

Pride had radiated through Lance then, and he experienced a surge of it now. He glanced back at Charlotte again, wanting to celebrate together. Needing it, really.

Her gaze remained on her computer.

She hadn't even gotten out of her seat to celebrate. The woman who'd spun around on the beach and squealed or high-fived after every phone call. She'd been willing to give up a quarterback most people were clamoring over each other for so that they'd land Fox.

And nothing.

Which was how he felt, too, come to think of it. They'd restructured this team together, and in spite of being well on his way to getting everything he wanted, instead of happiness, he felt...empty. Hollow.

That hole that'd been punched through his chest remained, and there was only one thing that'd fill it.

And she refused to even look at him.

Everything inside of him was unraveling, coming undone at a rapid pace, and it sent the phone call he'd been trying to keep out of his head rushing to the foreground again.

Yesterday afternoon Mitch had called and asked about Charlotte—funny enough, Lance had only answered because he figured he'd be the one member of his family who *wouldn't* ask about her.

When he told Mitch they weren't together anymore, his brother asked what the hell was wrong with him that he'd let a girl like that go.

"It was one week," Lance had said. "One amazing week, but still." He'd held back that it was the best week of his life. That he relived the amazing moments in his sleep and woke up to the harsh reality it'd ended and everything was different now.

"What does time have to do with anything?" Mitch had asked. "I knew Stacy was the girl for me on our first date."

"You were together for two years before you got engaged, and it was another year before you got married."

"Because planning a wedding in the limited off time

both of us have wasn't easy, not because we didn't want to get married. Plus, I was trying not to scare her off by proposing too soon. But trust me, I wanted to put a ring on it within a week."

Lance hadn't known what to say to that, but it turned out Mitch hadn't been finished anyway. "Have you ever asked Dad when he knew Mom was the one?"

"Can't say I have."

"Well, after I announced to the family that Stacy and I were engaged, Dad got all nostalgic. He told me that he was pretty sure Mom was the one when he asked her out and she told him she didn't date football players. By their second date, Dad went from pretty sure to sure, and within a month, he'd asked her to marry him."

Lance had heard the story about them only dating a month before getting engaged, but he'd always thought it was more the way it was back when his parents were dating, or that they'd simply been fortunate it'd worked out so well.

"Sometimes you just know," Mitch said.

It hit Lance hard, the words ringing over and over in his head. It wasn't just fortune or luck, and time didn't have anything to do with it. He knew he'd never find anyone like Charlotte and that he'd screwed up and that he wanted her back. Part of him had known that since he'd woken up that morning after their blowout, before he'd even found out Gavin's mom had leaked the story to the press.

"Okay, the other team snatched up a quarterback within five minutes, and they're just about to announce who's on the Giants' ticket," Williams said. "Then we'll be up again."

Right. The next draft pick. That was where his head was supposed to be. He was still debating between two players, not sure if he wanted a running back or wide receiver more. The coach and GM were split.

He found he didn't care, not even a little. Because

sometimes you just know.

"Charlotte," he said.

No response.

Screw his pride. It was time to go big. He said her name louder, loud enough that everyone in the war room looked at him, too.

"You need stats?" she asked, her eyes going to the board instead of him.

"I need you," he said, and the whole room went deadly quiet.

"We're on," Williams shouted. "Who's it going to be? The running back from Penn State or the wide receiver from Bama?"

Lance cleared his throat. "I've made a decision. I'm not picking until Charlotte hears me out."

Her head snapped up, her green eyes finally focusing on him. "Don't be stupid."

"Why stop now? I was stupid for assuming I could take you to my brother's wedding without anything changing between us. Even stupider to fall so hard for you in such a short amount of time." He took a step up the aisle, his gaze locking on to hers. "But the stupidest thing I did *by far* was to let you go. To not fight harder for you. So I'm abandoning my pride and throwing myself at your mercy. I'll drop to my knees if that's what it takes. This is the war room, and I'm ready to go to war for what I want—and that's you."

He took another step up, slowly moving toward her, his heart pounding so hard he felt it in every inch of his body. "Actually, it's more than want. Like I said, I need you."

Around them, people began squirming in their seats, frantically glancing at the ticking clock up front.

"Brett," Charlotte said. "Call it in."

Lance spun and pointed a finger. "Call and you're fired. I lose my mind and make brash decisions like that all the time—ask Charlotte."

"You're being ridiculous," she said, that fire inside of her finally igniting as she shot to her feet.

"You're one to talk. You won't even hear me out. Won't even let yourself be alone in a room with me."

"We already went through this. It didn't work. We never should've broken the rules in the first place." Exasperation roiled off her, reminding him of their first few meetings in his office, only this was magnified by everything they'd been through together since then. "And you doing this right here in front of everybody breaks so many sections of the handbook I don't even know which one to start with."

Lance raised his voice and addressed the room. "Apparently we're not supposed to make you guys uncomfortable by discussing our relationship in front of you. PDA is also out, but I'd give up my first draft pick next year if that was even an option."

A collective gasp went through the room, and in any other situation, it might strike him as comical.

"Is anyone uncomfortable?" he asked.

Blank stares and gaping mouths followed, all except for Coach Bryant, who made a rolling motion with his finger, encouraging him to keep on with this crazy-ass play he'd made. He'd launched the ball, now it was up to her to catch it.

Just like with a long-shot pass like that, panic hung heavy in the air—but he could tell that was more due to the clock hitting the halfway point than the fear of PDA.

"Talk or kiss or do whatever the hell you need to do," Williams said, pinching the bridge of his nose. "Just hurry up about it so we can make the call."

Lance turned back to Charlotte. "See. They're fine with it. Now, where was I?"

"I think you were in the middle of proving that you're a pompous asshole who doesn't think the rules apply to you."

"I won't even bother denying that. Charlotte, I fu—screwed up," he said, deciding he'd at least *try* to follow some of the rules in case it'd help his predicament. "I was falling so fast and hard, and I told myself it was too good to be true. I let my doubts overtake my common sense. I've been burned by people I thought I could trust before, and I let my past get in the way of my future."

He climbed up those last few steps, until they were on the same tier. "To be clear, *you're* the future I want. We've worked so hard building this team together, and the last couple of weeks have shown me that it means nothing if I don't get to share it with you. Losing my football career sucked, but I knew I could move on. Losing you… I can't do it." Adrenaline pumped hard and fast, the kind of spike that preceded a devastating crash or a moment of everlasting glory. "I know we have a lot to talk about, and I'm not even asking you to forgive me right here and now. I just need you to say you'll consider it—"

"The clock's at four minutes," Charlotte said, gesturing toward the red numbers. "I know you're not really going to let us run out of time. You and I can discuss this stuff later."

"Nope. You and I are the most important thing to me, even today. And if it takes missing a pick to prove that to you, I swear to God I'll let that clock hit zero. There's always next year— That's a football fan's motto, right?"

"We're more than fans," Charlotte said, a hysterical edge to her voice. "This is our team and our livelihoods, and we can't afford to let another shitty year pass us by."

He shrugged, as if he was powerless to do anything about it. "It's in your hands now."

"Three minutes!" someone yelled, and everyone began muttering to please just hear him out.

"This is against every single rule!" Charlotte pressed her fingers to her forehead. "It *definitely* breaks the terms of the agreement we signed."

In the background, a sports reporter said, "Still waiting for the Mustangs to call in…"

"Lance, you have to let him make the call," Charlotte said.

"I will if you agree to at least have dinner with me." He tried to keep his voice steady even as everything in him began deflating. This was supposed to work—*it had to work*. "Just give me another chance to prove I'm the guy for you."

"Come on, Charlie," Coach Bryant said. "We all can see how miserable you both are without each other."

"We talk about it in the break room," the offensive coordinator added.

"Also against the rules," Charlotte said.

"Love doesn't give a shit about the rules." Lance closed the last few feet of space that remained between them, stopping right in front of her. It hit him hard, how in love he was with this stubborn, amazing, beautiful woman. "That's why I can't let this go—why I'm willing to risk so much on a second chance. I'm in love with you, Charlotte James. I think I fell a little bit in love with you that day you stormed into my office and rattled off the list of offenses against me, and every day we spent together I fell that much harder. It's killing me to see you across the office and not be able to tell you how much I care. Or how much I want to kiss you.

"Agree to have dinner with me. I can finish apologizing then." With every second that ground out in the air the wound in his chest gaped wider, and he forced out one last word, putting every ounce of the rawness he felt into it. "*Please*."

"O-okay." Her voice was shaky, and he wasn't sure if it was from affection or anger, but all he cared was that he'd finally gotten some emotion. He'd work on making it the right one later.

"Tonight? I can't wait another night."

"Yes! Just make the damn call!"

"One more thing," Lance said, and the entire room groaned. "Nitrofanov, the running back from Penn State, or Morris, the wide receiver from Bama?" She rattled off stats for both guys, the words running into each other as if she were auctioning off their skills.

"I need an answer."

"My gut says Nitrofanov, even if his stats aren't quite as strong. He has more heart."

"Make the call," he said, glancing at Williams, who frantically dialed and shouted their pick across the line with twelve seconds to spare.

Charlotte dragged a hand through her hair and left her hand resting on the top of her head. "You're crazy."

"Crazy about you," he said, not caring that it was cheesy. He reached out and took her hand, relief flooding his veins when she curled her fingers around his instead of pushing him away.

Did he dare hope? He gave her hand a slight tug, bringing her body close enough to bump against his.

She braced one hand against his chest and slowly tipped her face to his. "Do you really love me? Or were you just saying that so I'd cave?"

He cupped her cheek, savoring the feel of her soft skin and inhaling her intoxicating scent. "I meant every word, I swear. I tried to tell myself it was too soon, but it doesn't change anything." He brushed his thumb across her cheekbone. "I'm in love with you."

Her eyelids fluttered closed, and she let out a long exhale before her eyes reopened and focused on his. "I'm kinda in love with you, too."

"Kinda?"

She laughed. "All right. 100 percent. I did my best to cling to my denial, but it was no use."

"Does this mean you forgive me for being the biggest idiot in Texas, where everything's already huge?"

"If I say yes, does that mean I forgo groveling over dinner?" She said it lightly, her words a balm to that gaping hole in his chest.

"I'm sure I'll screw up enough that most of our dinners will include groveling."

The corner of her mouth turned up, and a smile slowly spread across her face— Man, he'd missed that smile.

"Kiss already!" someone yelled—he was pretty sure it was Bryant—and her smile widened, a flush of pink creeping across her cheeks.

Lance raised his eyebrows, silently asking if she was okay with fudging the rules a bit.

"Admittedly," she said, "my brain is shouting the same thing about you kissing me already."

He crashed his lips over hers, not wanting to waste another second not-kissing her. Whoops and hollers filled the room, the cheers even louder than after they'd secured their new rookies.

He lifted her off her feet, wrapping her tighter in his arms and kissing her deeper.

"Now go make use of one of the empty offices so we don't have a repeat of this during the second and third rounds," Williams said. "If you hurry, you'll be back to get the updates on who everyone else has scooped up."

Charlotte scowled at their GM, and Lance could see the protest about his being inappropriate on the tip of her tongue. He also could tell by her sigh that she'd decided to let it go. If anything called for a celebratory night of rule breaking, it was this.

"Actually," Lance said, lowering her to her feet but using his arm to keep her tucked next to him. "We've got the rest of our options mapped out pretty well, along with backup options, so you can text me updates, and I'll be here bright and early tomorrow morning so we can do it all again."

He looked down at Charlotte, unable to resist giving her a kiss on the cheek. "Ready to get out of here?"

• • •

This day hadn't gone at all the way Charlotte thought it would. Well, being in the same room as Lance *had* been as tortuous as expected, but for him to lay everything on the line like that? With the entire staff watching?

And he loved her...

Which led her to say something she'd never expected to say in the middle of the draft madness. "Beyond ready."

Hand in hand, they left the war room. They made out in the elevator. They kissed their way out of the lobby and over to his car.

He tucked her inside, rounded the hood, and settled behind the wheel. "Name the restaurant."

"Actually, I was thinking we could order in. We already made enough people uncomfortable with our PDA, and considering what I want to do to you, it'd be best if we didn't have an audience."

The passion that flared to life in his eyes echoed through her, and suddenly she was worried she'd never survive the drive home without spontaneously combusting.

"My place it is," he said, firing up the car.

This time, she didn't complain about how fast he drove. Seconds after he'd parked, they'd climbed out of the car and resumed their kissing. During their private elevator ride up to his floor, they went from PDA to risqué. He ran his hands over her ass, her breasts, up her thighs, and under her skirt.

She was a panting, needy mess by the time they spilled into his penthouse.

Instead of peeling off her clothes, he took a step back, and an involuntary whimper came out.

"I'll take care of you, babe, I promise. I just wanted to take a second to soak in the sight of you standing in my place, your lips red and swollen from my kisses."

"Speaking of soaked…"

He made a strangled noise in the back of his throat. His eyes drank her in from head to toe, heat licking every place they touched, and she couldn't wait for his hands to do the same. "I also want to make you a promise. I'll never doubt you again. Never treat you the way I did the night of Mitch and Stacy's wedding." His blue eyes implored hers. "I need you to know how sorry I am."

She opened her mouth to respond, but he dragged his thumb across her lower lip, and her mind went hazy with desire.

"This life—our life if you stay with me—is going to be crazy busy. There will be a lot of traveling and stressful decisions, but it doesn't scare me as long as I know you'll be by my side every step of the way."

"I will be," she said, then she tipped onto her toes and lightly kissed his lips.

"I didn't get to the rest of my promise."

"Well, get to it already," she teased, pinching his side.

He clucked his tongue at her. "Patience."

"We've established I don't have any of that."

He grinned, his thumb swiping across her lip again. "I love that about you. Love everything about you. Which is why I promise that you'll always come first. And if I'm not putting you first, you have my permission to smack some sense into me."

"I've been doing that without your permission, so I think I can handle that." She leaned closer and dragged her nose across his cheek. "I appreciate it, though." She kissed the scruff she'd missed, enjoying the scrape against her sensitive skin.

"Now..." She skated her hands down his chest to the center of his stomach to the bulge in his pants.

A ragged groan ripped out of him as she squeezed over the fabric.

"Your groveling debt has been paid in full. Groping time is on."

His low laugh echoed through her, and then his hands were on her ass. He hauled her against him so that her core lined up with his erection, and he ground against her as his mouth descended on hers.

He boosted her into his arms and walked them toward where she assumed his bedroom was.

Sure enough, a king-sized bed greeted them.

"Oh, before this goes any further," she said, "I should probably get my laptop and update our love contract." His face dropped, and she laughed. "Only kidding."

He tossed her on the bed and crawled over her. "I'm going to make you pay for that." He parted her lips with his tongue, sliding it inside her mouth and stroking her into a frenzy.

While they'd had a lot of great sex, this time was different. Deeper, more meaningful, their bodies so perfectly in sync. He whispered *I love you*s as he painted kisses across her skin and imprinted himself into every nook and cranny of her heart.

At one point, she'd cursed the day Lance Quaid had walked into her life and made such a mess. But as they lay in bed cuddling afterward, she realized that in a lot of ways, he'd put her back together.

Epilogue

If Charlotte didn't stop chewing on her nails, she wouldn't have any left. She wasn't even a nail bitter, but apparently the first game of the season—which would be starting in about seven minutes—had turned her into one. The preseason games had gone...okay. The dynamic of the new and old players with the new coaching staff took a lot of adjustments, and they were getting there, but they'd still had a few things to work on.

This was the first game that counted, and she told herself that it wasn't the end of the world if they lost.

She didn't voice that opinion aloud, though, because for all of Lance's replies about being "fine," she'd never seen him so high-strung.

She walked over to where he was sitting in the owner's box and put her hand on his shoulder. He started, almost as if she'd yanked him out of another world, and then lifted his hand to cover hers. "I'm fine," he said.

"I know. Just like I'm fine. In that way that I'm gonna puke and my heart is alternating between pounding too fast and forgetting how to beat."

He slid his fingers up to circle her wrist and tugged her around so she was sitting on his lap. There was a good chance cameras would flash on them, and the old her might've thought it too improper, but the current her needed to be in his arms and as close to him as possible.

The door swung open, and Maribelle and Chuck stepped inside.

"Charlotte!" Maribelle rushed toward her, and she stood and opened her arms for the hug coming her way. Lance's mom clung on like she never meant to let go, and it warmed Charlotte from the inside out. Enough to chase a bit of her nervousness away. "I'm so, so happy to see you."

"Right back at you," Charlotte said. They'd talked on the phone here and there over the past several months, but they hadn't seen each other since the wedding.

Charlotte hugged Chuck, and Maribelle turned to Lance and gave him a big squeeze before patting his cheek and telling him to relax.

He told her he was fine.

"Fine. Sure. Thank goodness you have Charlotte." Maribelle took her hand. "You've got a real keeper here, and you nearly gave me a heart attack when I found out you'd lost her. I thought I was going to have to fly down and knock some sense into you."

"That was months ago, Mom."

"Still." She put a hand over her heart. "Messing with your poor mother's emotions like that."

Charlotte smiled at him over his mom's head, and he winked at her. "I promise that I fully realize what I have, and how lucky I am that she gave my sorry ass a second chance."

"Language!" Maribelle said, which saved Charlotte from having to— They were in a professional environment after all.

Lance and his dad exchanged a quick bro hug and stifled their emotions together, and then they settled into their seats right in time for the coin toss.

Two minutes into the game, Gavin fumbled. Charlotte fought the urge to bury her head in Lance's shoulder while Williams strung together an impressive amount of swear words that no one dared to reprimand him for. Not when they'd all been thinking a variety of the same thing.

"He's getting there," Charlotte said, squeezing Lance's hand. "Everyone fumbles from time to time." Now that she knew Gavin Frost better, not only did she think he was the best quarterback for their team, she genuinely liked him as a person. He was funny and hardworking and a total team player. But he'd instantly won her over when he'd shown up for his first official day as a Mustang with his best friend since childhood in tow, an adorable blonde named Julie. They explained that she worked as a pathologist in Phoenix now, but that every big step one of them made, the other person showed up for if at all possible, and becoming a Mustang was a huge step. The two of them kept up via phone and computer, and Charlotte made a mental note to see about getting Julie to a game. Maybe that'd help steady him, and she cursed herself for not thinking of it before.

It's okay. He'll make up for his mistake during our next possession.

Lance glanced toward the door, and it hit her that he'd been doing that a lot.

"Are you expecting someone?" she asked.

He gave a noncommittal head wobble before scooting forward in his seat, his attention back on the game.

"That's our boy, shutting them down," Charlotte said as their first draft pick, Darius Fox, sacked the other team's quarterback, forcing them to kick off.

The door opened, and Charlotte did a double take when

her dad walked in. She slowly stood, blinking, thinking it might be a mirage. She felt Lance behind her. He wrapped his hands around her shoulders. "I'm here if you need me," he whispered.

"Hi, Dad," she said, and he walked over and hugged her. They'd met up a few times since she'd gotten back from her trip. He was doing well, working his construction job and going to meetings, but they still had some work to do on their relationship, and thanks to her crazy schedule, they hadn't seen each other much.

She introduced him to Lance, who leaned around her to shake his hand.

"We chatted on the phone," Lance said, "but it's nice to meet you in person."

Charlotte glanced over her shoulder at him.

"I thought it'd be nice to have our families at the game." He lowered his lips to her ear. "He said he wasn't sure he could come, so I didn't want to get your hopes up."

That explained why he'd been extra cagey.

A strange, extremely proper air seized the box for a minute or two, but then they started cracking jokes and cheering and coaching the players who couldn't hear them.

The game went back and forth. The other team would score, and the Mustangs would answer, but they never managed to take the lead.

"He's going for it?" Lance asked when Coach Bryant sent the offense out for the fourth down.

There were still four minutes to go, but they needed a touchdown to win. It was a risky play. They needed three and a half yards for a first, and if they turned it over on the other team's forty-yard line, they could—and most likely would—make a field goal that would put them far enough ahead that the Mustangs would need to score twice to have a shot at winning.

"We hired Sean because he takes risks," she said, despite worrying it was too great of one. Usually she was a go-for-it kind of gal, but they needed to start winning games to get and keep fans in the seat—not to mention to have a shot at playoffs—and the pressure was so much stronger now that she'd tied her life to Lance's.

Both the fan side and her professional side were internally screaming.

They erupted along with the crowd as Nitrofanov, the rookie running back the team had dubbed Nitro thanks to his explosive speed, broke through a gap she hadn't even seen and ran the three and a half yards…

Plus another ten.

Hit the twenty-yard line…

The ten…

"He's going to score." Charlotte slapped a hand over her mouth, scared she'd jinxed it, but her dad grabbed her free hand and squeezed tight.

"He's got it," Dad said.

They jumped to their feet as Nitro crossed the goal line. They cheered and exchanged hugs, and she turned to Lance, who planted a heated kiss on her lips.

"That was all you," he said.

She shook her head. "Um, that was you being ridiculous and making me choose someone with seconds to go. Plus, Williams was the one who snatched up our new fullback. I mean, did you see that block?" She spun and held up her hand to the GM. "Rockin' the picks, Williams."

He was a tad old-school and had definitely not known what to make of her, especially after the debacle in the war room on Draft Day, but he grinned and slapped her hand. "We make a good team."

She bounced on the balls of her extra-tall heels, putting her trust in Lance, who'd undoubtedly catch her if she wobbled out of control.

Not a single butt was in a seat as the last couple minutes of the game ticked down.

The clock hit zero, and their losing streak was officially broken.

Charlotte and Lance exhaled twin breaths. She placed a hand over her rapidly beating heart, telling it that it was okay to relax now. "One down…"

There was a lot to go, but they had more hope than they'd had in a long time. Especially considering they'd just beat the team that'd been ranked fifth after last season.

When she turned to Lance, he was down on one knee. A black box was open, a big-ass diamond ring inside, winking against the lights.

"Holy shit," she said, and he laughed.

"Isn't swearing at a professional work event against section three of the handbook?"

She threw her hands over her mouth.

"My mom made it clear she'd disown me if I let you go again, and like I told her, I have no plans of ever doing that. I love you, Charlotte James. You challenge me and calm me and make me better, and I couldn't ask for a better partner. As I've said before, you're my Sam, and there's no one else I'd rather go to Mordor with."

He grinned extra wide, and while she was sure everyone else in the room was slightly confused, a thousand butterflies erupted inside of her. It was the most perfect, nerdy thing to say, especially with the juxtaposition of all the NFL regalia in the background. It was so perfectly them. "Of all the deals I've made this year, that one to take you to my brother's wedding was by far the smartest, and the one I've gotten the best return on."

"Kinda making me sound like a hooker again," she said, and the people around them chuckled. "Probably shouldn't have taken that left at Mordor."

"Well, I didn't have you to help edit this speech for me." His blue eyes lifted to her face, the love shining in the depths enough to make her breath catch. "At one point, I didn't think I had time in my life for love, but now that I've experienced how awesome love can be, I realized I don't want to waste any more time not being married to you. What do you say? Wanna strike another bargain involving a wedding? This time it'll be ours."

She laughed. "Don't you need me to run some stats first? On you, on me. On you plus me."

"Go with your gut."

"My gut says you have a deal." She smiled down at him and added, "Of course I'll marry you, Lance Quaid. Even though I'm not sure you technically asked."

"Oh, I asked, and you already said yes, so no taking it back now." He slid the ring on her finger. He stood and planted a kiss on her that would've knocked her on her butt if he hadn't also wrapped his arm around her waist, and judging from the feedback in the room, she was pretty sure their proposal had just been telecast wide.

Good. Now everyone will know that he's all mine.

"Is it too hasty to request they hurry and strike your name from that eligible bachelor list?" she asked against his lips. "Like right now?"

"I'll have my people call their people."

"I'm your people." Technically it'd probably go to PR, but she'd be the one who'd talk to them, so really it was just cutting out the middle man.

"You're mine, that's for sure." He skimmed his hands down her sides. "I'm guessing this means we're gonna have to fill out some more forms?"

Charlotte shrugged. "I don't know what you're talking about. Don't tell me you're some kind of uptight rule-follower."

He laughed, low and deep, and his lips found that spot on her neck that drove her crazy. "Only for one woman."

She grinned and kissed him again, letting herself fully fall into it. Then she pulled back so she could peer into the face of a man she was so in love with that it made it impossible not to believe in true love and the one and a whole mess of things she thought she'd never believe in again. Which made it all that much more fun to surprise him and say, "Well tonight, Mr. Quaid, I'm thinking a little rule breaking is in order."

Want more from Cindi Madsen? Turn the page to start reading *Just One of the Groomsman* by Cindi Madsen. Available in Mass Market Paperback everywhere books are sold May 28th.

Chapter One

The boat house came into view and Addie's excitement level went from its already high seven to a solid ten. An emergency meeting had been called, and all of the guys were going to be in attendance. Every single one, including the guy she'd been dying to see for so long that she'd almost worried their sporadic phone calls, texts, and messages were the only way they'd ever communicate again.

Addie pulled up next to the sleek, compact car she'd have to make fun of later—right now it meant that Tucker Crawford was here in the flesh, and within a few minutes, the whole gang would be here as well. She wasn't sure why Shep had called the meeting, but it took her back to high school when so many of their evenings and weekends were spent here at the Crawfords' boathouse. Lazy afternoons and countless poker games. Nights spent celebrating team wins or commiserating over losses, whether it was the high school team that the guys had all played for, Crimson Tide football, or our NFL teams, on which they were a house divided—it'd led to some of Tucker and her most heated exchanges.

The scent of Cypress, swampy lake water, and moss hit her as she climbed out of the beater truck she often drove, and since she was hoping for a minute or two with Tucker before everyone else showed up, she rushed up the pathway, her rapid steps echoing against the wood once she hit the plank leading to the boat. "Tucker?"

"Addie?"

She heard his voice but didn't see him. Then she rounded the front of the boat, where the chairs and grill were set up, and there he was. Even taller and wider than she remembered, his copper brown hair styled shorter than he wore it in high school, although the wave in it meant there were always a couple of strands that did their own thing, no matter how much gel he put in it.

A laugh escaped as she took a few long strides and launched herself at him, her arms going around his neck. "I'll be damned, you actually made it this time."

Using the arm he'd wrapped around her lower back he lifted her off her feet and squeezed tight enough to send her breath out over his shoulder. "I'm sorry for accidentally standing you up a few times. It's stupid how hard it's been to get away this past year."

"That's what happens when you decide to go and be some big city lawyer." She pulled back to get another look at one of her best and very oldest friends. She had so much to tell him that she didn't know where to start. Thanks to his crazy work schedule, even their phone calls and texts had slowed to a trickle. Despite working at the law firm for nearly two years, he was still one of the junior attorneys, which meant he ended up doing all the time-consuming research for the partners. Before that he'd been busy with law school, and while she wasn't usually the mushy hugger-type, she didn't want to completely let go, just in case she had to go another year without seeing him.

Only now that she was focusing on every single detail, from the familiar blue eyes to his strong, freshly-shaven jawline, to—holy crap, when did he get jacked shoulders and pecs and arms like that? Was lifting bulky legal files muscle-building. If so, maybe she needed to recommend it as part of her clients' physical therapy regimens.

His gaze ran over her as well, most likely assessing the ways she'd changed—or more likely hadn't—but for a quick second, her body got the wrong message, a swirl going through her stomach and her pulse quickening.

And before she thought better of it, she reached up and ran her hand through his hair, loosening the hold the gel had on it. He could definitely pull off the clean-cut lawyer look, but she preferred the more-relaxed version. Maybe that version would also help her keep from looking at him as something other than...well, him. Tucker Crawford. The boy who'd once landed her in detention because he'd dared her to put super glue on the teacher's whiteboard makers while he distracted him with a question; boy who'd challenged her to a deviled egg eating competition at the town festival—to this day the sight or scent of a deviled egg made her stomach roll.

Tucker's hand went to her hip, a shallow breath fell from her lips, and time froze...

"Crawford? Where you at?" Shep's booming voice broke whatever weirdo vibes were trickling into the reunion she'd been awaiting for what seemed like forever, and she dropped her hand, just in time for Shep, Easton, and Ford to come around the corner to the deck of the boat.

"Murph!" They yelled when they saw her, and then they exchanged some high fives and a few bro-hugs on their way to give Tucker the same treatment. She saw the rest of the guys around town now and then, but it was harder to get together now that everyone had careers and other obligations, and they hadn't hung out in way too long. Funny how in high school they couldn't wait to get older so they could do whatever they wanted, and instead they ended up having less free time than ever.

Shep placed two six packs of beer on the desk railing. "Before we get this party started, I guess I should let you all know what we're celebrating." The hint of worry she'd felt since getting the urgent meeting text evaporated. The message had been so vague—typical guy, although her mom and sister had often accused her of the same thing.

Addie sat on the edge of the table, and when Tucker bumped her over with his hip, she scooted. Then the table wobbled, and Tucker's hand shot out and wrapped around her upper arm as she worked to rebalance herself.

He chuckled. "Guess we're heavier than we used to be."

"Speak for yourself," she said, shoving his arm, glad things were back to normal. With a hint of noticing the firm press of his shoulder and thigh and the warmth radiating off his body.

"So, you guys might recall I've been seeing Sexy Lexi, going on a year now."

"How could we forget?" Addie quipped. "You talk about her non-stop." She glanced at Tucker. "Seriously, we go to get a beer and it's just Lexi this, and Lexi that."

Shep didn't scowl at her like she'd expected, grinning that twitterpated grin he now wore instead.

"She's actually very lovely." Addie curled her hands around the table. While his southern belle girlfriend worked to hold it at bay, she didn't think Lexi was her biggest fan, and she hated always having to calm down her friendship with the guys in order to not upset the balance of their relationships. Hopefully a little more time and getting to know each other, and Lexi would understand that Will Shepherd was more like a brother than anything.

All of the guys were.

Tucker's hand covered hers and he gave it a reassuring squeeze.

Okay, maybe she was questioning the past tense of that *were* the tiniest bit.

Crap, she didn't know. But she could say for sure that she and Shep were more sibling-like than the rest. It wasn't the first time her friends' girlfriends were wary of her, and she doubted it'd be the last. Sometimes she worried she'd get left behind, just because she was a girl in a group of guys. That was a technicality, though. It wasn't that she didn't have female friends or that she didn't know a lot of great women; it was that she'd grown up with these guys and forged memories and they liked to do the same things she did.

It was why she'd gone by "Murph" more often than Addison Murphy, or any other variation thereof. Thanks to her love of comfy, sporty clothes, she'd been voted "most likely to start her own sweatshirt line" in high school, a title she was proud to have, by the way.

Easton had been voted "most likely to end up in jail," and ironically enough he was now a cop, something they all teased him about. Which reminded her...

"Don't let me forget to make fun of your prissy car when this meeting is over with," Addie whispered to Tucker.

He opened his mouth, assumedly to defend himself and then Shep cleared his throat.

"*Anyway*, last weekend I asked Lexi to marry me." A huge grin spread across his face. "And she said yes."

They offered their congratulations, and after a few claps on the back and obligatory jokes about ball and chains, Shep said, "I want you guys to be in my wedding. To be my groomsmen."

Addie's stomach dropped. "You guys" usually included her, but she knew the word "groomsmen" didn't. "Ha! You guys are all gonna have to wear stuffy penguin suits and take hundreds of pictures. Have fun with that."

Shep looked at her, and a sense of foreboding prickled her skin. "Before you go celebrating too much, you're in the wedding party, too. I told Lexi that I wanted you as one of my groomsmen."

While his girlfriend—make that fiancée—was pretty patient and understanding of Shep's crazy, out-there ideas, she was also *extremely* girly. Like she wore dress and heels more often than not—including to the local bar, which wasn't a dress-and-heels kind of joint—and belonged to one of those societies that threw things like tea parties and galas. "I'm sure that went over about as well as coming out as a vegan in the middle of Sunday dinner."

"She understands that you're just one of the guys," Shep said, and a hint of hope rose up. She hated that lately she felt left out. Add to that the spinning-wheels sensation and her life needed a shakeup.

Maybe I should've taken that job. It would've meant moving over three hours away from Mom, Dad, and Nonna Hutchins, but she still wondered if she'd missed an opportunity. She'd witnessed the sorrow of her sister moving a state away. They'd been so upset, asking if they'd done something wrong, because how couldn't you want to stay in Uncertainty, Alabama, where everyone knew everyone, and they all thought that entitled them to being all up in your business?

"But she's also more traditional, her family even more so."

"I understand," Addie said. "I don't think I'd look very good in a tux anyway, and my own mother would probably die twice over it."

"Which is why…" Shep straightened, his hazel eyes on me. "Lexi and I came up with a compromise. You'll be a groomsmen in name, and when it comes to all the usual pre-wedding stuff, but in order to be part of the wedding party you're going to have to wear the same dress and shoes as the bridesmaids." The rest of the words came out in a fast blur, like he hoped if he talked fast enough I might miss them. "And you might have to dress up one or two other times, like at the rehearsal dinner and maybe even the bridal shower."

The guys burst out laughing. "Murph in a dress and heels," Easton said. "That'll be the day."

Addie picked up the nearest object she could find—a coaster—and chucked it at his head. It bounced off but didn't deter him from laughing.

The table shook, and when she looked at Tucker, he had a fist over his mouth to try to smother his laughter.

"You too?"

"Please, Addie," Shep said. "I know it's not your thing, but I can't imagine you not being part of this." He shot a challenging glare at the group of them. "And spare me the jokes about actually caring about my wedding. I never thought I'd be this happy, but I am, and I want you guys there. I need you guys with me on this."

This time, the "you guys" definitely included her. Which made it that much easier to say, "I'm in. I'll do whatever you need me to."

• • •

Man it was good to be back in town, even if only for a quick weekend. Tucker had been working hours and hours on end, thinking that after putting in two years at the law firm he'd have enough experience and clout to slow down a little. It never slowed down, though, his work load multiplying at an impossible-to-keep-up-with pace. He'd had to cancel his last two trips home with lame, last-minute texts and calls, but now that he was seated around the poker table with his friends, all felt right with the world.

"You're bluffing," Addie said when Easton threw several chips into the pot. She matched his bet and then they laid down their cards, her full house easily beating his pair of Aces. "Read 'em and weep, sucker." She leaned over the table to gather her winnings, and Tucker's gaze ran down the line of her body. Okay, so maybe one thing felt a little off, but it didn't exactly feel not-right, even if he knew he should shut down all thoughts of Addie's body and how amazing she looked.

He cracked a smile at the thought of her in a dress and heels, bouquet in hand. It wasn't that they'd never seen her wear a dress; it was that she loathed them, and she'd once slugged him in the shoulder for even mentioning her dress-wearing at her sister's wedding. The skirt had been long and baggy, and the real tragedy was that she couldn't toss around the pigskin—her mom said it'd ruin her nice clothes, and then added that it was an "inappropriate wedding activity, anyway." So then they'd *both* had to sit there with their hands folded in their laps and it was boring as hell, an emotion he'd rarely experienced around her.

"Your poker face is crap, Crawford. I know you're thinking about how funny it is that I just agreed to wear a freaking bridesmaid's dress, and if you don't want me to jam that beer you're drinking where the sun don't shine, I suggest you wipe the smirk off your face." She pointed her finger around the table. "That goes for all of you."

"I appreciate you going along with it," Shep said. "I told Lexi that you'd probably punch me or kick me in the balls just for suggesting it."

"Lucky for you, you were too far away and wearing that love-struck grin that makes me take pity on you."

"When someone basically says thank you, maybe don't follow that up by insulting them." Shep began dealing the cards he'd just finished shuffling. "Just a suggestion."

"This is why so many guys in town are scared of you," Easton said with a laugh.

She clucked her tongue. "They are not."

All of the guys nodded, and Tucker found himself nodding even though he hadn't lived in town for the better part of a decade. It'd been like that since high school, and the selfish part of him was glad that no guy had come in and swept her off her feet. Not that Addie would ever let some guy do the sweeping. Still, with her blond hair that was forever in a high ponytail and the smattering of freckles across her nose that drew you right to them and her big brown eyes, it was surprising she'd stayed mostly single. Or maybe she hadn't told him about her boyfriends, the way he'd never really discussed his girlfriends with her. There weren't many to talk about since he'd been so busy, but he also didn't want anything to get in the way of getting back to them when they managed to find time to talk.

Ford pinned her with a look. "Addie, when guys come in for physical therapy, you tell them to stop crying over something your grandma could do."

"Well, she could! My nonna is tougher than most of the dudes who come in whining about their injuries. Then they don't want to put in the work it takes to get over them. Telling them my grandma could do the things I'm instructing them to do is motivating."

"Not to ask you out," Ford said, and snickers went around the table.

"Very funny. Being scared of me and being undateable are two different things."

"You're hardly undateable," Tucker said, the words similar to exchanges they'd had in high school.

"Yeah, but it's nearly impossible to find someone who doesn't already know too much about me—or me about them—and even if I manage that, then I introduce him to you guys, and things unravel pretty quickly after that."

"Maybe with one of us getting hitched, we'll be less intimidating." Shep tossed in the ante and everyone else did the same.

"I'm sure it's me," Addie muttered. "Now, do you guys want to talk about my pathetic dating life, or do you want me to take all your money?"

"Wow, what great options," Tucker deadpanned. "Not sure why anyone would be scared of you. Couldn't be all the threats."

She turned those big eyes on him and cocked an eyebrow. "Listen, city boy. Maybe you can just flash your shiny car and some Benjamins to get your way where you live, but here we still live and die by the same code."

He leaned in, challenge firing in his veins. "And that is…?"

"Loser buys beer."

Shep revealed the flop and Tucker watched everyone's faces for signs of what cards they had or were hoping for. They did a few more rounds of betting as more cards were revealed, and at the end it came down to him and Addie.

She called his bet and then proceeded to take the last of his chips.

They played until Addie had pretty much cleaned everyone out, then one by one they left, save the two of them.

"Are you staying at the boathouse tonight?" she asked as she gathered her keys off the table outside.

He wasn't sure if she was offering him a place to crash or just curious. His parents had relocated shortly after he started law school, and he'd hated how uprooted he'd felt even though he didn't technically live in Uncertainty anymore. He'd asked them to hold off on selling the boathouse, and when Dad claimed he couldn't, Tucker bought it himself. Having to visit them in a different city made it that much harder to get back here, and he'd already seen repairs that would need to be made. "I like it out here on the lake, so I would prefer it even if my parents' hadn't sold their place."

A smile curved her lips as she ran her hand over the deck railing. "I love this mini-house and all of our memories here."

"Me, too." He folded his forearms on the railing and looked over at her, watching the breeze stir the strands of hair. "Tonight was the most fun I've had in a long time."

Her grin widened, and it lit up her whole face. The moon glowed off her features—pretty features he couldn't help gazing at. Growing up with her had left him so used to how she looked that he'd forgotten how beautiful she was, and he didn't really notice until he'd gone somewhere else and realized how unique she and the relationships they had was. No one else was like her. It was why she was one of his very best friends, and that meant stifling the urge to ask her to stay the night with him. He wanted to think it could be just like old times when they'd crash out on the couch or tiny bed.

Except now he might be tempted to curl her to him, and not just for warmth or minor cuddling. It must just be that he hadn't had time off in forever, the fun he'd admitted to leaving him more buzzed than the beer. Or that he hadn't been out with a woman in so long that his thoughts were running wild. Either way, he needed to leash them before they ruined one of the purest, best relationships he had in his life.

"Good night, Tucker." She turned to go, but then abruptly spun around and hugged him tight. "I understand that your job is demanding, but don't be a stranger."

He squeezed her back, taking a whiff of her shampoo—something fruity that smelled good and made him want to bury his nose in the silky strands, another sign that he was drunk and nostalgic, and he should definitely let her go now.

"At least with Shep getting married you've got another

excuse to come down and spend more than a weekend here," she said.

He nodded. "Yeah, it's good to have an excuse." What he wanted was an excuse not to go back to his cold, generic apartment and mind-numbing job.

What he wanted was to return to his friends and the town he loved, and he wasn't sure how he could possibly go back and be satisfied with his old life after tonight showed him everything that was missing from it.

Acknowledgments

Since this book is all about football, I just have to say thank you to my parents and grandparents for making me a born and raised Broncos fan. I learned to yell at the TV from a very young age. Still haven't quite learned how to get the players, coaches, and refs to listen, though… LOL

With every book, the people who always sacrifice and support me the most are the members of my family. To my husband and my kids, thank you for being so supportive, even if I switch books and plotlines partway through conversations without telling you.

To my wifeys, Gina L. Maxwell and Rebecca Yarros, you know I adore you. Thank you for always being there to talk plotlines and answer editing questions and to make me laugh when I need it most. I love our very structured Monday morning video meetings and how we can attend in our yoga pants. I don't even have words for how grateful I am to have you both in my life.

Thanks to the entire staff at Entangled Publishing. To my editor, Stacy Abrams, who has edited book after book after book with me. Some of our longest comment threads have been about football, so it was only fitting that we do a football series together. To Liz Pelletier for supporting me and being a champion for my books—thank you for believing in me. Big thanks to Holly and Riki for publicity awesomeness, to Heather Riccio for her ninja skills, to Katie Clapsadl, Jessica Turner, the cover designers and formatters, and everyone else on the Entangled team who helps my book get into readers' hands.

Shout out to my agent of awesomeness, Nicole Resciniti. You're a rock star, and I can't thank you enough for all you've done for my career. Xoxo.

Last, but certainly not least, thank you to my readers for supporting my books and sending me messages that keep me going. My FB group, Cindi Madsen's Banter Babes, is full of amazing people who are also some of my loudest cheerleaders. Come on over if you'd like to join us—we mainly talk about books and life and how books make life better.

And thank you, dear reader, for picking up this book. You help make dreams come true.

About the Author

Cindi Madsen is a *USA Today* bestselling author of contemporary romance and young adult novels. She sits at her computer every chance she gets, plotting, revising, and falling in love with her characters. Sometimes it makes her a crazy person. Without it, she'd be even crazier. She has way too many shoes, but can always find a reason to buy a pretty new pair, especially if they're sparkly, colorful, or super tall. She loves music and dancing and wishes summer lasted all year long. She lives in Colorado (where summer is most definitely NOT all year long) with her husband, three children, an overly-dramatic tomcat, & an adorable one-eyed kitty named Agent Fury.

You can visit Cindi at: www.cindimadsen.com, where you can sign up for her newsletter to get all the up-to-date information on her books.

Follow her on Twitter @cindimadsen.

Discover more Amara titles...

STORY OF US
a novel by Jody Holford

Declan James has been Brockton Point's most ineligible bachelor, but now that his closest friends have found their happily-ever-afters, he can't help but wonder what that might be like. And then Sophia Strombi shows up on his doorstep. Sophia's life is a mess. Since she's working hard to get her life back on track, she's desperately trying to ignore the fact her boss makes her heart pound in a good way. Besides, she has a huge secret she's keeping from everyone—one that's a life-changer.

TOMBOY
a *Hartigans* novel by Avery Flynn

Ice Knights defenseman Zach Blackburn has come down with the flu, and my BFF begs me to put my nursing degree to use. But paparazzi spot me sneaking out of his place, and accusations that I slept with him fly faster than a hockey puck. At first, all of Harbor City wants my blood—or to give me a girlie-girl makeover. Then the grumpy bastard goes and promises to help raise money for a free health clinic—but only if I'm rink-side at every game. Suddenly, remembering to keep my real hands off my fake date gets harder and harder to do.

Screwed
a novel by Kelly Jamieson

Cash has been in love with his best friend's wife forever. Now Callie and Beau are divorced, but guy code says she's still way off-limits. Cash won't betray his friendship by moving in. Not to mention it could destroy the thriving business he and Beau have worked years to create. But this new Callie isn't taking no for an answer. He's screwed...

One Wedding, Two Brides
a *Fairy Tale Brides* novel by Heidi Betts

Jilted bride Monica Blair can't believe it when she wakes up next to a smooth-talking cowboy with a ring on her finger. Ryder Nash would have bet that he'd never walk down the aisle. But when the city girl with pink-streaked hair hatches a plan to expose the conman who married his sister, no idea is too crazy. And even though Monica might be the worst rancher's wife he's ever seen, he can't stop thinking about the wedding night they never had. What was supposed to be a temporary marriage for revenge is starting to feel a little too real...

Made in the USA
Monee, IL
20 July 2020